NIGHTSHIFT

NIGHTSHIFT

KATE DOUGLAS
CRYSTAL JORDAN
LYNN LaFLEUR

APHRODISIA
KENSINGTON PUBLISHING CORP.
www.kensingtonbooks.com

APHRODISIA BOOKS are published by

Kensington Publishing Corp.
119 West 40th Street
New York, NY 10018

All Kensington titles, imprints, and distributed lines are available at special quantity discounts for bulk purchases for sales promotion, premiums, fund-raising, and educational, or institutional use.

Special book excerpts or customized printings can also be created to fit specific needs. For details, write or phone the office of the Kensington Special Sales Manager: Kensington Publishing Corp., 119 West 40th Street, New York, NY 10018. Attn. Special Sales Department. Phone: 1-800-221-2647.

Aphrodisia and the A logo Reg. U.S. Pat. & TM Off.

ISBN-13: 978-0-7582-6936-2
ISBN-10: 0-7582-6936-6

First Kensington Trade Paperback Printing: December 2011

10 9 8 7 6 5 4 3 2 1

Printed in the United States of America

CONTENTS

DREAM CATCHER

KATE DOUGLAS

1

_____

In orbit behind Earth's moon—present day

Zianne? Is he the one? Is he strong enough? Smart enough?

I think so. He's very strong—I heard his voice over such a great distance, but I don't know. We've waited so long. How can I be certain?

We're dying, Zianne. All of us. There's no time to hesitate. There are hardly enough of us left to matter.

No. Don't say that. We matter. We must.

Then go. Even I sense this one. His world will nurture us for now, but this man . . . this one man will be our salvation.

Silicon Valley—April 1992

"Fucking chicken scratch." Mac Dugan wadded up yet another lined yellow page covered in pointless doodles, equations, and code. He reached overhead, aiming for the Sloan's Bar and Grill sign over the trash can.

Powerful fingers closed around his wrist.

Jerking his arm free, he spun around, prepared to take a swing at whatever idiot had interrupted his mini-tirade. When he saw who it was, he laughed. "Christ, Dink. Haven't seen you in ages. You trying to get yourself killed?"

"Nope. Just trying to save your stupid ass."

Mac grabbed the beer Dink handed to him. "Who says my ass needs saving?"

Dink grinned. His wide smile, along with the collar-length blond hair and thick dark lashes framing light blue eyes, made him almost too pretty for a man. "I do," he said. "That redhead, Jen? The one who was with you last month? She's all cozied up to the bar with your nemesis."

"You mean Bennett? Crap." Mac took a sip of his beer and fought the compulsion to glance over his shoulder. "I didn't know he was here. With her? Shit. Why'd I ever go out with her?"

"Because you were horny?" Dink snorted. "She keeps looking this way. Maybe she wants to get laid again."

Mac shook his head. "Not by me. What about Bennett? Is he watching us?"

Dink chuckled. "Nah. He's too busy staring at her cleavage."

"Fucking jerk. Weird she'd be here with him after . . . well, shit. Maybe I'm just paranoid." He avoided turning in his seat to stare at Phil Bennett. Even if the guy was responsible for totally fucking over his life, Bennett was more than welcome to the redhead. Except . . . It was like that stupid cartoon lightbulb flashed on in his mind. What if Jen and Phil had been an item before she came on to Mac? What if she'd been using him to get stuff—like his project notes?

"Of course you're paranoid." Dink was obviously reading his mind. He took a swallow of his beer and cocked one eyebrow. "You have a right to be, after what happened." He glanced once again at the couple. "On the other hand, you sure you don't want to get laid? She looks interested, and she's hot."

Mac laughed. "How do you know? You like guys."

Dink flipped him off, but he didn't deny it. At least his sexual preferences had never gotten in the way of their friendship. "I know gorgeous when I see it, male or female. She definitely fits the description."

Mac shrugged. "I know the red hair's not natural."

"It didn't seem to matter at the time."

It hadn't. He'd met her just a couple of days before the shit hit the fan. She'd come on to him, made it patently obvious she wanted to get laid, and it had been too damned long since he'd gotten a piece of anything but his right hand. "What can I say? She caught me in a weak moment." He waved his hand at the pile of discarded notes in the trash. "That's what counts. I know what I want, how it should look and what it needs to do, but I can't get the damned program to work."

Dink held up both hands and shook his head. "Hell, don't look at me. Starving grad student, future TV news guy here, not developer of weird software. You're so far past me on all this computer shit I wouldn't know where to start. What about the guys in the lab? I hear they're doing amazing stuff."

"I'm barred from the lab after what happened." He practically snarled. "Bennett's lies got me booted out of the program, cost me the grant and the rest of my scholarship. I'm just about out of cash." He held up the beer Dink had bought him. "Thanks for this, by the way."

"Well, fuck." Dink glared at him. "They were wrong, Mac. You know he stole your work. I still think you should fight it."

Mac forced a quick smile. "Thanks, man. Unfortunately, Phil had the notes, not me. In his handwriting. My originals are missing. Even the floppy disks are gone, so there's no reason to believe me. Besides, his uncle's the dean of the department."

"And Bennett's a lying turd."

"I agree, but it earned him a clean shot at the grant we were competing for." Mac shrugged, but he couldn't let it go. When he lost his access to the campus computer lab, he'd lost his only link to the new World Wide Web and contact with other software developers. His scrapped-together computer was too limited to test the programs he hoped to design, the ones he knew could bust him out of obscurity.

Right now, his future was totally fucked.

Keeping his back to Bennett and the redhead, Mac finished off the rest of his beer and shoved away from the table. Then he carefully stuffed his notepad in his backpack and looped the pack over his shoulder.

Dink tossed back his beer and rose as well. "Not so fast, brain-boy. You're coming with me."

"Where?" Mac folded his arms across his chest and gave Dink the kind of stare that generally intimidated most guys.

Except Dink, who just laughed. "Don't try that 'death to evildoers' look on me, big guy. My computer crashed. That's why I was looking for you. I want you to retrieve a paper I just finished. Gotta have it for tomorrow, man, or I'm screwed."

"That I can probably do." What threw Dink for a loop was usually a simple fix for Mac. He loved computers, and with the way technology was improving, it was obvious the twentieth century was going out with a bang.

Mac intended to be part of the explosion. He'd built his own system—and Dink's, for that matter—from scratch, but Mac's wasn't anywhere near as fast as the computers in the lab on campus. He needed faster, more complex equipment to accomplish his goals. It was so damned frustrating, living in Silicon Valley where everything was happening at warp speed, aware of so many new innovations, and yet stuck on the fringes without the equipment he needed to handle his ideas.

Shit. Just one more thing totally out of his control.

He glanced at the bell tower marking the center of the campus he'd thought of as home for the past seven years, and fought back a surge of anger. The dean had accepted the project Phil Bennett turned in, decided Mac was lying when he accused the bastard of theft, and then had the balls to say they'd let him drop out of the postgraduate program rather than formally charge and expel him.

He'd lost his scholarship and access to the lab. Lost any chance of qualifying for the grant he needed to continue his work. Lost everything because that little weasel had somehow stolen his project, lied about it, and gotten away with it.

Even worse, the incident was going on Mac's record. A black mark against his name, against the honor and integrity he'd always valued so much. No matter how bad it got, he'd never compromised. Never. Now this.

Why the fuck was it always an uphill battle? He was so damned tired of fighting life on his own, but other than Dink, he'd been alone since the foster care system booted his ass out at eighteen. The academic scholarship to the university had saved him. Until Bennett screwed him over.

If he could just get his life in order, maybe things wouldn't look so damned bleak, but now—right now—it all sucked.

Big time.

"Dinkemann, you are such a horse's ass." Mac kept his voice down as he stopped to throw a blanket over Dink's prone form on the couch. He stood over his sleeping buddy, remembering. They'd been through so much together. Growing up with a guy in the same crappy foster home created a link like nothing else. Even though they were complete opposites, Mac loved Dink in a way he couldn't explain. There was nothing he wouldn't do for him.

Well, almost nothing, though Mac couldn't deny he'd thought about it. Dink was gay and loved Mac, and while the thought of sex with his buddy had crossed his mind, Mac himself hadn't crossed the line. Yet.

Maybe it was all the beer he'd had tonight, but for some reason the thought of loving Dink *that way* didn't bother him as much as it had. *You've had way too much to drink, Dugan.*

It was definitely time to go home. Quietly, Mac closed the door to Dink's tiny apartment. Fueled by more beer than he'd needed, he hoped he'd be able to make it back to his apartment without getting arrested for public intoxication.

He rarely drank this much, but seeing Jen and Phil together tonight had thrown him. The more he thought about it, the more he was sure she'd stolen those pages of notes the night they'd fucked like bunnies until he finally fell asleep. She'd been gone when he finally dragged himself out of her bed and went back to his own place. Maybe she hadn't slept as soundly. Was she the one who'd ripped out the pages that had turned up in Phil Bennett's precise handwriting?

Had Phil used those hours to break into his apartment and steal the floppy disks with the research and all his notes?

There was no way to prove it. The pages were gone, along with the disks, something he hadn't noticed until it was time to prepare the grant application. And then it was too late.

Only Dink believed him, but their bond went deeper than mere friendship, sometimes so intensely visceral it was barely a step away from sexual attraction. Sort of how he'd felt tonight.

Except Mac knew he was straight. He'd never questioned his own sexuality, never doubted how much he loved women. In fact, tonight he'd gone off on a riff, rhapsodizing over the ultimate fantasy female. He could still see her—tall and athletic with long black hair and violet eyes. Dink had thrown in a computer nerd personality. What had he called her?

"A nerdette." Mac laughed, his voice echoing in the quiet night. "Just what I need."

Mac figured he was nerdy enough for two.

Dink, of course, had fantasized over the ideal guy—a guy who sounded suspiciously like MacArthur Dugan—tall, lean build, thick waves of caramel hair, a killer smile, and sapphire blue eyes—Dink's terms, not Mac's.

Dink had never hidden his feelings from Mac. So why did Mac feel as if he were keeping secrets from Dink? He loved Dink. Just not *that* way. Or did he? Damn. Mac stopped, grabbed the front of his jeans, and adjusted the crotch. Why the hell was he getting hard? Thoughts of Dink, or of his fantasy woman? Shit.

He focused on Bennett and the stolen project, and fury spurred him on. With his gait not quite steady, Mac made it up the stairs to his fourth-floor apartment in a matter of minutes.

Still pissed.

He and Dink had discussed how absurd it was. Why would Mac lie? If he didn't know the material, his ignorance would prove him wrong, but the dean refused to allow Mac to defend himself.

He'd never cared much for the dean, and the feeling had obviously been mutual, but the man's response to Mac's claims went beyond mere dislike. He'd been absolutely irate with Mac and had immediately taken Phil's side. What could Dean Johnson gain from his nephew winning the grant instead of Mac? Family unity or something stupid like that? Was that worth risking his tenure? Possibly, but probably not. But what else? Shit . . . Mac knew the program inside and out, with or without the notes and floppies. Did Bennett? No. No way.

Yet Mac still hadn't been allowed to defend himself.

Which left him guilty with no recourse. Cursing, Mac dug through his pants pocket for the key, fumbled with the damned thing, and promptly dropped it.

He leaned over to pick it up and almost fell on his face when the world spun a little too fast. "Oh . . . shit." He grabbed the key, stuck it in the lock, and after a couple of fumbles, got the door open. Moving very carefully, he managed to get inside his apartment without falling on his ass.

He leaned against the closed door a minute and let the world right itself once more. Then he tossed his backpack on the floor and slipped out of his jacket, but when he turned to dump his coat on the chair, something sweet tickled his senses.

He sniffed the air.

"What the hell?" Mac inhaled again, drawing the rich scent into his lungs. Vanilla? Honey? It was vaguely familiar, but he couldn't quite place it. Flipping on the light in the kitchen area, he glanced around to see if he'd left anything out.

The counters were clean, the sink empty except for a coffee cup and a cereal bowl. He sniffed the air again, but the scent that had seemed so pervasive eluded him now.

Yawning, seriously regretting those last few beers, Mac headed to the bathroom for a shower. If he relaxed enough and went to sleep thinking about the new graphics program, maybe he'd dream a solution. With any luck, his subconscious—what Dink called his lizard brain—would figure it out.

Except once he'd stripped and stood beneath the hot spray, his damned lizard brain focused on his dick instead of the program. Mac glanced ruefully at the tip of his cock.

The broad head with its dark slit stared up at him as if begging for attention. "Shit. You're supposed to be ready for bed." Grinning like an idiot, he wrapped his right fist around his shaft and cupped his testicles in his left hand. "Wonder what it means when a guy has conversations with his cock?"

He refused to answer himself. Instead, Mac leaned against the tile wall with the hot water beating down on his chest and shoulders and stroked himself with a firm grip, stretching soft, pliable skin over hard meat with one hand, rolling his balls between the fingers of the other.

His mind wandered as the pressure grew. He wanted a visual, but the redhead just pissed him off and her image quickly faded. He thought of Dink, but that was more than a little unsettling. Then his fantasy morphed into a woman with long black hair and intelligent violet eyes.

She smiled at him, and he knew her. The one he'd described earlier to Dink—the perfect woman. Mac's ultimate fantasy.

His cock actually jerked within his grasp. He was leaking pre-cum now, almost faster than the shower could rinse it away. He tugged harder on his balls, rolling the solid orbs between his fingers, squeezing his fist tighter around the base of his dick, finding a rhythm he knew couldn't last.

His balls sucked up close between his legs. He tightened his grasp and squeezed them almost painfully as his fantasy woman floated just inside his field of vision. He concentrated on her face, on the deep, violet eyes and cascade of coal black hair curling around her shoulders.

She was too real, too perfect for him to have invented her, but Mac had no idea where he'd seen her. She was beyond gorgeous, miles beyond any woman he could recall. The scent of honey and vanilla filled his senses and raised his temperature. She gazed up at him with the water cascading over her shoulders, across the fullness of her perfect breasts. Her nipples were a deep rose against porcelain skin, their tips drawn tight.

She smiled and then slowly dropped to her knees and nuzzled his groin as the spray slicked long, dark hair back from her face and steam filled the shower stall. The tip of her tongue slipped between full lips and she licked the side of his shaft, nipping daintily just at the juncture where his cock rooted to his groin. His entire body tensed.

The room spun. Too much beer, too much sensation, but her mouth on his dick anchored him. Deep crimson lips encircled the broad head. He groaned, thrust his hips forward, and she took him deep. His hands dropped to his sides as she worked more of his cock into her sweet mouth.

"Fuck." The curse slipped out on a whisper. He slapped his

palms flat against the wet tile to stop the walls from spinning when the muscles of her throat tightened around his sensitive glans.

"Shit. Holy, holy shit." Mac squeezed his eyes shut. His knees went weak, his head spun. Cursing steadily, he leaned his head against the tile as his hips rocked forward into the hot, wet clasp of her mouth. Her teeth scraped the sides of his shaft and the muscles in his buttocks clenched. He struggled for control, but she hummed deep in her throat and the vibration was a shock of pure fire running the full length of his shaft.

"Fuck. Oh . . . fuck." His hips jerked and his climax boiled up and out. He tried to open his eyes, to watch her, to prove she truly existed, but it was impossible to fight the pulsing throb of orgasm. Just as the woman was impossible. There was no one kneeling at his feet. That wasn't the flick of her tongue licking away the last drops of his seed. No, it was merely the most vivid sexual fantasy he'd ever had in his life.

What else could it be?

Legs trembling, breath heaving in and out of his lungs, Mac opened his eyes. He was alone. His cock lay soft and flaccid over his throbbing balls. He'd come without touching himself. Shot his load into an imaginary mouth and felt every lick of her tongue, every deep, sucking draw of her lips and cheeks.

Still too damned drunk, definitely spaced, Mac stared at the empty shower in front of him. At the spot where the woman had knelt. Slowly shaking his head and seriously doubting his sanity, he scrubbed the stink of the long day off his body. Then he turned off the water and toweled dry with trembling hands.

The scent of vanilla and honey teased his nostrils, but he refused to consider the connection. Half-asleep, physically drained, he crawled into bed and turned out the light. He'd barely pulled the covers over his bare shoulders before sleep claimed him.

2

There it was again, that sweet scent that made him think of warm vanilla wafers. Crawling out of a sublimely sexual dream featuring his latest fantasy female—a dream that faded away as consciousness returned—Mac sniffed the air. Had the smell of cookies awakened him?

He really wanted to get back to that dream.

The room was still dark, but the same tantalizing sweetness he'd noticed earlier filled his nostrils. Stronger now. Closer.

He reached for the lamp on the bedside table. A soft hand stroked his chest. Mac sucked in a gasp of air.

Scrabbling for the switch, he flicked on the light and shoved himself back against the headboard.

Blinking beneath the bright light, he stared into the face of a woman too perfect to be real—eyes so purple they sparkled like amethysts beneath thick, sooty lashes, and hair as black as night. Her skin was fair, her lips full and lush. If he'd dreamed her into existence, she couldn't have been more perfect, and that was the only way she could have gotten here, because he sure as hell hadn't invited anyone in tonight.

"Who the hell are you?"

She frowned. Her dark brows knotted, and two tiny lines appeared between them. "I'm Zianne," she said, as if he should know. "Don't you remember? And you are Mac."

She spoke with a soft accent he didn't recognize, in a voice that was low and sort of raspy. Hinting of sex and secrets, it raised shivers along his spine.

He shook his head. He'd been so damned drunk when he left Dinkemann's place—had he met her somewhere tonight? He'd never had an alcoholic blackout in his life, but if this was the result, he'd definitely been wasting his time.

He flashed on the fantasy he'd had in the shower. The same woman beside him in bed? No. That wasn't real. She wasn't real. He'd imagined that. Hadn't he? Was he imagining her here, now?

Impossible to imagine her scent, the weight of her warm body against his. Her touch. He inhaled a deep, shuddering breath. "Where'd you come from?"

She shrugged as if he were a complete fool for asking, and for a minute he thought he must be, because there was no way in hell he'd ever forget bringing someone like Zianne home to his apartment. There wasn't enough alcohol in the world to make him forget a woman like her.

A memory flashed through his mind, of Zianne kneeling before him in the shower, her mouth . . . *Dear God. Her mouth!*

She smiled with those perfect, lush lips and stroked his cheek with her fingertips. Her touch was soft and warm. Perfect.

"You brought me here." Her scent enveloped him, stealing his thoughts from the question.

Fresh-baked cookies. Vanilla and honey . . . why does she smell so familiar? And then it came to him, the memory so subtle it held a dreamlike quality. Comforting smells from a childhood he'd long forgotten. A time when his parents still lived, when he'd had a real home, a real family.

A time before he was four years old and the world as he knew it ended. No matter. He couldn't go back, couldn't change the car accident that took his mom and dad's lives, the accident that left him unharmed and alone. Quickly Mac blocked the actual pain he experienced whenever that time intruded.

He couldn't change what was, though he could enjoy the spark of memory from before. Could enjoy the warm scent of Zianne in his arms. Mac took a deep breath and stared into those unbelievable violet eyes. Who in the hell was she?

Zianne smiled, leaned close, and kissed him, enveloping Mac in more of that subtle, sweet perfume. Her lips moved slowly, warm and soft, over his mouth. Sex personified.

Need blossomed. Need on so many levels, so many different wants and desires. Love. Sex. Companionship. Friendship. Other than Dink, he'd been alone for so long he'd forgotten what it felt like to have someone close, someone who mattered. Zianne's kiss promised to fill needs Mac had forgotten he ever had.

Her taste was even sweeter than her scent. Zianne's mouth moved over his, tasting, nipping, licking. She slid closer until she lay atop him, until her lips covered his and her tongue probed the sensitive flesh above his teeth, inside his mouth. Her hands were in his hair, her fingers separating the strands and sending shivers of pure fire along his spine. She held him and kissed him deep; explored his mouth with her mobile tongue.

He remembered the way her lips had felt around his cock. It had to have been her, but how? He couldn't have imagined something as real as her mouth on him then. On him now. She'd sucked him deep, taken his seed and swallowed every drop. Now she made love to his mouth, the intensity of her kiss pulling all he was, all he had to give—just as she'd done before.

Mac's body grew hard beneath her long, supple length. His cock rose between her thighs, his muscles rippled beneath his skin. The weight of her breasts on his chest made him strangely angry. He wanted to see them. Wanted to nuzzle his lips and face against their softness, but she'd taken control and he didn't fight her for dominance. He had no will of his own. None.

He couldn't fight her. Could only lie here beneath her perfect body as she made love to him. As she took him, raising up on her knees, grabbing his turgid length in her fist, placing the broad head between her thighs.

There was the briefest awareness of soft, damp curls, of even softer, wetter lips. Then she arched her back and came down on him, all in one smooth, flowing motion that drove him deep inside. He felt heat and the ripple of flexing muscles, then a smooth, wet channel gripping him in an unforgivable vise, pure sensual pleasure personified in this perfect woman.

He raised his hips and thrust hard against her, reaching now for those breasts she so proudly displayed. His palms cupped their weight, his fingers found the taut nipples and he pinched them. She moaned and he twisted the sensitive tips, waiting for Zianne to beg him to stop. Instead, she moaned her pleasure and her hips moved over him until he and she caught the same rhythm.

He stopped pinching and lightly stroked and teased the rosy tips, then cupped her breasts fully in his hands as their bodies danced to an unseen orchestra, to the beat of the heavy drum of thundering hearts, to the song of blood rushing through veins and the discordant harmony of straining lungs.

Caught in a maelstrom of unimaginable lust, he thrust into her, grabbing her by the waist, lifting her up, pulling her close. The slap of flesh against flesh echoed, of lungs gasping for air as they raced each other to the finish. Zianne's body was hot and alive, quivering beneath his hands, her eyes hooded beneath their dark fringe of lashes, her full lips parted. She watched him. Watched him with an intensity that might have frightened him at another time.

Not now.

Now Mac was trapped in a delirium of need, his body connected at a visceral level he'd never experienced, his heart and soul held by too many emotions he couldn't identify. Emotions he didn't try to name, because they couldn't be. They couldn't exist in his world. Hadn't existed in MacArthur Dugan's life since that long-ago time before his parents died.

He'd not known true happiness since then. Nor had he felt real love, and he couldn't feel it now. This could not possibly be love, not this amazing sexual experience with a woman he didn't know, a woman he might never see again.

The thought left him bereft as it flitted through what little bit of his mind still functioned on a conscious level. Then everything fled, wiped out by the full-on experience of orgasm. By the overwhelming sensation of everything he was, everything he had to give—all of it flying out of him, leaving him entirely. Leaving Mac, and entering Zianne.

She arched her back and pressed close. Took his heart, took his soul, took his seed. She cried out as her long nails dug into his ribs, leaving red furrows behind. He welcomed the pain. Added it to the sensations ripping him in two as he practically came apart, pumping his seed deep into her welcoming body.

Mac's heart thundered in his ears. He felt its counterpart in Zianne's racing heart when she collapsed against him. Her tangled hair covered his mouth, her lips were pursed against his sweat-slick chest, blowing tiny puffs with each escaping breath.

It took everything he had to raise his right hand and stroke her smooth shoulder. Enervated, he was weak as a kitten, yet his mind seemed unnaturally clear. Impossible, considering how much he'd had to drink tonight, but he was more aware of this woman, more aware of his body and the way it connected to hers, than he'd ever felt with anyone before.

Her inner muscles still pulsed in a slow, rhythmic clench and release around him, and he wanted nothing more than to make love to her again. To repeat what had been a singular experience, something he'd never once felt in his twenty-six years. They'd shared more than mere sex. There'd been something else, a connection he couldn't explain. A feeling of *knowing*, as if Zianne knew and understood him in ways no one else ever had.

Or ever could. As if he knew Zianne the same way. Except Mac knew nothing at all. Who she was. Where she came from. How he'd met her. How she'd come to be in his apartment.

In his shower?

So many questions. So much he wanted to talk to her about, but his eyelids grew heavy and his heart rate slowed. His breath no longer huffed in and out of his lungs as if he'd run a mile.

Zianne lay across him, apparently asleep with his softening penis still buried deep inside her. He knew there were things he should wonder, but her body was soft and warm over his and her perfume took him back to that childhood he barely recalled.

With the scent of honey and vanilla, and Zianne's thick, black hair tickling his nose, Mac tightened his arms around her waist and drifted closer to sleep. They'd talk in the morning. For now, though, his world felt right. As if the problems bedeviling him for so long weren't problems at all. Not with Zianne in his arms. As long as he had her beside him, Mac imagined he could do anything. Anything at all.

3

Shaken, Zianne stood for a moment beside the bed. Her fingers drifted softly across his shoulder, over skin damp from their loving. Her body, this unfamiliar form, still trembled from the force of his passion, her passion. It had left her energized in ways she'd not expected.

And confused in a manner she'd never experienced. She whispered his name. "Mac." Rolling the sound on her tongue, she gazed at him with hope, and with more than a little guilt. She'd touched his mind tonight. Touched his memories, discovered his needs, and then she'd filled them. Such a simple thing, to return the fantasy after he'd shared so much delicious energy.

There was untapped depth to this man. Reservoirs of strength she'd not expected, and he was not nearly as alien as his form suggested. He was more like her than she'd imagined. Not merely his intelligence—no, it was more than that. Emotions she'd thought only the Nyrians possessed, needs very similar to her own. A need for family, for connection. For love.

She'd touched those needs on a level deeper than she'd expected. Had shared even more with MacArthur Dugan than she'd planned. Was that why she felt so unsettled and confused? So filled with emotions and, curiously, with regret?

She didn't understand why she regretted the simple manipulation of his thoughts—she'd merely given him the feelings he needed. Maybe the elders could explain. She hoped so. An entire race of sentient beings depended on her success.

A shaft of morning sunlight cut across Mac's closed eyelids. Blinking against the pain of daylight and too much alcohol, he slowly rolled to the edge of the bed and pushed himself upright. What a night. And what a weird bunch of dreams.

He sat there a moment, cataloging all the things about him that hurt. The list was longer than usual.

"Damn." It hurt to blink. Hurt to move. Even hurt to breathe. He ran his fingers through his mussed hair and tried to think. That hurt, too.

He scratched his chest and ran his fingers down the ribs on his left side. "Shit. What the hell . . . ?"

Blinking owlishly, Mac raised his left arm and stared with bleary eyes at the red lines running across his ribs. Frowning, he twisted slowly and painfully and focused on the matching scratches down his right side. Snapped his head around and stared over his shoulder at the rumpled sheets on the bed.

He thought he'd dreamed her. Sex in the shower, in his bed. It had all been a dream. He was alone. He should be alone.

Except he hadn't been alone last night.

Memories flashed, exploding so fast and furious they made his aching head spin. The woman. The sex. The thick, black curls tickling his nose. *The sex.* Her mouth around his dick. The flick of her tongue across his sensitive glans.

Her fingers. He groaned. Those long, mobile fingers, stroking. Tugging. Twisting and squeezing. Pain and pleasure and more pleasure. Arousal so intense it almost fried his brain.

A connection unlike anything he'd ever experienced with a woman so perfect she would be forever imprinted on his mind.

Images raced through his head. His semi-aroused morning wood rose up into action mode. Mac groaned. He lay back down on the bed with his feet still planted on the floor. *Zianne.* She'd said her name was Zianne, but where the hell was she?

He sniffed the air, and caught it—the faint scent of vanilla and honey almost lost in the pungent odor of sex and sweat. "Zianne? Hey, Zianne?" He listened to the familiar sounds of an empty apartment. Dripping faucet, neighbor's shower, cars passing by four floors down. "Zianne? Are you here?" Nothing.

Rubbing his fingers across his belly, Mac sighed. *Where the hell'd she go?* If not for the scent lingering in the air, the raw scratches across his ribs, he'd chalk her up to too much beer or an overblown wet dream. Or both. But she wasn't a dream.

Good God . . . how many times had they screwed last night?

Made love? No. MacArthur Dugan didn't do love, but what they'd shared went so far beyond mere screwing he wasn't sure what to call it. So unbelievable that if not for the scratches across his ribs, he'd think he'd imagined her. It. The sex.

Damn. The sex. He absentmindedly stroked his erection, remembering the feel of her lips on him, the way her violet eyes had somehow looked right inside him. He and Zianne had hardly talked, but he'd felt a connection to her unlike anything he'd ever experienced.

How the hell did you explain something like that?

And where the hell was she this morning?

Just thinking about her made him harder, so he kept stroking and squeezing his dick with his right hand, reached beneath to cup his balls with his left.

She'd sucked on them last night. Sucked first one ball and then the other between those gorgeous lips. She'd used her tongue and the pressure of her cheeks to take him just to the point of pain, just to the place where he'd felt the first frisson of panic that she might actually hurt him.

But she didn't. No, she'd held him there, torturing him on the edge of pure bliss, sucking and stroking and somehow knowing exactly how much pressure it took, how hard to squeeze, how lightly she could lick and taste until he couldn't take any more. Just thinking about her now had him on the edge. Had him gripping his balls tighter, stroking faster, breathing harder.

She'd explored his slit with the tip of her tongue, stretched the tiny opening and lapped up every drop of pre-cum. She'd used her teeth, nipping at the edge of his glans and along the thick vein on the underside. Short, sharp little bites that, along with the sucking and squeezing and licking, made him nuts.

He tried to remember exactly how it felt and what she'd done, and suddenly he was groaning, coming all over himself, shooting thick streams of ejaculate over his hand and wrist and making a mess.

After so much sex the night before, he couldn't believe there was anything left. His orgasm seemed to take forever, not that he wanted to rush it. His cock continued to pulse in time with his racing heartbeat long after the flow stopped.

So now he was hungover and covered with spunk, without a clue who the hell Zianne was, where she'd come from, where she'd gone. Well, he was damned well going to find her.

If only he knew where to start. Groaning, Mac rolled back to a sitting position and shoved himself off the bed. A shower first. And coffee. Lots of coffee. Then he'd search for Zianne.

"Crap." Mac slammed the cupboard door and rubbed his pounding head. No coffee. Grabbing his backpack, he headed for the coffee shop across the street. Dink was there, sitting alone in the back, leaning forward with his head in his hands.

He looked as rough as Mac felt, which, for some reason,

made Mac feel better. He dumped his pack on the chair across from Dink. The loud *thunk* when it landed earned him a curse and a bloodshot glare. Smiling innocently, Mac walked to the counter and bought a cup of French roast and a blueberry muffin.

Still grinning, he carried his breakfast to the table. "Rough night?"

Dink still glared at him.

Feeling better by the minute, Mac sat. "You get that paper printed out? I left the file on a floppy on your desk." He sipped the coffee, imagining little caffeine soldiers racing into his bloodstream, and wishing they would hurry.

"Yeah. Thanks." Dink stared at his coffee. "I turned it in first thing. Thank God I don't have another class until after lunch." He groaned. "Crap, man. Why do you let me do this to myself?"

Mac took another swallow. "I'm not your mother."

Dink grinned at him. "Fuck. You'd make one ugly mother."

Mac popped him a middle-finger salute. It was the best he could come up with, at least until the caffeine did its job. He took another swallow. "Dink? You ever hear me mention a chick named Zianne? Dark hair, violet eyes?"

"Not the name." He shook his head. "That sounds like your fantasy woman, remember? We might have been almost sober when we were into that part of the conversation."

"'Almost' being the descriptive word here." Mac sighed and took a bite of his muffin.

Dink didn't say anything. He just stared into his coffee cup. Finally he raised his head and narrowed his gaze. "You've got bigger worries than women. What're you going to do about Bennett? I saw the bastard again this morning."

"I have no idea. The project notes are gone. All of them." He snorted his disgust. "No way I know of to prove I'm innocent if Dean Johnson won't let me argue the project in front of the committee. That's the only way I can possibly prove it's mine."

"That sucks. You know it inside out. I doubt Phil Bennett knows his ass from a hole in the ground. Have you thought of going directly to the grant committee?"

"It might work, if I could get to them." Mac leaned back in his chair and stared at Dink. "Any grand ideas, smart guy?"

"Can't you just make an appointment?"

Mac shook his head. "Won't work. Dean Johnson's not just on the committee. I could offer to meet with the chairman, but the dean's got a lot of power in this—he administers the funds, and he's convinced I'm guilty. I'm screwed."

Dink finished his coffee, stood, and tossed the cup in the trash. "It wouldn't hurt to ask, Mac. Think about it." He slapped Mac on the shoulder as he left. "This is your entire professional future we're talking about."

Mac watched as Dink left the coffee shop. Times like this he almost wished he were wired like Dink. Wished he could go home with his best friend and fuck until he didn't care anymore. Dink's devotion was the one constant in Mac's life, the one thing he knew he could always count on.

But he couldn't be what Dink needed. He could only be who he was, and that was one fucked-up bastard. Mac sat alone, sipping his cooling cup of coffee, thinking of Dink's comment. "Entire professional future. Fuck." He stared into his cup and sighed. "Like I have one?" After a moment, he tossed the cup in the trash and headed back to his apartment.

No scent of vanilla and honey greeted him this time. If he didn't know better, he'd wonder if he'd imagined the whole scene last night, but there were those long scratches on his ribs and the fact he knew his imagination wasn't good enough to have conjured up someone like her. Hell, she even had a name. Zianne.

So much for fantasy, but who the hell was she? Would she ever come back? Like, maybe tonight? "Yeah. Right. Get real."

Mac dumped his pack out on the desk and fired up his computer. The small screen flickered to life while he flipped through the lined yellow pages of his legal-sized notepad.

Page after page of code and comments, all of it close to but not exactly what he wanted. His vision seemed so clear when he imagined the program—something that would give users a "what you see is what you get" experience working in a simplified graphics program with the ability to create complicated visuals. WYSIWYG that was beyond intuitive. He could almost touch it, but for some reason it wouldn't come together the way he imagined.

He flipped to the last page, the most recent set of notes, and stared at the figures covering the yellow lined sheet. Something wasn't right. He ran his fingers over the neatly written code. Shivers raced up his spine.

That wasn't his handwriting, except no one else had access to his notes. The tablet was with him all the time, especially after the mess with Bennett. The stuff he'd tossed last night hadn't been complete enough to give anyone an inkling of what he was working on, but someone had made notations here that . . .

Mac studied the additions, excitement overriding paranoia. He knew he hadn't written this. Knew it was someone else's work, but damn it all, it made sense. He rolled his chair over in front of the computer, opened a DOS window, and typed in the code. It wasn't all he'd been planning to do, but it was a start. A damned good start, and it was working.

Working like he'd dreamed it would. Lost in the amazing process of creating something out of nothing but symbols and numbers and hope, Mac's fingers flew across the keyboard.

Mac limited himself to one beer. No more. He really didn't need or want another hangover like the one that had totally wasted him all morning. He munched on a leftover piece of pizza as he wandered through the apartment, checking the lock on the door and even the windows to make sure they were secure.

No way was anyone getting his notes. Not now. Not when he was so damned close. He pulled the floppies out of the computer and stuck them under the mattress, then pulled them out just as quickly. "Shit. That's not gonna work."

He stared at the floppies in his hand and laughed. Yeah, like a gorgeous woman was suddenly going to appear in his bed again. Well, a guy could hope, and if Zianne came back tonight, he hoped like hell the mattress got another workout like last night. Not good for floppy disks.

He stuck them in his dresser drawer, under the socks. Damn, but he hoped she came back. He wanted to see her when he was sober, not blinded by booze. He wanted a clear-eyed view of her perfect breasts and sleek, round hips and those amazing violet eyes. Desire sliced through him, a surge of pure animal lust so hot and sweet he almost groaned. Damn. If she didn't come back tonight, he wasn't sure how he'd handle it.

Wasn't sure he could. One night and she'd become an obsession. He'd thought of her all day. Sniffed the air, searching for honey and vanilla to no avail. He couldn't get past the fact he'd not gone down on her once last night, and now he wondered if she'd taste as sweet as she smelled. If he'd find the same magic with those intimate feminine lips that he'd found when they kissed.

Which meant he'd spent the better part of the day hard as a post, which hadn't helped his concentration. But he'd had those amazing additions to his notes—bits of code that got him closer than ever to his goal. But who? How?

Zianne? Who else? She was the only one who'd been in his apartment, the only one to have access to his work, and it would have had to be while he was asleep.

Before or after that amazing sex? But how would she know what the program needed?

How did she know anything about him? About his work?

A blinking light caught Mac's attention. Shoving papers off the answering machine, he wondered how long the message had been waiting. He was forever turning the phone's ringer off and forgetting to check for messages.

Mac pressed the button and Dink's voice came through. He sounded upset. Beyond upset, but at least the message was recent. "Answer your damned phone, Dugan. It's Thursday. Four o'clock. I'm at Sloan's. Bennett's spilling his guts, only it's his version. He's saying you stole his research and tried to pass it off as yours. The idiots believe him. Mac, you're gonna be so screwed if you don't fight this. Totally screwed. You know how gossip travels. No one will hire you. Not in this town."

Mac didn't remember sitting, but his butt was planted on the edge of the bed and he had his head down, between his knees, hoping like hell he wasn't going to throw up. *Fucking Bennett.* That wasn't the deal. The dean had promised confidentiality if Mac went quietly. Mac had gone. Bennett had no right, especially when it was untrue. Shit.

The bastard had been out to get him for the past six months, ever since he'd learned Mac had applied for the same grant money. It was a lot of money, but didn't he understand the concept of competition? That's how things worked in academia.

Fair competition. For whatever reason, Phil Bennett didn't think the rules applied to him, and he'd used his uncle's position as dean to back him up. Mac wondered how the hell he'd be able to fight such blatant nepotism, but if he didn't, Dink was right. Mac was screwed.

What were his options? Could he bypass the dean? Go directly to the committee?

Shit. Would it even matter?

4

A shower wasn't the same by himself. There was no reason to expect Zianne, but depression swamped Mac as he toweled off in the empty bathroom. There was no sign of her anywhere. No scent of vanilla and honey, no beautiful woman with violet eyes.

Nothing but the usual—an empty bed with rumpled sheets. Bone weary and dejected, Mac lay down and tried to relax, but the work he'd done today wouldn't leave him alone. He was assuming Zianne had added the bits of code to his notes, but what if she hadn't? She was the only one he knew of who'd had access, but he still knew nothing about her. He wanted to talk about the program with her, find out if she was the one, or if he was just losing it altogether.

Did it even matter anymore? His reputation was shot. Who'd be interested in working with someone they thought was a liar and a thief?

Of all the questions haunting him, that was the hardest to ignore. That and the fact he was alone, and he'd much rather think of Zianne. Mac lay there in the darkness, remembering the feel of her lying warm and naked beside him. He recalled her sweet scent and the soft whisper of her breath against his chest when she'd climaxed, those amazing violet eyes and the way they'd gone all hazy and unfocused in the aftermath of orgasm.

Where was she tonight? Would he ever see her again?

"I'm here, Mac."

"Shit!" He lunged out of bed, ripping the blankets with him. Zianne lay there, her body sleek and naked, her hair all tousled and tangled as if she'd been out in the wind.

Or making love.

"How the hell did you get here? I'm still wide awake. Why didn't I hear you?" He stood there beside the bed, staring at her, wondering if he'd truly lost his mind. His place was locked up tight as Fort Knox. No way she could have gotten in. Not without his knowing.

She reached for him and ran one long, slim finger across his chest. "You called me and I came. Don't you remember?"

Mac stared at her, caught between bliss and the utter shock of Zianne in his bed. How the hell did she sneak in here while he was lying in bed, awake and thinking about her?

Unless he'd fallen asleep without realizing it? No. He was tired, but not that tired. Mac wrapped his fingers around her hand and stopped her sensual exploration of his chest as he slowly eased back into bed. She curled her fingers around his and tugged, as if she wanted to pull him close. Mac wasn't about to give in. Not until he had some answers.

"I didn't call you, Zianne. My phone's turned off. Even if it were on, I don't know your number. So, I'm asking you again. How the hell did you get into my apartment?"

She blinked. Her huge violet eyes disappeared beneath sooty lashes. Reappeared. Disappeared again. He was fully aware he was falling into the hypnotic rhythm of her thick lashes, her amazing eyes. Her lips. She ran her tongue over her full lower lip and Mac groaned.

Fully aware, and yet unable to stop, Mac leaned closer, drawn to her as if they were connected by a powerful, yet invisible thread.

Instead of answering, Zianne shrugged. Even that slight twist of her shoulders turned him on. God, he was such an idiot.

Zianne pursed her lips. She felt his concentration waver even more when she ran her tongue over the surface of the bottom lip, and then the top. Mentally she pushed harder. His was such a powerful mind and so difficult to control, but she'd quickly figured out the instincts of this body. She used them, used her knowledge to attract him at his most basic level.

She knew that as powerful as his energy was, Mac's sexual energy was even stronger. She needed every last bit. Scraping her teeth over her lower lip, she chewed on the fullness, holding his gaze on her mouth. Then she sent the image of her teeth scraping over his dick last night. She felt him waver.

She hated the subterfuge. Hated the fact she manipulated him, in essence, lied to him. He was a good man. Not only was his mind the strongest she'd ever touched, he had an inner core of honor and integrity that made her ruse more painful.

She'd discussed it with the others before returning. If not for the fate of her people, she would tell him everything, but they'd all agreed, the truth could easily turn him away. She couldn't afford the risk. As her people's emissary, she had to gain his trust first. That meant she needed his love.

Zianne pushed harder. Silently she begged Mac's forgiveness the moment she knew she'd won this round.

Mac felt his defenses fall. "I can't," he whispered. "But why?" Whenever he tried to question her, it felt as if something held him back. His emotions were all tied in to his need to question her, and yet he hardly knew her. He had no idea who she was, where she came from, how she got here. How had she taken control of such a huge slice of his heart, of his life?

She'd spent one night in his bed—just one amazing night. That was all. Why did he feel a connection with Zianne he'd never felt with another person?

The closest friend he had was Dink. Mac loved him, but it was the love a man felt for a friend. Enough for Mac, but not what Nils Dinkemann wanted. He needed more than Mac could give.

Mac loved him enough that he'd tried. A kiss. Jerking each other off. Curiosity on Mac's part, blind need on Dink's. Mac had definitely been aroused and he might have followed through, but something was missing. Something important. That connection that tied heart and mind and soul into a perfect package.

How, after only one night with Zianne, did he feel as if he held that package in his hands? It made no sense. None at all.

"Tell me about your day, Mac. Did your work go well?"

Ignoring his questions, she trailed her fingertip across his chest. He caught her hand and kissed her fingers, but then he tightened his grasp, locking her hand to his. Had this same hand written those perfect and precise notes? "How do you know anything about my work?"

Her smile blossomed. "But I know these things. I see them." She leaned close and pressed her lips against his forehead. "I know that you are brilliant. That your mind struggles to create new programs for your computer. I know that you have a vision of what can be and the ability to follow it."

He felt his eyes growing wider with each word Zianne spoke. She'd not nailed anything specific, and yet she spoke as if she read his mind. He shivered, caught in that perfect violet gaze. Who was this woman?

A loud thump against the apartment door ripped him away

from his questions. "What the hell?" He turned so quickly he almost tumbled out of the bed, grabbed a pair of sweatpants off the floor, and slipped them on. "Wait here. I'll see who it is."

He ran into the front room and glanced through the small peephole in the door. "Holy shit. Dink?" Ripping the door open, he caught his friend as he stumbled into the room. Blood poured from a gash in his forehead. His lip was split, one eye almost swollen shut. His clothing was torn and bloodied. "What the fuck happened?"

Dink's legs went out from under him, and Mac stumbled to the floor with his buddy wrapped in his arms. Zianne was suddenly at his side, wearing his old robe and holding a stack of clean towels.

"What happened to him? Who did this terrible thing?"

Dink raised his head and stared out of his one functioning eye. "It was Bennett," he said. At least that's what Mac thought he said, but Dink's lips were swelling even as Mac watched. Zianne spun away and went into the kitchen. A moment later she was back with a plastic bag filled with ice cubes. She wrapped it in a towel and held it against the side of Dink's face.

"Let's get him to the couch," she said, and it seemed perfectly right to follow Zianne's lead and half carry, half walk Dink over to the sagging couch and help him sit.

"Bennett's a little squirt," Mac said. He had to make a joke out of something. If he didn't, he wasn't sure he could handle this, handle Dink beaten to a bloody pulp. "Don't tell me he did this to you by himself."

Dink squinted and focused on Mac with the one eye that wasn't swollen shut. "He had help. A lot of it, and they're not students. They worked me over like professionals. Something else has to be going on besides that damned grant and your project."

Mac sat back on his heels. "What do you mean?"

Zianne handed him a glass of water. Dink took it, and for the first time seemed to notice she was even in the room. "Who are you?" He swung his head around and stared at Mac. "Who is she? She's the one you were talking about, right? The one with the violet—"

"Yeah." Mac interrupted Dink and grabbed Zianne's hand. "This is Zianne. And this is Nils Dinkemann. Call him Dink."

Dink stared at Zianne for a moment and then flashed a bloody but approving smile at Mac.

"Get your shirt off," Mac said, ignoring his unspoken opinion. "I want to take a look."

"I've waited years to hear you ask me that." Dink's attempt at a cocky grin was more of a pained grimace.

"Stuff it, Dinkemann." Mac lowered his voice and asked, "How're your ribs?"

"They hurt like hell. Everything hurts, but nothin' feels broken."

"You need a doctor? I can call a cab, get you to the ER."

"No. No doctor." Emphatically, Dink shook his head.

"Okay." Mac nodded. They could always go later if he needed medical care. Mac carefully helped him out of his shirt. Bruises and bloody contusions covered his chest and back, but Dink's attention was on Zianne, not the damage to his body. He stared at her first, and then at Mac, but he didn't ask the obvious.

He didn't have to. How much, if anything, did Zianne know about the grant? It wasn't a secret anymore. Bennett had announced Mac's downfall loud and clear, according to Dink, but Zianne wouldn't know that. She shouldn't know anything.

As if he'd asked her, Zianne rested her fingers on Mac's shoulder. "I know Mac has been unjustly accused of a falsehood. This Bennett? The one who beat you? He is involved?"

Mac couldn't have hidden his surprise if he'd wanted to. His head felt as if it might explode with all the unanswered questions when he focused on Zianne. When he stared into those innocent violet eyes and dared her to tell him how she knew.

Zianne smiled gently, but said nothing. Then she brushed her fingers across his forehead. Again, that unreal sense of connection. Somehow, with her touch, Mac knew she understood what was going on. But how? He felt dizzy from so many questions—more questions than he knew how to ask—but the most important ones wouldn't leave him alone.

Who, exactly, was Zianne? Had she heard about the scandal from Bennett? If not, then how? How could she be so certain of his innocence? He'd been ready to ask her about the notes when Dink arrived, but hadn't had a chance.

He frowned. Would it have done him any good? When he actually asked her things, she never really answered. Did it matter so much how she knew? Or did it merely matter that she believed his innocence?

His questions spun so fast they made his head ache.

Dink leaned back against the couch with the ice pack pressed to the side of his face. What if Mac were to tell him how he and Zianne met? How Zianne just appeared in his bed . . . hell, in his fucking shower?

Dink was hurting because of Mac's problems with Phil Bennett. Somehow, Zianne knew about the scandal, yet she didn't seem the least bit concerned Mac might be a liar and a thief.

Which raised another question: Could he trust Zianne? He knew nothing about her. A weird thought flitted through his mind, and he wondered if he might be falling in love with her. Impossible. Why would he think that? How could you love someone you didn't even know?

He stared at her, his thoughts in turmoil, his heart as confused as his head. None of it made sense. No sense at all.

5

Zianne stood in front of the kitchen sink and rinsed Dink's blood off her hands. She'd quite literally escaped to this room, though anywhere would have worked so long as it took her away from Mac's probing questions. She wasn't ready to answer them, but she couldn't hold him off much longer.

She and the elders had talked of this. They'd decided it was best Mac not know her true identity. Too often, other life forms had been unable to accept the fact they weren't the only sentient beings living among the stars. Such egocentricity made no sense, but Zianne bowed to the greater wisdom.

She wanted to think Mac would accept her, but she couldn't take the risk. He had no idea what she would ask of him. She wasn't ready to tell him that, either, though she had no doubt he could and would do what she needed. He was a good man with an inquisitive mind of immense power.

Humans truly were exquisite creatures. She'd taken on shape and form before, using the mental energy of sentient beings, but nothing like this. She'd reached out and caught the stunning energy of his mind light-years beyond the far side of his world's sun. He had drawn her here with his power—power he'd unknowingly shared with Zianne. When the ship had drawn close enough, MacArthur Dugan's vivid sexual fantasies—complete with a startling visual of his ideal woman—had literally blasted her into being.

And what a being it was. One never knew when assuming another creature's form if the acts inherent to a particular species would be pleasing to her Nyrian sense of joy. She'd quickly discovered that pleasing Mac pleased her as well.

Everything she and Mac did together gave her joy.

Everything, except when he questioned her. She disliked pushing his thoughts in other directions, the sense of guilt she felt. She knew her evasiveness was no better than the lies of that one named Bennett, though she'd been as honest as she could when she said Mac had called her.

The lie was merely in how one defined a call.

And he had called her. She'd been searching for a powerful mind, and his compelling fantasy had been strong enough to pull her through both time and space. She'd never dreamed anyone like Mac existed in this quadrant of the endless, timeless universe.

Had never imagined how she would begin to feel about him after so short a time. And she did feel. Strongly.

"Zianne? Will you help me carry Dink into the bedroom? If you grab his feet . . ."

She went to help. The injured man was either sleeping or unconscious, though he groaned when Mac carefully lifted him beneath his arms and, with her help, carried him in and laid him on the bed.

Mac raised his head and shrugged. "I'm sorry, Zianne. It's the only bed, but I can't leave him on the couch." He gazed at his friend and then once again smiled at Zianne with definite interest in those gorgeous eyes of his. "Believe me, you have no idea how sorry I am."

She smiled to let him know she understood. She felt regret as well. "It's okay. He's badly hurt." She moved closer to the bed and stroked Dink's hair. His appearance pleased her as much as Mac's, yet he was different. "This should not have happened. That other, the one called Bennett. His lies bring you trouble."

She felt Mac staring at her. Dear Nyria, this was so hard. She wanted to tell him everything. She'd tried to think of how she could help without giving herself away, but without honesty, she was no better than those who conspired against him.

Even so, Mac wasn't ready to accept the truth. He gazed at her now with those beautiful blue eyes of his, and she felt the questions circling in his mind. She closed her eyes and pushed.

Amazingly, Mac's mind pushed back even harder than before.

Startled, she jerked, and then quickly composed herself. Did he even know what he was doing? What she was doing?

Mac tilted his head, studying her much too closely. "How do you know so much, Zianne? We only met last night. Who are you?"

Fighting a need to be honest, she faced him.

And lied by omission. "I'm someone who wants very much for you to succeed." She glanced away, well aware he followed her every move, her every word. She felt the need in him. He fought it now. Held it under iron control as he watched her.

"That's not enough," he said. "I need to know more. I need answers." He dared her. His focus on her was absolute.

She took a deep breath and glanced away. Why was it so hard to meet his gaze? "It's all I can give, Mac. For now." Even as she said it, she knew this wasn't enough. He demanded honesty.

He wanted to trust her. She'd felt it last night when he took her, when he joined their bodies and made her feel things she'd never experienced in her long, long life. She wanted to feel those things again. Wanted him to love her enough that when she finally admitted who she was—what she was—he would have no choice but to accept.

Could he do that? Love her without knowing the truth? She'd pushed as much as she dared, but the future of the last of her kind depended on MacArthur Dugan and his brilliant mind—and on technology he hadn't even begun to create.

Once again she faced him, locked her gaze to his.

The truth hit her like a shock out of the heavens. She quickly looked away. Lies. All lies. She was lying to herself even more than she lied to Mac. This wasn't for her people. Not at all. She wanted Mac to love *her*—to know what she was and love her anyway. To love her, not as a creature from another world, but as a woman.

To love her as she already loved him.

Mac stared at her, at her perfect profile as she turned away. What the hell was going on? Damn, he wanted to trust her, but how? Why was she so damned evasive? And how could she look into his eyes with such truth and sincerity, and yet refuse to answer the simplest questions?

She stood there gently stroking Dink's bruised and battered face, and Mac's anger with Zianne shifted. Damn. This was just wrong. Dink shouldn't have had to fight to protect Mac's honor. That was Mac's job, and he'd failed miserably.

"I need a beer." He glanced at Zianne. She still watched Dink, still brushed his cheek with her fingertips, and Mac was unaccountably jealous, that she should be touching his friend and not him. "Do you want one?"

"No, thank you." She raised her head, frowning—probably at his tone of voice. "You go ahead. I'm fine."

He left her and stalked into the kitchen. They'd been as intimate as two people could be, but it was all physical. He knew nothing about her. She told him nothing, yet when he thought of sending her away, he couldn't do it.

"God damn it!" Mac slammed his palms down on the counter, trembling with rage and frustration. "Focus, Dugan." Zianne wasn't the issue. Dink getting beat up was. His future was.

Tomorrow he'd go directly to the university's chancellor. Screw the dean—if he didn't clear his name, Mac's success in the nascent yet already incestuous computer industry was screwed.

The inertia that had gripped him was gone. In its place, anger surged—so much anger Mac struggled to contain his rage. Anger at Zianne and her damned secrets, anger that his friend had been a target for Mac's problems. He grabbed a can of beer from the refrigerator and popped the top with shaking hands. He gulped a few swallows and then carefully set the beer down, took a few deep breaths, and forced a calm he really didn't feel.

Then he noticed the bloody towels and Dink's torn and bloodstained shirt lying on the floor in the front room. Mac took another deep, calming breath, stalked out of the kitchen, and gathered up the bloody mess. He stuck the towels and shirt in the kitchen sink to soak and turned on the cold water.

Taking one deep breath after another, he stared at the water as it turned from pale pink to deeper red with Dink's blood. He finished off his beer while he waited for the sink to fill. Finally, he forced his anger under control, grabbed a second cold beer, and went back to the bedroom.

Dink sat on the edge of the bed.

"What the hell are you doing?"

Dink's face was still bruised, though not as swollen. He grinned at Mac and slowly shook his head. "I vaguely remember getting in a fight and coming here. I never expected to wake up in your bed. Please tell me we, uh . . ."

Mac laughed. "Shit, man. I thought you'd be out for hours. And don't get your hopes up. Zianne and I carted your ugly carcass in here less than half an hour ago." He handed Dink the beer he'd just opened. "Here. You need this more than I do."

Dink grabbed the can from him and took a swallow. Even his split lip looked better, though the bruises along his ribs were still a mottled purple and red. "Thanks." He shook his head. "I was hurting like hell, but I feel a lot better now. Thanks for . . ." He glanced at Zianne, returned her smile, and then shot a confused look at Mac. "For whatever."

Shoving himself to his feet, Dink stood beside the bed and rolled his shoulders, as if testing for injuries. "I actually feel pretty good." He looked almost as surprised as Mac felt.

Dink had been in bad shape not that long ago. Now he looked like he'd played a rough game of football or taken a fall, not like a guy who'd been beaten half to death by thugs.

It made no sense. None at all. But neither did the reason he'd been beat up in the first place. "Dink, when you first got here, you said you thought more than Bennett was involved. What did you mean? What happened?"

Dink shook his head. "I'm not sure. I was minding my own business, having a beer at Sloan's. Bennett was drunk on his ass. He knows we're friends and he got in my face with a bunch of crap about you. I called him on it. He said you never had a shot at the grant anyway. That he had an 'inside line directly to the big bucks.' His words, not mine."

"An inside line? What the hell could he mean by that? And how'd that lead to you getting beat up?"

"A couple of older guys came over and told him to shut the fuck up. He said something to them I didn't catch, called me a fag and then threw a sucker punch I really wasn't expecting. I got up and flattened him with my first swing, but the other guys jumped in. They knew what they were doing. I don't remember much after that."

Zianne's light touch on Mac's shoulder startled him. He

jerked his head around and caught the quizzical expression in those amazing violet eyes. "Bennett's uncle is the dean of the department. Could that be Mr. Bennett's inside line?"

"Dink and I talked about that, but what's he got to gain?"

"There is a lot of money in grants for postgraduate students. Am I correct?"

Mac nodded.

"Is there enough money that the dean of the department might want to manipulate its dispersal? If he had a willing student, someone to make the application . . ." Her voice trailed off. In a stronger tone, she added, "The money is funneled through the head of each department."

Dink's eyes flashed from Mac to Zianne and back to Mac. "She's right. It makes sense, Mac. We've been assuming all along that Dean Johnson is honest. What if he's in league with his nephew? If the money is awarded to that jerk, the dean is the one in charge of disbursing it. You're only familiar with the one grant, and it's a big one. What if they're running a scam? What if they set it up so that Phil Bennett is awarded the money from numerous grants and they share the profits?"

"It's going to show up in audits, don't you think?"

Dink shrugged. "Depends on who's in charge of the audit. This university has a huge budget. There's a shitload of money going through the computer science department right now. I doubt they've got that tight a lock on who's getting what."

"And if the applications are manipulated to show that Bennett's the most deserving of the applicants, then it's conceivable he could be raking in a lot of grant monies."

Zianne interrupted Mac. "You need to get your case before someone outside of the department. Even if it means replicating the project that got you into all this trouble, it would be worth it to prove your honesty, don't you think?"

Mac nodded. "Makes sense. But how do we go about this?"

Smiling, Zianne leaned forward and kissed him. "Leave it to me. Dink? You stay here with Mac. I will return in the morning."

Still wearing nothing but Mac's old robe, she left the bedroom and walked out into the front room. Mac shot a quick, confused glance at Dink and then followed her, still frustrated by the questions she'd not answered, the things she knew, and how she knew them.

He needed answers. Now.

The room was empty. His robe lay on the couch. "Zianne? Zianne, where the hell are you?" He checked the front door. It was still bolted. The kitchen was empty. So was the bathroom.

Dink met him in the front room. "Gonna tell me about her?"

Mac sat on the arm of the sofa and shook his head. "I wish I could. She's done it again."

"Done what?"

"Disappeared. Not just as in leaving . . . I mean, she's literally disappeared. Gone without using a door or even a window, you get my drift? It's not the first time, either." He glanced at the robe lying on the couch and choked back a laugh. "Only this time she was naked."

"That's impossible." Dink sat down on the opposite end of the sofa from Mac. "You sure you're all right?"

"No," Mac said. Laughing harder, he grabbed a pillow off the sofa and threw it at Dink. "I was just about to get laid when you showed up. Not only am I sober, I'm horny and I've lost my woman. Again."

He waited for Dink's snort of laughter. When it didn't come, Mac turned and looked at his friend. Dink stared back at him for a long, silent moment. Then he sighed, and the sound was unnaturally loud in the quiet room. He didn't break the direct gaze he focused on Mac. "I'm not a woman, but I'm here for you, Mac. You know that, don't you? You've always known that."

A shiver raced across Mac's spine. Apprehension or desire? He wasn't sure, but Mac knew how Dink felt about him, how he felt about Dink. Somehow, the feelings were stronger tonight than they'd ever been. Maybe it was the fact his friend had defended him and suffered for it. Maybe it was the way Zianne confused him, or his own convoluted needs and fucked-up desires.

Whatever the reason, what had seemed uncomfortable in the past, what had felt like a line he shouldn't cross, seemed to be the right thing to do now. Tonight. The right step to take.

Zianne filled his mind, but ruthlessly he shoved her image away. He had no idea what they had, if anything. Without honesty there was no trust. Without trust, no relationship.

Honesty and trust defined what he had with Dink. Their friendship was too strong, their ties too complex to turn away from the powerful need in his friend's unspoken plea.

And, to be perfectly honest, his own need. Standing slowly, Mac held out his hand. Eyes wide with both hope and surprise, Dink slowly wrapped his fingers around Mac's.

Without a word, Mac led Nils Dinkemann into the bedroom.

6

Mac didn't know what to expect. He certainly hadn't imagined how easy it would be to cross a line he'd never crossed before, to allow himself to fall into Dink's fantasy of the two of them as lovers.

Tonight. This was only for tonight, and maybe that unspoken boundary was the reason it was so simple to slip out of his clothing and stand there, studying Dink with the knowledge the two of them could take this as far as they wanted this one time, without any regrets.

It was almost as if they'd given themselves permission to let arousal and desire rule. Dink was more uncomfortable looking than Mac. Maybe because he'd dreamed of this for so long without ever expecting it to actually happen; now that Mac was standing here naked and aroused, Dink seemed unable to proceed.

So Mac took the lead, and the moment he reached for his friend, the moment he pulled him into his arms and held him close, everything felt the way it should. It felt perfect.

They were both heavily aroused, two young men of equal

height and breadth. Dink's bruises had almost faded, which raised a question for another time. No one healed that quickly, not from the kind of injuries he'd had when he arrived.

Now his bruises were forgotten. When their chests came together, when the line of contact spread from chest to belly to thighs and the solid length of two hard cocks rode high against one another, Mac wondered why he'd waited so long to share this act, this amazing connection with his oldest, closest friend.

Dink groaned and thrust his hips close. He grabbed Mac's face in his hands and kissed him on the mouth, forcing entry with his tongue. At first Mac was uncertain—this was a guy he was kissing. Another man with callused hands, beard-roughened jaw and stubble across his upper lip, but his breath was warm and tasted of yeast and hops, and the press of his tongue tangling with Mac's had him panting and wanting more.

Dink's kisses trailed across his chest and down his belly until he fell to his knees in front of Mac. He turned his face and nuzzled the thatch of dark hair on Mac's groin and his fingers dug into the thick muscles of his butt.

Just last night, Zianne had knelt in front of Mac. She'd taken him in her mouth, but it had been nothing like this. Her touch had been gentle, feminine, and sweet. Dink swallowed him down, sucking Mac's cock, tugging at his balls with one hand, stroking the sweaty crease between his buttocks with the other.

There was no subtle, teasing foreplay with Dink. Mac felt the firm pressure of one thick finger against his ass. It was an entirely new sensation, and Dink's intent was both direct and obvious. Mac clenched tight and fought it at first, but the suction on his dick wasn't going away and he widened his stance, opening himself to Dink's exploration.

Mac tangled his fingers in Dink's thick blond hair and held him close against his groin. He struggled to master his needs, to fight the unforeseen lust shredding the last remnants of control. He'd not expected this much sensation.

Dink pushed hard and forced a finger through Mac's tight anus. Cursing, Mac clenched against the fiery burn of entry, the unexpected pain. Then Dink swallowed Mac's cock.

Too much! The wet slide down his friend's throat, that long finger probing deep and rolling across his prostate, Dink's free hand tugging and squeezing Mac's balls, his mouth and throat sucking Mac's cock like a damned Hoover. Too much, too fast.

Mac didn't even have time to savor the moment. His climax exploded hard and fast and he clutched his fingers in Dink's hair and thrust forward. Dink took him all the way, swallowing the thick rush of seed, probing deep inside Mac's dark channel and putting even more pressure on that sensitive gland.

"Shit. Holy shit, Dink . . . don't stop. Fuck, don't stop." Mac's legs gave out and he collapsed backward onto the bed, but Dink went with him, still sucking and licking his slowly shrinking cock, then licking his sac and the sensitive skin behind his balls.

It took forever to come down, and when he did, Mac caught the look of triumph in Dink's eyes and laughed. "Shit, man. That was . . . I had no idea. None. Did you plan that?"

Dink wiped his lips and stretched out on the bed beside him. "Not exactly." He laughed. "I knew if I ever got you to agree, this was what I wanted to do."

Mac rolled his head to one side and looked into Dink's eyes. "What about you?" He waved his fingers loosely in the direction of Dink's cock standing tall and proud. "What're you gonna do with that thing?"

Dink raised one eyebrow. Mac knew exactly what Dink wanted, and while he wasn't entirely sure it was what he wanted, fair was fair. "Lube, man. You'd better use a lot of fucking lube."

"Roll over." Dink stood up, and he was somehow larger now, taller and broader, and his cock was definitely more than

Mac wanted. He didn't say a word—merely rolled over so his belly was on the edge of the mattress, his ass pointing in the air.

Mac had never felt more vulnerable in his life, yet he trusted Dink. And that was the crux of the matter, wasn't it? He still didn't trust Zianne. They'd had amazing sex, but how could he have felt so connected without trust? And he had felt it—a powerful connection to a woman he hardly knew.

But thoughts of Zianne faded—his cock was rising against the rumpled blankets, but not for her. This was for Dink. Mac hadn't expected to feel so aroused, not by the thought of his buddy plowing his ass, but already he was aching and ready.

Dink disappeared into the bathroom and returned with a tube of hand lotion. "This the best you got?"

Mac gazed over his shoulder. "It's not like I make a regular habit of this."

"I know." Dink smiled, and it was so tender, the look so sweet that Mac sucked in a surprised gasp. It was easy to forget just how beautiful his friend was. "Hold still."

Mac looked forward and rested his chin on his folded arms. Dink was behind him, close enough that Mac felt the warmth from his body and the brush of wiry hair where his thighs rubbed against Mac's butt. Then Dink's hands lifted his hips, pulling him up on his knees.

The sense of vulnerability increased with his butt in the air, but he waited for Dink's intimate touch with a growing sense of anticipation, yet no solid idea what to expect.

When it came, even though he was ready, Mac's body still jerked. "It's okay," Dink said. "This stuff is cold. I'm trying to warm it in my hands." He ran his fingers along Mac's tailbone, raising shivers across his spine. Then he used one hand to separate his butt cheeks. Mac felt the blush rising over his face and chest. It was as embarrassing as it was arousing to know Dink was looking at him so closely. Even more embarrassing to know that taut little muscle back there was flexing in unexpected anticipation as Dink got him ready.

Warm fingers slowly traced the line from Mac's perineum to his tailbone. The pressure against his sphincter was a surprise, the way he reacted, the number of nerves clamoring for more. He'd never realized how sensitive he was back there, but then he'd never had anyone pay this much attention to his ass.

He closed his eyes. It was easier this way when he couldn't see the rumpled sheets where he and Zianne had been lying just a short time ago. He didn't want to think of Zianne. It somehow seemed unfair to Dink, and that was the last thing Mac wanted. If he was going to do this, he wanted it to be all about Dink.

So why did it feel as if it were all about Mac?

Dink's fingers gently rubbed a surprisingly soothing pattern back and forth over that amazingly sensitive bundle of nerves guarding his ass. Mac's balls ached, his cock felt like a steel rod slapping against his belly, and he fought his body's need to press against Dink's teasing touch and force him through that sensitive ring.

Obviously, Dink didn't need his help. Mac grunted. He hadn't planned to, but the thick finger pressed close and passed through so fast it caught him by surprise. Dink paused. "Push out," he said. "Don't fight me. I don't want this to hurt you, bud." He added another finger, and then a third, but he did it so slowly and carefully, Mac's body adjusted just fine. There was no real pain, not even the sharp burn he'd felt earlier from just one finger.

This time there were three. Crap. Dink's cock was still bigger than three fingers, but he slipped his fingers out of Mac so fast, replaced them with the head of his cock so smoothly, that he'd pressed forward and was through before Mac had time to panic, or worse, tighten up.

This time Mac didn't just groan. He moaned, a long, deep moan of absolute pleasure. There was pain, but it felt right, and he spread his knees and tilted his hips to give Dink a straighter shot. Damn, but he'd never felt stuffed so full of anything in his life, and still Dink pressed forward.

Mac's breath was stuttering in and out of his chest and Dink was groaning and cursing, a soft litany of sound that turned Mac on even more. After what felt like forever, Dink clasped Mac's hips in both hands and leaned close, so close that his breath tickled the back of Mac's neck.

"You okay? I'm not hurting you, am I?"

Mac didn't trust himself to speak. He shook his head.

"You're sure? Because I can't hold on, Mac. I need to move. This is killing me, going so slow."

Mac chuckled. Took a deep, controlling breath. "Well," he gasped, "don't let me be the one to stop you."

"Fuck you, Dugan." Laughing, Dink pulled back, and the sensation of that long, thick cock drawing almost entirely out of his ass had Mac clutching the blankets in front of him and holding on for dear life.

Then Dink slammed back in, sliding smoothly deep inside Mac. Slipping even farther than he'd gone before, pressing harder. Mac grunted and locked his knees to hold his position on the bed. Dink picked up the pace, driving deep, pulling out, going deep again with a pounding, driving rhythm that had Mac cursing in time with each thrust.

"Fuck, fuck, fuck . . ." Gritting his teeth, waiting for pain and experiencing nothing but pleasure, Mac took everything Dink had to give. Took it and reveled in the sense of connection, the purely sexual experience of getting fucked by a guy he knew almost as well as he knew himself.

Almost. Until now, Mac had never allowed himself to know this side of Dink's life. Now, with Dink taking control, with

Dink fucking him to within an inch of his life, Mac saw a new, more powerful side to his friend. Felt a new sense of connection with someone he would never again see in the same way.

It was amazing, surprising, unbelievably satisfying.

"I can't hold on, Mac. I can't . . ." Dink cried out. At the same time, he shoved Mac down on the mattress, pumping his hips forward in short, sharp jerks and then thrusting hard and deep.

Mac pressed back against Dink's rigid body and tightened his muscles around the thick, pulsing length filling him. He'd never felt so full, so connected to another man. Hadn't imagined what it would feel like as the recipient of another man's seed.

This was Dink—his oldest, closest friend, sharing something Mac had denied both of them for whatever reason. He couldn't remember now why he'd always told Dink no. Sex with Dink was unlike anything he could have dreamed. Better, stronger, more powerful—an orgasm that seemed to last forever.

And ended all too quickly. Long moments later, Mac became aware of the stickiness beneath his belly. He'd come at the same time as Dink. Shit. He hadn't expected he'd come, not taking the bottom like this, but the friction of his erect cock rubbing back and forth across the bedding, the amazing sensation of Dink plowing into his ass like they'd done this for years . . .

He let out a huge gust of air. Dink had collapsed across his back, and his chest heaved with each breath. Mac lay there, cocooned in Dink's warmth, sticky with his own release and knowing there'd be more when Dink finally pulled free, but he'd never experienced feelings like this after sex with a woman.

Was this how Zianne felt when he came inside her?

Like a vessel. He felt as if he held something precious that belonged to his friend. Mac almost laughed. Who'd have thought he'd be lying here after sex with Dink, analyzing it?

Didn't women do that? Mac rarely thought about sex. No, he usually just enjoyed it, but what he'd shared with Dink had been special. Unbelievably so. Suddenly it didn't seem important that this be a one-shot deal.

No, they'd definitely do this again.

He had no doubt Dink would want to, but he'd probably be afraid to ask. Typical of his buddy. Not so typical were the tears Mac felt against his shoulder. Dink's tears. Mac hoped they were from happiness. From the same sense of satisfaction Mac was feeling.

He reached over his shoulder, grabbed Dink's shoulder, and gave him a squeeze. "Bud? You okay?"

Dink sniffed. "Yeah. That was amazing, but what about you? I'm sorry, Mac, if I hurt you. I . . ."

Hurt me? Who's he kidding? Mac lost it. Laughter bubbled up and out of him, laughter neither he nor Dink expected. He laughed even more when he realized Dink was hard again.

Then neither one of them was laughing at all. No, they were back into that amazing rhythm, that unexpected sharing, fucking like they'd done this forever.

7

Mac rolled over, startled the moment he realized Dink was the one snuggled up against his back. Then the last few hours came surging back into his mind, and he relaxed.

Who'd have thought?

The first rays of early morning sunlight cast pale shadows against the walls. His body still thrummed with arousal, but his heart was the organ that appeared to have been affected most deeply. He loved Dink the way he'd always loved him, but it was somehow more. He'd expected to feel guilt, but there was none. No sense of dismay or discomfort over what they'd shared during the long night. It was what it was.

He loved Nils Dinkemann. Period. Maybe not in the romantic way Dink wanted, but this was still good. Damned good. Sighing, Mac rolled back to his left side. Violet eyes stared into his.

"Shit! Zianne? How the hell . . . ?"

She smiled innocently and snuggled close against his chest, sandwiching him between Dink's masculine warmth and her own feminine softness. "I didn't want to wake you."

Her soft, sexy whisper teased all Mac's nerve endings, and he was suddenly, inexplicably, aroused. Again. Dink's body pressed a bit closer behind him, and Zianne's fingers found his cock. Somewhere, deep in the sane recesses of his mind, Mac wondered if this was just some perverted fantasy, but Zianne was stroking his cock and Dink was coming to life behind him.

"I'm awake." He almost choked on his response to Zianne.

Dink's lips traced a pattern across his upper spine. "Good," he said. "Damn, Mac. How can I still be horny?"

"You're not. You're dreaming." Mac's brain sort of fizzled and short-circuited as Zianne's sweet honey and vanilla scent overwhelmed the masculine stink of semen and sweat. Dink's fingers slipped along the crease in his ass. Without thinking, Mac rolled his hips back to meet his buddy's touch.

Then Zianne's fingers tightened around his cock and he whimpered. Hell, did she even realize Dink was in bed with them? Did Dink know Zianne was here? Had anyone even opened their fucking eyes to figure out what was going on? Mac rolled over on his back with one hand on Zianne, the other on Dink. "Hold it. Both of you. Dink. Are you aware that Zianne is in bed with us? That she's playing with my cock? Zianne? Do you have any idea what Dink's planning right now?"

Zianne popped up on one elbow and brushed her hair out of her eyes. "Good morning, Dink. How are you feeling?"

Dink leaned across Mac's supine body and planted a big kiss on Zianne's full lips. "G'morning. Much better, thank you. I have no idea what you did to me last night, but it worked. I feel wonderful." Then he turned and smiled at Mac. "Good morning to you, too." He leaned over and planted a kiss full on Mac's mouth. "I know exactly what you did to me. Wanna do it again?"

Caught in what had to be the most surrealistic experience of his life, Mac kissed him back. "Shit! What the hell am I doing?"

He shoved Dink away and sat up. "Can someone please tell me what the fuck is going on?" He glared at Zianne and then at Dink, but the two of them just looked at Mac as if he were totally insane.

Maybe he was. How else could he explain the erection that was so far beyond morning wood that his mind found it difficult to contain his need? He wanted Zianne. He wanted Dink just as badly, just as powerfully, but he couldn't want both. Could he? A guy was either gay or straight—right?

Try telling that to his cock.

What the fuck was going on? Dink on one side, Zianne on the other, both of them grinning at him like he was a damned fool when he was obviously the only sane one here.

Mac consciously struggled to bring his pounding heart under control, slowed his frantic breathing, and sighed. Feeling as if the world as he knew it was crumbling around him, he took Dink's hand in his right and Zianne's in his left, anchoring himself between the two people he loved most.

Except he was furious with Zianne, right? He glanced at her, at those beautiful violet eyes, and crumbled. "What's happening? You. Both of you. Me. I don't get it."

"What's there to get, Mac?" Zianne scooted up against the headboard and touched his chin with her fingertips, forcing Mac to look at her. "We both love you. You love both of us."

He stared into those violet eyes, and the questions in his mind forced their way to the front. "I don't know you," he whispered. "How can I possibly love you?"

"How can you not?"

She was so damned sure of herself as she leaned close and kissed him. Her lips were soft and warm, her taste so sweet he groaned against her mouth. How could he not love her? She'd appeared in his life when he needed her most. While Dink had always been there for him, Zianne had come when he called.

Or so she said. Why, though, when he questioned her very

existence, did the need to know seem to fade from his mind? Who was she? *Why* was she? But her tongue was stroking the sensitive roof of his mouth and her fingers were stroking his cock. Slowly she slid back down on the bed, her lips and tongue making all his questions go away.

Dink chuckled and scooted close as Zianne pulled Mac on top of her. Mac's cock slid between her legs and then he was slipping easily inside. She was tight, her channel hot and wet, the muscles rippling along his length. He was vaguely aware of Dink moving around behind him and then intimately aware of those now familiar fingers stroking his butt, stretching his tender anal ring, making everything ready for penetration.

He sighed when Dink pressed the head of his cock against his ass, groaned when he forced his way through the tight muscle. He was still sore after all the activity last night, but when Dink surged forward, Mac went with the flow, thrusting deep inside Zianne. She smiled and he could have sworn her violet eyes were twinkling in the early morning light.

She raised her long legs, locking her heels against Dink's hips, not Mac's. Linking the three of them for a slow and easy ride as they rocked together. Passion seemed to rise like a gradual tide, an almost dreamlike sense of climax growing, arousal peaking, their bodies coming together in a soft yet glorious orgasm that tipped them gently over the edge together.

This was no frantic coupling, not a rush to the finish but instead a joining of hearts and souls that left Mac feeling satiated and quietly replete.

Zianne's body rippled around him and he felt Dink's heart thundering against his back. Easing down to one side so he wouldn't crush Zianne, Mac kissed her cheek and closed his eyes.

There was so much to think about. He'd never considered anything like this and he couldn't help but wonder how this part of his life could be so perfect while so much of it was so fucked up. Thank God for Dink, and for Zianne as well. They'd somehow managed to give him back that sense of self he'd felt was missing.

Today he'd go back to the campus. He was ready to take a stand and prove his innocence. Later. After he slept some more.

Mac heard someone moving near the bed and slowly opened his eyes. Dink had just showered. He had a towel wrapped around his slim hips and was going through Mac's closet, obviously looking for something to wear that wasn't covered in blood.

There was no sign of Zianne. "Where ya goin'?" Mac shoved himself up and leaned against the headboard.

Dink smiled at him, and there was so much love in that look that it made Mac feel guiltier than ever. "I've got a freshman class to cover for the professor. It's almost eleven."

"Did you see Zianne leave?"

Dink shook his head. "She was gone when I woke up." He sat on the edge of the bed next to Mac. "That was really something, wasn't it?" His soft laugh was filled with a sense of wonder.

Mac swallowed back a flip answer. "Definitely." Damn, he was so screwed. "Dink? You know I love you. You know I want to do this again, but . . ."

Dink tilted his head and shot a lop-sided grin at Mac. "I know, Mac. You're never going to feel the same for me that I do for you. I get that. I'm okay with it. But last night . . . this morning." Slowly he shook his head. "It's more than I ever imagined. I do hope we do it again. You okay with that?"

"You know I am." He smiled at Dink. Then he looked closer. Where were the bruises? The split lip? The black eye? "Dink? Do you have any idea how you managed to heal so quickly? I mean, you were a mess last night, and now . . ." His voice trailed off as Dink quickly stood.

"It was Zianne. I don't know how, but when she touched me last night . . ." He shrugged and moved away from the bed. "I dunno, Mac, but if you ever figure out her story, I want the details. Hey, I'm going to borrow some of your stuff, okay? I need to get moving or I'm gonna be late."

Obviously Dink wasn't ready to talk about it. Mac nodded. "Meet me at Sloan's this afternoon, okay?"

Dink nodded. "I can't get there till after four. That work for you?"

"Yeah. That's cool." Mac watched as Dink grabbed a shirt and a pair of jeans and quietly slipped out of the bedroom. Then he flopped back down on the bed. *Zianne.* All the questions he had always came back to her, but why? And why, when she was near him, did he quit asking? Shit.

She'd left last night to find something that was supposed to help him with the mess surrounding the grant, but she'd never mentioned a thing when she came back. Of course, none of them had done much talking. "Who am I kidding? The three of us didn't talk at all."

He sat there a moment longer, thinking of Zianne, thinking of Dink, but all of his thoughts merely confused him more. Finally Mac rolled out of bed and headed to the shower. His head was spinning, and it wasn't from the sex. It was spinning around the mystery that was Zianne.

It felt strange being back on campus. He should be heading to class or working in the computer lab, not walking toward the complex where the chancellor's office was. What did he have, other than suspicions?

"Mac? I was looking for you."

What the hell? "Zianne? What are you doing here?" Damn. She was so gorgeous in tight black jeans and a purple long-sleeved T-shirt. With her black hair flowing over her shoulders and those amazing violet eyes, she took his breath away.

"Like I said, looking for you." She grabbed his hand and tugged him over to a small group of tables beneath a large oak. "Now I have found you. Remember? I told you last night I had some things to check into." She smiled and sat on top of one of the tables. "When you go to see the chancellor—"

Mac interrupted. "Wait. How do you know I'm planning to see the chancellor? I haven't told anyone I was coming here."

She shrugged. He tried to remember if he'd said something, but Mac knew he hadn't. They'd been too busy screwing.

"This is important," she said. Ignoring his question, she tapped a finger against his chest. "You must tell him you were set up, that you suspect there is a scam being played out under his nose. That Dean Adam Johnson, Phil Bennett's uncle, has been collecting grant monies for years under false pretenses. That he has now involved his nephew in the scam, and if they're not stopped, they're going to bring shame on the entire university."

Suddenly his concerns didn't seem as important. "Are you sure? How do you know this? Crap." He laughed. "I'd love to tell him, but without proof, I'm afraid our dear chancellor would throw me out on my ass. With good reason."

Zianne reached into her back pocket and pulled out a thick envelope. "You cannot say where you got these papers, but they are the proof you need to catch the chancellor's attention."

Frowning, Mac took the envelope and carefully opened it. "These are bank statements. A personal account of the dean's." He raised his head and stared at her. "How did you get these?"

Again, she ignored him. "Compare the figures to this list, which is available as part of the department's fiscal records." Zianne handed him another sheet of paper.

It took only a few moments to make the comparison between the deposits of grant money into the school account, the regular payment checks made as the money was supposedly disbursed to the student of record, and matching deposits into Dean Johnson's personal account.

When he finished reading, Zianne handed more pages to Mac. Copies of checks from the dean, made out to Phil Bennett. The link was complete. Mac finally raised his head and focused intently on Zianne. "How did you get this information? How did you even know to look? The guy's obviously a crook, but you . . ."

Shaking her head, Zianne held up a hand to stop him. "I can't tell you, so please don't ask. These are copies of actual records you have received anonymously." She wrapped her fingers around Mac's. "Enough to prompt an investigation. What they find will clear your name. That's what you want, isn't it?"

He stared at the papers in his hand and then at Zianne. The questions pounded in his mind—questions he knew she wouldn't answer. "Zianne . . . I . . ." He let out a huge breath. "Thank you." Carefully he folded the papers and stuck them in the envelope. She was right. He had what he needed to at least start the investigation that could clear his name.

Then he'd clear things up with Zianne.

She leaned close and kissed him. "I'll meet you at your apartment tonight." She stood and cast a flirtatious glance over her shoulder. "I hope we'll have something to celebrate."

He watched her walk away, but celebrating was the furthest thing from his mind. Frowning, he turned away and headed for the chancellor's office.

Zianne turned and watched as Mac climbed the stairs to the office building. Her heart pounded, her palms felt dry, and there was a strange feeling in her stomach. It took her a moment to identify the sensations as fear. Not for herself, but for Mac, but it wasn't merely because he needed freedom from the dean's accusations in order to be able to help her people.

No. It was more than that. Again, that tendril of guilt tied her in knots. She wanted him free of the charges for his own sake. Not because of what he could do for her.

This was just for Mac.

She'd spent hours finding the records he needed. How could she tell him that she'd become a stream of pure energy, that she'd gone inside the bank's computer system in order to recover the information? He would look at her with disgust if he knew she wasn't human. He might still be willing to help her people, but he would never be able to love Zianne.

She hoped he could love the woman she'd become, the one he'd created with his beautiful sexual fantasy and his powerful mind. He'd never love the creature of energy she truly was.

Or could he? She wiped unexpected tears from her cheeks and wished him well. And fantasized her own special dream, of Mac knowing who and what she was, and loving her anyway.

And that was suddenly more important than it should be.

8

Mac stopped at Sloan's for a beer. He took a table in the back and sipped his brew, silently celebrating.

"Hey, Mac. I was hoping you'd still be here." Dink slid into the seat across from him. "You look like the cat who ate the canary. What's up?"

Mac raised his glass in toast. "All's right with the world, my friend, though you might want to steer clear of Phil Bennett and his merry band of idiots for a while. He's gonna be pissed."

Dink leaned back in his chair. "Tell me all about it."

"I decided to go straight to the chancellor's office. It turns out there's an ongoing investigation of Dean Johnson."

"Embezzlement, right?" Dink's grin stretched ear to ear.

"Yes and no. It appears the man's running a number of scams. One involves illegal student visas and stolen software. Another has to do with distribution of illegal drugs. The chancellor said they weren't even looking into embezzlement of grant monies. Yet. No wonder it's so hard to get an appointment with the dean. He's a busy boy." He laughed, amazed by how much his situation had suddenly improved. "Anyway, I met Zianne on campus this morning, and . . ."

"What was she doing there? She's not a student, is she?"

Mac shook his head. "Hell, I don't know and she won't tell me. But she had paperwork that proved a lot of our suspicions, and no, I have no idea how she got it. The chancellor was quite interested. He said he'd have to get warrants for the originals, but the copies told him what to look for."

"Which is?" Dink took a sip of his beer.

"An unlikely connection between the disbursement of grant monies, and like-sized checks showing up in the dean's personal account. Oh, and regular payments to his nephew."

"How the hell did Zianne get information like that?"

Mac shook his head. "No idea, and she's not talking."

Dink laughed. "Do you know anything about her other than the fact she's gorgeous and good in bed?"

"Don't go there. Whatever Zianne's secrets, they're her business." He stared blankly at Dink. "Shit. I can't believe I'm defending her. Her secrets make me crazy." Except he owed her for helping him clear his name, didn't he?

Dink gazed steadily at Mac. Finally, he exhaled, long and slow. "Never mind. Back to the chancellor. What else happened?"

"My scholarship's being reinstated. I have full access to the computer lab while the investigation is ongoing. It's been kept quiet, but he expects it to break open when the warrants are served, maybe even this afternoon."

"That soon? Wow . . . but what about the grant? You need that income, don't you?"

"I'm back in the running and there's still some scholarship money left. I'll have to replicate my project, but without the notes, it'll take me a while. He said he'd speak with the committee and make sure they gave me enough time. Dean Johnson's been pulled from it, so I don't have to go through him. If

I can replicate the project, it'll prove that Phil stole my work."

"Can you do it?"

Mac shrugged. "I think so. It shouldn't be too hard. It was a fairly simple program."

"Shit. I wonder how Zianne got the information?"

Mac stared at his beer a moment before he raised his head. "How's she do anything? How does she get in and out of my locked apartment without a key? How does she heal your injuries with merely a touch? How the hell does she know so much about me?"

"Have you asked her?" Dink sipped his beer, but he kept his gaze locked on Mac.

"I try. It's like I can't think of the questions when I'm around her. I dunno, Dink. It's freaky, but at the same time I feel like an idiot, wanting to question everything."

Dink steepled his fingers and rested his chin on their tips. "Mind control? Is she somehow controlling your thoughts?"

Mac jerked back in his chair. Then he laughed and hummed a few bars from the opening theme to *The Twilight Zone*. Dink didn't even crack a smile. Mac shook his head. "I don't know. She could be doing something. I can't get her out of my head."

He stared toward the front of the bar, at the lights beginning to come on outside, and wondered if Zianne was waiting for him at the apartment. She'd said she'd be there tonight, that maybe they'd have something to celebrate.

Just being with her. Touching her. Seeing her . . . that's all it took. There was no other explanation. No way to convince himself he was making up feelings he'd never experienced before. Mac turned his attention once again to Dink, almost afraid to say the words out loud. He sighed. He honestly didn't know if he should be laughing or crying or running for the hills. "I don't know jack shit about her. I think I love her. How stupid is that?"

Dink's smile was more sympathetic than anything else. "I

figured that much. I'd have to be blind and mentally deficient not to have guessed how you feel about her. It's all over your face." He laughed and sat back in his chair. "Shit, man. You have the same look on your face when you're with Zianne as I probably do when I'm hanging out with you."

"Aw, Dink . . ."

"No." He held his hand up. "Don't feel bad. I'm over the worst. Of course, fucking until your eyes cross tends to help."

"Fucking works." Leave it to Dink to put things in perspective. Mac toasted him with his beer. Might as well spill it all. "There's more. It's so bizarre I feel sort of stupid bringing it up, but you know the program I'm working on? Someone else has added code to it. Stuff that I never would have thought of, but it works. It makes the program better, more stable, less apt to crash."

"What do mean, someone else? You're never away from those notes of yours. They're in your backpack now, aren't they?"

"Yeah." He grabbed the pack off the back of the chair. "Right here. Always with me. There was more fresh code today. It's not in my handwriting and I haven't had a chance to test it yet, but I think it's going to fix some issues I was trying to deal with." He opened his pack and pulled out the yellow legal pad. "Look. See the different handwriting?"

He set the tablet on the table in front of Dink and waited while his friend studied what, to him, was probably incomprehensible gibberish. After a moment, Dink raised his head. "I have absolutely no idea what this shit means, but you're right. The handwriting is definitely not yours. It's actually legible."

"Thanks loads." Laughing, Mac stuffed the legal pad back in his pack. "I think it's Zianne's."

"What? Is she a geek? That's a relationship made in heaven, though she doesn't look like any geek I've ever seen. Of course, neither do you."

"Gee, thanks. Hell, I don't know, but I started noticing the additions to my work the morning after I first met her. How else do I explain it?"

"Have you asked her? Asked about her? Checked to see if she's enrolled in any classes, if she's listed in the employee registry?"

"Dink, do you even know her last name? Because I sure as hell don't."

Dink looked disgusted. "I repeat. Have you asked her?"

Mac shook his head. "No. I kept thinking I'd look at her wallet, check and see if she's got a driver's license, but she doesn't carry a purse. Do you know any woman who doesn't have a purse, or at least a backpack? No lipstick, no makeup, no hairbrush."

"No clothes, at least not this morning. Damn, she's hot."

Mac laughed. "You're not supposed to notice. You like guys. You're supposed to think I'm hot."

"I do. Damn, you know I do, but you have to admit, she's a truly gorgeous woman." He got a totally dopey expression on his face. "I mean, this morning was . . . it was . . . damn, Mac. What was that? Have you ever . . . ?"

"Hell, no. And I bet you haven't either." Mac finished his beer and stood. "C'mon. She said she'd meet me at the apartment. You coming?"

"Oh. Yeah. I'm coming. Hopefully more than once."

"Jackass."

"Love you, too, sweetheart." Dink shoved Mac's shoulder. Laughing, Mac stumbled, grabbed Dink to keep from falling, and pulled him off balance.

The sharp staccato of gunshots filled the room. Glass covering a photo on the wall behind their table shattered.

"Down!" Still hanging on to Dink, Mac threw him to the floor. They scrambled on hands and knees into a hallway that led to the restrooms.

Another burst of gunfire sent chips of wood flying over their heads. Women screamed. Someone cursed. A man shouted.

"What the fuck? What's going on?" Dink leaned toward the open doorway. Mac dragged him back.

"Idiot! Get back here. Those are real bullets."

"Shit." Dink flattened himself against the wall. A minute later, the sound of a siren grew closer and then stopped out in front. The two of them stayed hunkered down in the dark hallway, listening as law enforcement entered the bar.

"You two in the back. Police. Come out with your hands up."

"We're coming." Mac stood up and pulled Dink to his feet. That was when he noticed blood dripping from his right arm. "Shit. I must have been hit."

The police officer lowered his gun once they'd stepped out of the hallway. "My buddy's been shot," Dink said. He glanced at the pattern of bullet holes on the wall. "Crap. We were sitting right here. Did you catch whoever was shooting?"

"No." The officer shook his head and glanced at his partner questioning patrons in the front of the bar. "Whoever it was took aim from the doorway. No one got a good look. They were all too busy diving for cover."

He checked the red slash running across Mac's bicep. "Looks like it just grazed you, but I bet it hurts like a son of a bitch. You're damned lucky."

Mac's arm was beginning to throb. He caught Dink's eye. "We were just getting up to leave. I stumbled. We were screwing around. Dink shoved me; I tripped."

"And you pulled me down."

"One of us could have ended up dead."

The cop walked over to the wall and pointed to a pattern of holes in the wood paneling. "Would have been head height if you hadn't ducked." He turned and looked at both of them.

"You're right. One—or both—of you could have ended up dead."

Mac climbed the steps to his apartment. His arm throbbed, but the paramedics had treated him at the scene. He'd decided he really didn't need to go to the ER. Dink had chosen to stay.

Once the news crews showed up, he'd been in his element. Dink was definitely aiming for the right career—he came to life when someone shoved a microphone in his face. Mac, on the other hand, couldn't wait to get away once the police had gotten all they needed from him for now.

He wondered if Zianne was waiting. He hadn't meant to be this late, and his head was so screwed after the shooting that he honestly didn't know if he wanted to see her or not.

She met him at the door, her eyes filled with worry, a whispered curse on her lips when she saw the bloody bandage on his arm. When she drew him close and kissed him, Mac decided he was glad she'd waited.

And just as glad Dink hadn't come home with him tonight.

Their lovemaking was fierce, as if part of Mac realized he could have died. As if Zianne knew the same. Fulfilling and frantic, an act that left both of them gasping and shaking, bodies replete yet wanting more. Mac's mind was at ease for the first time in days, in spite of the fact someone might have tried to kill him.

The wound on his arm was completely healed.

He didn't ask Zianne how. Pulling her close against his chest, Mac nuzzled her thick, dark curls. "Thank you. Because of you, it appears I've got another shot at the grant, but it will be administered by someone other than Dean Johnson."

"I'm glad. Now you can concentrate on your work. You have much to do. It will be easier with access to the faster computers they have in the lab."

"How do you know this?" Mac brushed Zianne's hair back from her eyes. Damn those eyes. He looked into their violet depths and was lost. But not tonight. Tonight he needed answers. "How is it you know me? That you know so much about my work? I've never discussed it with you, and yet you know things."

Always she looked him directly in the eye. Always. But not now. Zianne's eyes weren't meeting his. She looked away, and he wondered what she was thinking. If Dink was right, she already knew what was on Mac's mind.

"Not yet, Mac. I promise I will answer all your questions, but not yet. Can you give me time?"

He pulled away from her, drawing her gaze until she focused on him once again. "I want to trust you, Zianne. But I feel as if you're hiding something important. Something that could be a deal breaker."

She smiled, but it was a lost and sad-looking smile. Then she gently touched his cheek with one fingertip. "Are we dealing, Mac? Is that what this is? I tell you things you might not want to know, or the deal's off? We're off?"

"Who are you, Zianne? Can you tell me that?"

This time her smile lit up her entire face. "I am the woman who loves you. The one you wanted. You called me with your dreams and gave me form. As long as I exist, I will love you."

He sighed, and yet he lacked the will to question her more tonight. Mac pressed his forehead to hers. "You're talking in riddles again, but it's been a long day and I'm too tired to figure out what you mean. God help me, woman, I love you, too. Will you be here in the morning?"

She tilted her chin enough to kiss his lips. "No. But I will return by evening. And I will help you with your project, if you'll let me. I have some ideas you might like."

"You've been helping me all along, haven't you?"

She shrugged and glanced away. "Yes. But unlike that other woman with the fake red hair, I will never steal your work."

"What?" He grabbed her shoulders and forced her to look at him. "How do you know about that? What do you know?"

She nibbled on her bottom lip, the way she did when she was nervous. "I know that the one named Jen ripped pages from the tablet while you slept, and that the other, Phil Bennett, stole the soft disks filled with your notes. I cannot tell you how I know, but . . ."

"I know. If you tell me you'll have to kill me."

She frowned so seriously, Mac burst into laughter. "I'm teasing." He rolled over on his back and brought Zianne with him. "Some day, you're going to tell me how you know this stuff. I know one thing, though. You're a computer nerd at heart."

She sprawled across him, all warm and womanly, rested her chin on her folded arms and gazed into his eyes. "You have no idea, MacArthur Dugan. No idea at all."

"You're not kidding," he said. Then he kissed her, and once again put his questions aside.

9

Zianne carefully slipped from beneath Mac's heavy weight. Sitting beside him on the rumpled bed, she watched him sleep. She clasped her hands tightly and rested them in her lap. It was the only way she could keep from brushing the tangled strands of dark blond hair away from his face.

Would she ever have enough of touching him? Of loving him? She hated the lies. Hated holding back who and what she really was, but the elders stood fast on this point, even though Zianne no longer agreed with them. She'd told them Mac's suspicions were close enough to the truth, and he appeared more curious than disgusted. Still, so close now, they feared his reaction.

Mac demanded the truth. Zianne wanted him to know. She hated pushing his questions away, controlling his ability to question her, but was her desire purely selfish? Would the truth end what had been the few surviving Nyrians' best chance at freedom since the Gar destroyed their world?

Was it so selfish of her to want what Mac offered? Love, a chance at a real life—even if it meant forsaking immortality?

Yes. No. She closed her eyes, surprised by the quick burn of tears. She would not forsake her people. No matter how much she loved Mac, her feelings were unimportant when held up against the needs of her entire race. Sighing, almost certain this strange human heart was breaking, Zianne shimmered into a column of pure energy and disappeared.

Where the hell did Zianne go during the day? Mac studied his notes, including some new additions from Zianne, and wondered if it really mattered. She was absolutely brilliant, the way she took his ideas and expanded on them. He didn't mind working nights for results like these.

Zianne had no concept of rules, of what should and shouldn't work, thank goodness. No, she merely knew what *would* work, and between the two of them, they were already doing some amazing stuff.

"At least I know you're not a vampire." He muttered it as a joke, but realized he was glad he could toss that worry aside. He'd seen her in broad daylight a couple of times, and while it sounded pretty stupid, he was relieved. Still, he wished he could get the damned theme from *The Twilight Zone* out of his head.

Or thoughts of Area 51, courtesy of Dink.

He glanced at the clock. It was almost time to meet Dink and Zianne at Sloan's for dinner. Dink had been looking into the investigation on campus, and Mac was anxious for news.

Once the warrants had been served, the dean had been arrested. Of course, he'd immediately made bail, but Dink was closely following Dean Johnson's legal hassles. His investigative techniques were sometimes unorthodox, but he'd discovered stuff even the police hadn't known to look for.

Mac wondered what else, if anything, Dink had found. Tucking his notepad and disks into his backpack, Mac slung the bag over his shoulder and headed down the stairs.

Dink and Zianne waited on the sidewalk. "What are you guys doing here? I thought we were going to meet at Sloan's?" Mac took Zianne's hand, tugged her close and kissed her. He wrapped an arm around her waist and tucked her close against his side.

"Zianne was just headed up to your apartment. I was early, so I grabbed her. By the way, I'm buying." Dink tossed the invitation over his shoulder as he headed toward the bar.

Now that was unexpected. Mac laughed. "You? What's the catch? I know it's not out of the goodness of your heart."

"Enjoy the moment, my friend. You're spending an evening in the company of Channel Three's new morning beat reporter."

"You're shittin' me! Really? They're actually going to turn you loose in the City by the Bay? With a cameraman and a mic?" Laughing, Mac caught up to Dink, shook his hand and pulled him into a hug.

"Yep!" Dink hugged him back before turning away to grab Zianne. He wrapped his arms around her and planted a big kiss on her mouth. "The news director called this morning. Said he liked the way I handled myself on the air when I got interviewed after the shooting. I've been sending them updates on what's happening with the investigation since, and their reporter's been in touch. I told him a week ago that news reporting was my goal. They've got a spot opening up in a couple of weeks and asked if I was interested. I don't even have to interview."

"Dink, that's wonderful." Zianne hugged him again. "But the job is in the city. That's a long way."

He kissed her cheek. "I'll need to get a place in San Francisco. I'll be low man on the roster, mostly working their cable channel, but it's a start."

They'd reached the bar. Mac opened the door. "After you,

news guy. When you're rich and famous, will you still remember your lowly friends?"

Dink snorted. "You're kidding. If anyone here ends up rich and famous, I imagine it'll be you and Zianne, especially now that you're working together. C'mon. Let's eat. You can tell me what new stuff you're building. You know I'm expecting something capable of blowing up the known universe."

"Not yet," Zianne said, laughing. "That's next week."

Mac glanced at her and sighed. He trusted her, and yet he couldn't help but wonder. When he really thought about what they'd developed in just a matter of weeks, their concepts and ideas were so alien, so unheard of, that Mac wondered where they came from.

He'd come up with a basic concept, but Zianne would run with it. Mac followed her lead but they worked together, taking the programs as far as they could. Mac thought of himself as the nuts and bolts guy. Zianne's job was fine-tuning the software. Her abilities were incomparable.

Their work had quickly drawn a lot of attention. Government attention, which meant large sums of money in their future, yet Mac still knew nothing about her. He knew he loved her, but even that powerful emotion was clouded in questions—questions that remained there, hovering in the back of his mind, as if their noise had been muted, as if his need to know wasn't strong enough for him to risk alienating Zianne.

What the hell was she doing to him? He might as well be bewitched. He raised his head and caught her watching him with a sad little smile on her lips.

And once again, Mac realized he didn't need answers. Not now. He leaned over and kissed her, and the three of them found a table in the back of the crowded bar.

It was the same table where he and Dink had sat not so long ago, the night they'd almost been shot. Mac glanced at Dink. "Recognize this spot?"

"Yeah. At least they patched the holes in the walls."

"The guy's still out there. They haven't caught him yet."

Zianne glanced from Dink to Mac. "This is the same table where you were shot?"

"Yep." He glanced around, but the place was full. "There's no place else to sit. You okay with it?"

"I guess." She smiled at him. "As long as you are."

He thought about it and realized he was fine. The attack seemed like it had happened to someone else, and in a way, it had. He'd changed since then. His entire life had changed, and it was all for the better.

After dinner, they headed back to Mac's. He glanced at Dink, walking next to Zianne, laughing at something she'd said. Damn, he was going to miss him, but it was probably for the best. He loved Dink, but not the way Dink needed to be loved. Maybe once he got to San Francisco he'd find a guy who put him first. A romantic kind of love, not just a best friend who happened to swing both ways.

"Damned light's burned out again." Mac stopped at the bottom of the stairs to his apartment. "Can you guys see okay? I can go up for a flashlight."

"It's fine. Just don't let go of the handrails." Zianne went on ahead. Dink was right behind her.

"You can trust me. I'll catch anyone who falls." Laughing, Mac took up the rear, but it was like walking into a damned cave going up to the fourth floor. He stuck his key in the door.

It clicked open before he had a chance to turn the key in the lock. "That's weird. Must have forgotten to lock it this morning." He reached in and flipped on the light as he opened the door enough for Zianne to walk in ahead of him.

She screamed. Mac grabbed her arm and pulled her back as two men rushed them. Dink swung at the first guy and connected, but the huge man barely responded to the impact. Instead he cursed, shifted to one side, and punched Dink in the midsection.

Dink went down hard as Mac grappled with the second man. Someone on the floor below shouted. Mac couldn't tell what he said—he was too busy trading blows with his assailant. The guy was strong, though, and fighting scared. It took a few punches, but Mac's fist finally connected with his jaw and he toppled.

Spinning around, Mac kicked at the one who'd just punched Dink. He missed the man's soft belly and connected with his thigh, but it was enough to make him stumble. Mac grabbed him by the collar and planted his fist in the man's face, but he twisted out of Mac's grasp and broke free. Blowing hard, with blood running from his nose, the guy crouched beside Dink's supine form with a knife clenched in his right hand.

Blood poured from a wound in Dink's belly. Mac's gaze flashed from the bloody knife to his bleeding friend. He glanced up just as the thug came at him with the knife. The flash of the blade caught Mac off guard, but he twisted out of the way just in time. Grunting with the missed attack, the guy shoved past Mac and raced out the door.

Somehow, in the dark, he must have missed the step.

Mac heard the scream as he went over the railing. The solid thud when he hit the ground had a sickening, final sound to it, but there was no time to appreciate the victory. The one Mac had knocked down was up again, coming right at him. He was big, but he moved fast.

This one didn't bother with a knife. He whipped out a gun, but before he had a chance to fire the thing, what looked like a bolt of lightning slammed into him. He screamed, dropped the gun, and fell to his knees. Stunned, Mac backed away as the crackling energy circled the man like a flaming rope and dragged him out the door.

Another scream, another dull thud as the body hit the ground four floors down. Mac fell to his knees beside Dink, blotting the impossible out of his mind. There was no time to consider what he'd just seen, not now with blood pouring from a deep knife wound in his friend's belly. Mac applied pressure, but it was obvious a main artery had been severed. Hot blood pumped out between his fingers.

"Zianne? Where are you? Can you apply pressure? I need to call nine-one-one."

"I'm here, Mac." She fell to her knees beside Mac. "Oh, Dink. Poor baby." She glanced at Mac, took a deep breath, and softly whispered, "Please, Mac. I love you. Don't hate me."

He didn't have a chance to respond. Zianne disappeared. Mac was blinded once again by a crackling bolt of pure energy, a flash of searing light that filled the room before it coalesced into a miniature tornado and dove deep inside Nils Dinke-mann.

Stunned, Mac sat back on his heels and stared at Dink. Light seemed to flicker behind his closed eyelids, and his horrible wound closed as Mac watched. Dink's blood had pooled on the floor around his body, but even that blood was disappearing, flowing in reverse as if something sucked every drop back inside. He'd almost bled out—now Dink's color was returning, his chest rising and falling slowly as he took first one breath, and then another.

Sirens wailed in the distance, but Mac didn't move. He couldn't. What he watched was impossible, and yet the questions he'd not been able to ask were finally making a strange and horrible sense.

Zianne. The question really wasn't who she was, but *what* she was. And no matter what, she was saving Dink's life. In so many ways, she'd saved Mac's as well. He'd give her time. Give her a chance to explain. This would all make sense. It had to.

Most of the blood was gone. Dink's eyelids fluttered but

didn't open. A flash of light surrounded his body and then Zianne was sitting beside Mac. Not a hair mussed, her clothes only a bit rumpled from the first few seconds after the attack.

"That was you," Mac said. He glanced over his shoulder. "You threw the second guy over the railing."

She nodded. "The first one, too, but I hadn't shifted yet."

"Pretty impressive." He glanced at her and almost laughed at the confusion in her eyes. "Ya think maybe you can answer some of my questions tonight? Without making me forget to ask them?"

She lowered her gaze and stared at her clenched fingers. "I promise I will answer all your questions."

"Good." Mac heard voices and glanced over his shoulder. A crowd was beginning to gather at the open door. His neighbors, the apartment manager. He heard the sound of doors slamming and knew the police had arrived. Probably an ambulance. He wondered if either of the guys on the ground needed medical care.

Probably not.

Dink stirred. Mac touched his fingertips to his forehead. "You okay, buddy?"

"I dunno." Frowning, he ran his fingers over his belly. "What happened?"

"A couple of thugs were waiting for us in the apartment. One of them . . ." He glanced at Zianne. "Punched you really hard." He touched the pink flesh on Dink's belly that had been a mortal wound only moments ago. "I'll tell you about it later. After the police leave."

Dink frowned. "After?"

Mac nodded and glanced at Zianne. Her violet eyes were swimming in tears. He realized he'd never seen her cry before. There was so much he didn't know, but he'd find out later. After the police left. "Yeah. For now, all the police need to know is that we were attacked by those two guys in my apartment, and we fought them off. They went over the railing during the fight. And Dink? For what it's worth, you were right. Zianne's one hell of a healer."

He turned and smiled at her. The surprise in her violet eyes was almost his undoing. What had she expected? That he'd run screaming in fear? He leaned close and kissed the shock right off her lips. "I love you, Zianne. No matter what."

And then he rose to his feet as armed police officers dressed in SWAT gear barged through the open doorway.

10

Mac scrubbed at the bloodstains in the carpet while Zianne and Dink righted the furniture and cleaned up the mess they'd made fighting off their assailants. "Too bad you can't remove stains as well as you heal wounds, Zianne." He glanced her way.

Zianne merely looked at him, lifted an eyebrow in Dink's direction, and shrugged.

"Oh." Mac ducked his head and concentrated on the stain. Obviously there were many things she could do. Things she wasn't comfortable sharing with Dink, no matter how close they were. The moment he'd made the decision to keep Zianne's secret—whatever it was—to himself, he knew he'd made the right choice.

"Crap. Is there any place the cops didn't dust for prints?" Dink headed into the kitchen carrying a wadded-up roll of filthy paper towels and cleaning spray.

Mac sat back on his heels. "They want everything they can get to build a connection between organized crime and one of the dean's scams. These two might be direct links to the counterfeit student visas, according to the detective. He recognized one of them and thinks prints will ID the other."

"Dead direct links, thank goodness. Bastards." Dink tossed the dirty towels and rinsed his hands in the sink. He turned and leaned against the counter. "At least now you can see why they were able to beat the hell out of me in that fight at Sloan's."

"We got lucky," Mac said. He hadn't told Dink about Zianne's part in the fight. Another secret, but he really had no choice.

Dink shoved away from the counter. "As much as I'd like to stay with you guys tonight, I've got an early ride into the city tomorrow. I think I've used up all my adrenaline, because I'm really tired. I'm going to head home."

Mac quickly glanced at Zianne and bit his lips to keep from laughing at her innocent expression. Adrenaline was the least of what Dink had used tonight. If he were a cat, he'd be working on his ninth life. Mac pushed himself to his feet. "I'm beat, too. Hell of a way to celebrate your new job. I'm sorry."

"I'm not." Dink swaggered over to Mac. "We got rid of the bad guys, right? Just think of what might have happened if I hadn't been here tonight. Who'd have saved your ugly butt?" Laughing, he added, "I just wish I could remember the fight. Thanks. Whatever you did, thank you."

"You got in a couple of punches before you went down." Mac felt his throat tighten. Damn but he was going to miss this guy.

"Well . . ." Dink glanced from Mac to Zianne. "At least I'm not going to be that far away." He sighed and wrapped his arms around Mac. "Damn, I'm going to miss the hell out of you guys."

Mac hugged him back. "I'll miss you, too, Dink. We've never been apart, not since we were, what? Seven?"

"Yep. Second grade, when my parents got busted and social services stuck me in the same foster care with you. We've been through a lot together. These last few weeks . . . they've been the best. I love you, Mac. Good luck." His eyes shimmered as he turned and pulled Zianne into a warm hug. "Take care of him for me, okay? He loves you. Don't hurt him."

Zianne kissed Dink and rested her arms loosely on his shoulders. "I will take care of him. You have my promise. Don't forget to come back here. I've learned there is nothing I love more than two gorgeous men in bed with me."

"That works for me, too." He took a deep, shuddering breath. His eyes glistened. "I need to get moving."

"Good luck." Zianne kissed his cheek one more time. "Let us know what time to watch for you on the television."

Dink paused at the open door and tipped a salute. "If you figure out a way to raise the ratings, a little help wouldn't be remiss."

"Gotcha." Mac laughed. "I'll have Zianne get right on that."

"You do that."

Then Dink closed the door behind him and was gone.

Mac turned and leaned against it. Sighing, he locked gazes with Zianne. "I'm really going to miss him, but this is the right thing for Dink. It's time for him to make his break. As for us? Whatever you have to say . . ." He studied her closely. Noted the tension around her lips, the slump to her shoulders, as if she'd already given up. "I want you to know that I love you. Just promise me something, okay?"

She stood alone in the center of the room and faced him as if she were staring at a firing squad. "I will promise you anything, Mac."

"No lies. No head tricks. You will tell me everything. You know everything there is to know about me. I want the truth about you, Zianne. You can't build a relationship on a foundation of lies. Without a strong foundation, we have nothing. So that's the deal. If you want us to last . . ." He shrugged. "All of it. Understood?"

"Yes. I promise, Mac."

She looked so guilt-stricken that it took everything Mac had not to pull her into his arms and tell her it was all okay. It wasn't okay. He realized he didn't care who or what she was, but he had to have honesty. He had to know the truth.

Tears glistened on her cheeks. He held out his hand. She took a step toward him. He stepped closer to her. When their fingers met, he tugged and she came to him, wrapping her arms around his waist, burying her face against his chest and sobbing as if her world had ended.

Maybe it had. He hoped not. He wanted to see this as a beginning, as a new start for the two of them. He lusted after Zianne. That was a given. He loved her sense of humor, her quick smile, and the brilliant mind that was constantly miles ahead of his. He honestly loved her as much as he liked her, but Mac knew he needed more.

He needed to know the real woman behind the one he loved, the one who made him laugh and challenged his mind. The image of that flash of pure energy, a deadly lightning bolt dragging their assailant to his death, slipped boldly into Mac's thoughts. He pushed it aside. He had no doubt that was a part of Zianne, but there was more. Much more.

He peeled her arms from around his waist and led her to the couch. Sat down beside her and took both of her hands in his. Looked into those violet eyes still swimming in tears, and gave her an ultimatum. "Only the truth, Zianne. Nothing else."

She sighed. Bit her lips and closed her eyes. Then she looked at him, pulled her hands free of his, and folded them in her lap. "First of all," she said. "I'm not really human."

Mac burst out laughing. "No shit, Sherlock. Now tell me the stuff I don't know."

* * *

"But how?" Zianne felt as if her heart, that strange organ that constantly rumbled in her chest, thundered now, as if it had leapt into overtime. "How did you know?"

"Sweetheart, I may be a bit of a geek, but I'm not entirely stupid about women."

Mac cupped her face in his big, warm hands and looked at her with such loving acceptance, Zianne felt sick. "I didn't come here to lie to you," she said. "That was not my intent, but I couldn't tell you the truth because you would have refused to help me." She swallowed back the horrible lump in her throat. That was the main drawback with this human form—there were so many physical reactions connected to the emotions that seemed to be connected to every thought, every action. Some of them were good, others just created more misery.

"You don't know that." He kissed her and slowly pulled his hands away from her face. "Now tell me. Everything."

"I hardly know where to begin, but I have an idea that will help. I must ask your permission. Will you open your mind to me? I can read your thoughts, but I want you to see mine. It should help you understand, if you can see what I'm thinking."

"Show me how."

His eyes were so blue. So trusting. She linked with him, going into his mind as gently as she knew how. His eyes went wide. A perfect smile of surprise spread across his beloved face.

"I feel you."

Good. Do you hear me?

Holy shit! I do.

Can you see what I'm showing you? Do you have a visual?

Oh. My. God. He raised his head and stared at her with a look of absolute wonder in his eyes.

Excellent. You must see everything I show you, if you are to understand. This is the world I came from. A world that no longer exists. And that, my beloved MacArthur, is why I need you so terribly.

He'd loved science fiction as a kid. Grew up on *Star Wars* and *Star Trek*. He'd even been hooked on *Lost in Space*. He loved to play video games and he'd always hoped he'd never outgrow his sense of wonder, but what Zianne was showing him with the power of her mind went entirely beyond anything Mac had ever imagined.

This was not some Hollywood set or a screen with amazing graphics. This was Zianne's home.

A home she'd just said no longer existed. He grabbed both her hands, surprised by how icy they felt. He squeezed them and looked into those gorgeous violet eyes. "My mind's as open as I know how to make it. Now tell me everything. Show me."

She nodded. Then she changed everything Mac had imagined another world would look like. The image in his mind grew sharper, an unbelievable landscape of sparkling stone, of flowing rivers that were streams of multicolored liquid. Lights flickered everywhere. On the ground, in the air, clinging to the sides of strange structures that might be plant life of some sort. He wasn't sure how he knew, but he recognized the flashes of light as Zianne's kind. These were her people.

"We are called Nyrians. We are creatures of pure energy. We originated on the world you see, many, many light-years from your Earth, long before your world existed. Much of our history has been lost. Our legends say we are children of the sun, fathered by the star our planet revolved about, though we may have had corporeal bodies at one time. Now all that is solid about us is a physical soul of pure carbon, a substance you call diamond. By the time I came into existence, we were nothing more than pure, sentient energy with a diamond at our center.

What you saw when I went into Dink's body? That's me when I'm not in a body like this."

She glanced down at her long legs and shrugged, almost as if she were embarrassed. "Our planet was alive and her name was Nyria. We, her people, were proud of our heritage as the offspring of a sentient planet and a star, but that pride may have been our downfall. Eons ago, we were visited by another race. At first we welcomed the Gar—strange, bipedal creatures we were able to communicate with telepathically. They showed interest in learning about us and knowing about our world. What we didn't realize is that they used our fascination with them to seduce us, so that when they invited us, we willingly chose to enter their star cruiser."

There was a long silence until, in a soft whisper, Zianne said, "Once they had as many of us aboard as they needed, the Gar destroyed our planet. Our world was lost; millions of her souls—our family, our friends, our Nyria—disappeared."

Mac jerked, blinking at the image that filled his mind. He'd not expected the horrible sight of her planet and her people exploding into a fiery ball—he was seeing Zianne's last view of her world—a view she'd had from a portal within the alien ship.

She tugged her left hand free of Mac's grasp to wipe at the tears streaming from her eyes. He'd been so caught up in the violent destruction, in Zianne's emotional reaction at the thought of so many deaths, he hadn't noticed she was crying. Tugging a clean handkerchief from his pocket, Mac pressed it into her hand.

"Thank you." She sighed, wiped her streaming eyes, and twisted the fabric in both fists. After a moment, she seemed to gather her composure. "We had not realized that our visit, fueled by curiosity, would leave us stranded as slaves aboard the Gar's ship. We no longer had a home to return to. The Gar wanted our energy. Their scientists had figured out how it could be tapped to run their ships. Now we power their engines, all life support, the intricate ecosystem that keeps the Gar alive." She shrugged once again. "Their home world is gone as well, polluted beyond recovery. It can no longer support life."

"But where do you get your energy?" Mac's mind was spinning as he remembered how Zianne had looked, streaking inside Dink. And before, when she'd dragged the guy out of his apartment and tossed him over the railing. "You can't constantly produce without feeding on something."

"Originally, we drew our energy from our sun, but once the Gar enslaved us, we learned to pull it from distant stars, from the inhabitants of the sentient worlds we passed during our travels. Human energy is an amazing source of power."

Images filled his mind and he saw what had to be the inside of the alien star cruiser. It was too bizarre for words. "You're able to come here. Why haven't all of you escaped?"

She was wringing the handkerchief between her hands now. He felt her tension, the frustration she and her people must live with all the time. "The Gar have taken our souls. If we go too long without the diamond, we will die. At the beginning of each shift, they remove that crucial bit of carbon that links us together as a people, and they store it until we have used up our available energy. When we go back to our cells, when our shifts end, the diamond is returned. Half of our people are always providing energy, but they do it without their souls."

She took a deep breath and he saw the huge engine rooms deep within the bowels of the alien ship, the arcs of pure energy that kept everything running. Zianne's brethren.

"How is it you can be here with me?"

She shrugged again. Such a human gesture. How did she know to act human? How did she have this form, this body, this very human set of values and fears?

"Your mind called me. I felt you far, far from your world."
She smiled, reached up, and ran her fingers across his lips. He
kissed her fingertips and inhaled the sweet scent of honey and
vanilla—a scent, he'd quickly discovered, that was also her
most intimate flavor.

"I recognized your unique strength and followed the signal
of your mind. Once we found an orbit around your sun and we
began to drink from that powerful star, I was able to strengthen
the link I'd forged with you. The more I studied you, the more
I learned. You humans create an amazing form of energy tied
directly to your reproductive abilities, an energy so powerful I
can take this form merely from the power of your thoughts."

Her image blossomed in his mind, but it was a visual from
the very first night he saw her. Naked, on her knees in the
shower, taking his cock in her mouth. Mac burst out laughing.
"You're saying my sexual fantasy is what brought you here? I
imagined the perfect woman sucking my cock, and you popped
into my shower?"

She raised her eyes and nodded with an almost sheepish expression on her face. "I was actually in your apartment a bit
earlier. Your fantasizing with Dink gave me form."

"Oh, Zianne. Dear God, but I love you." He grabbed both
her hands in his again. He wanted her with an ache that went
beyond anything he'd ever known. An ache that was centered
in his heart and soul. He leaned close and kissed her. Tasted the
sweet honey and vanilla of her lips. "What do you need from
me? How can I help? That's why you're here, isn't it? Because
somehow you think I can help?"

Her beautiful violet eyes, no longer awash in tears, sparkled.
She nodded. "You already are. The programs we're developing
are the beginning. Not only have you called me through space
with your amazing mind, you have brought me through time.
The ship circles your sun both many miles and many years

from us. When I leave you each morning, I return through the time slip that links me to the ship, fully recharged after being with you and able to cover my shift of work. The nights I don't come to you are the nights I must connect with my soul, or I will die."

"But the risk . . . what if you're found out?"

She leaned close and kissed him, but she pulled away before he could deepen it. Probably a good idea. It was so easy to get off track with Zianne.

"I am very careful, and my abilities appear to be growing the longer I am connected to you. Because I had such a powerful link to you, my people chose me as their emissary, as the one to help you create the programs that would aid in our escape. You and I are working on them now, but much will depend on your world's technology growing more sophisticated, and that is something our software is already speeding up. I know, from the future I've seen, that you will succeed. It's going to take many years." She laughed. "It's also going to take much of your currency, but money will never again be a worry for you."

Mac's mind spun on overload; Zianne's images spilled into his head, illustrating the unbelievable story she'd spun. How she found the information about the dean and when she'd added to Mac's scribbled notes. Impossible, and yet he had to believe her. With the visual proof burning itself into his mind, with the unexplainably complex work they'd completed over the past weeks and the answers to questions he hadn't known to ask suddenly falling into place, it was all beginning to make sense.

And Zianne was right. Money was not an issue. The interest in their work was already coming with promises of more money than he'd ever dreamed. None of their ideas were close to marketable at this point, but Mac's reputation as a talented and innovative software developer was growing.

"How far in the future are we talking, Zianne? When will this rescue take place?"

"Almost twenty of your years from now."

"Twenty years! Shit, Zianne. I'm twenty-six now. I'll be in my forties by then. Isn't there any way to make it happen sooner?"

She shook her head and looked at him as if she were trying to explain things to a child. "It's difficult to explain. When I leave you, I am there, in that time. It's a new century in your world. There will be many changes between now and then, but we did not arrive in your orbit until that new century had begun. In 2012, to be exact. And it will take that long for your world's technology to mature to the point where we can expect a rescue to succeed."

She leaned into him and he wrapped his arms around her slim body. She felt warm and alive, and so damned real. How could he think of her as something fabricated out of fantasy?

"I am real, Mac. I'm flesh and blood. I have a mind and a conscience. I have felt so much guilt over my lies to you, the things I didn't think I could tell you, but I was afraid you would send me away, that you'd just think I was a freak. I hope you'll forgive me."

How could he not forgive her? Not if he believed her amazing story. Mac realized there wasn't a shred of doubt—not after what she'd shared—but he still needed answers. "Why didn't I question your existence? I'm not stupid, but you appeared in my shower, wrapped those gorgeous lips of yours around my cock, and I just accepted you. Were you controlling my mind? That bothers me. What did you do?"

She shook her head against his chest and he held her closer. "I'm not strong enough to completely control your mind. I used your desire not to know the truth about me. You doubted my existence from the beginning, but you didn't really want to know the details. I used that desire and strengthened it with just the slightest push. You wondered, but your need not to know something you couldn't accept was stronger than your desire for the truth."

He thought about that a moment. She was right. He'd been terrified he might learn something about her he couldn't deal with. "You nailed it. I hope you're happy."

When she frowned, he kissed her nose. "I'm teasing you. You're right. I didn't want to learn anything that would make you leave me. You're not going to leave, are you?" He leaned away and forced her to meet his gaze. "Does this mean I've got you for the next twenty years?"

She turned and straddled his hips. "I'm not going anywhere. Your sun is a great source of power, and the Gar are happy to stay in one place for a while. I've been able to slip in and out of the ship without too much risk. They actually have no idea how many of us there are, which makes it easy to confuse them with our numbers."

"But you're here without your soul. What if they leave while you're with me?"

"If I couldn't return in time, I would die." She sighed and kissed him. "Don't worry. My people can contact me. The signal is faint, but I would have time to return to the ship. There's no reason to think they'll be leaving. The main thing is to get the programs ready and the antennae built in time."

"What antennae?"

She grinned at him. "The antennae you're going to use to call my people here. We'll need a small group of men and women with very powerful minds—minds capable of broadcasting physical images via your antennae that are explicit enough to give form and substance to the other Nyrians aboard the Gar's ship."

"How come you don't need an antenna to hear me?"

"Because you, MacArthur Dugan, are one in a billion. Your

wonderful mind reached me in space, many light-years beyond the far side of the sun. You called me. Pulled me to this place and this time, and when I told my people about you, they were able to, well, shall I say, persuade the Gar to come this way."

"I love you, Zianne. Whatever you need, I'll do my best. If you're beside me, I don't think there's anything that can stop us."

"Love is an emotion Nyrians feel. I can honestly say I love you, too, Mac."

He looked at her, at the fantasy woman he'd created, and wanted more. "Show me who you really are, Zianne. I want to see your natural form. Will you show me?"

She stared at him from eyes gone wide, pools of amethyst that tugged at his heart. But then she stepped back, out of his embrace, and shimmered into a million sparkling lights. As Mac watched, the lights spun in a mesmerizing circle, drawing together into a single bolt of sparkling energy.

She pressed against him and covered him in light. He felt a sharp tingle—not really pain, but a feeling akin to static electricity that fired his nerve endings and had his hair standing on end.

Then she slipped inside, her shimmering energy melding with his cells, becoming, for that moment in time, a part of him. There was no way to describe it, no way to understand feelings so entirely alien, yet so unbelievably seductive, a connection unlike anything he'd ever experienced.

A few seconds later, Zianne stood in front of him as if she'd never changed. As if she'd not just rocked his world with more possibilities than Mac ever could have dreamed.

She kissed him. Her lips were soft and warm and oh so human. As they kissed, Mac's head filled with alien images of such amazing clarity, of such fascinating form and shape, that he felt as if he traveled the stars within Zianne's mind.

His body still shivered from their melding. His heart thundered in his chest as he pulled her even closer.

Twenty years. He could do this. Twenty years working beside Zianne with her people's freedom as their goal. Twenty years of heaven, and then, hopefully, the rest of his life with Zianne—his fantasy come to life.

TAKEN BETWEEN

CRYSTAL JORDAN

1

It was time to put up or shut up.

A spurt of adrenaline flooded Kira's veins, and she felt a feral smile pull at her lips. Her fangs pricked at her flesh, and she ran her tongue down one long canine to the wicked point.

The fox-shifter within her easily caught the scent of the man she wanted. He was a Between, like her. A shape-shifter. Max Delacourt. The rich masculine scent of human male edged with the animalistic scent of a red wolf. It was a smell she knew as well as her own, one she'd craved for far too long. And she would have him. Soon. Whether he knew it or not.

She was through waiting. Tonight she would have him.

A low moan sounded through the door she stood guard beside, and she smoothed her expression into a professional mask. If anyone knew how to wear a professional mask, it was her— she'd learned from her butler father. No one could poker-face like a butler born and bred in England.

Kira's replacement turned a corner in the hallway to walk toward the royal suite. The Between king and his fiancée had been closeted inside for the seven hours since Rhiannon had returned to the palace. Kira had to work to smother a smile. King Elan hadn't been able to hide his impatience to have Rhiannon back in the island nation of San Amaro. He'd barely managed to slam the door in his Guards' faces before the carnal sounds of mating had begun filtering into the hall.

In many ways, it was a relief to have Rhiannon here instead of running her health club in Oregon. The stubborn woman had insisted that she didn't need to be followed around by security guards if she wasn't royalty yet, so Kira had had to arrange for more covert means to assure the future queen's safety. As second in command of the King's Guard, Kira had been pulling double duty for months taking care of her normal job assignment, plus handling her unspoken position as the head of the future Queen's Guard.

With all the details of her business tied up and the wedding the next day, Rhiannon was on San Amaro to stay. Finally. The only person happier about that than Elan was Kira. No more juggling jobs for her. No more pretending. She was openly in charge of Rhiannon's security detail, which would officially become the Queen's Guard after the wedding ceremony.

"Everything okay?" Her replacement for the next guard rotation stopped in front of her, his face serious.

They both froze when a pleasured female scream echoed out of the king's room. Using every one of the skills she'd learned at her father's knee, Kira cleared her throat. "Yes. Everything's going just fine."

"So it seems," the man quipped, a faint grin on his face.

Kira clapped him on the shoulder as she headed down the hallway. "Enjoy your evening. Or something."

He snorted, and she glanced back to see him settling into place beside the door. Good.

Pushing open a side door, she stepped out into the cool night. The sea breeze off the Pacific carried the hints of salt and open water, mixing with the deeper scents of garden blooms and the people on the island. Even as the familiar environment encouraged her to relax, she did an automatic sweep of the area to make sure that the palace was as secure as it should be. They'd had several serious threats against the king's life recently—one in particular that had the entire Guard on alert—and it paid to be cautious. More than that, old habits died hard, and she'd been a cop for the LAPD before she'd joined Elan's Guard when he'd become king.

It had been a crazy time for the Between. The former king had outed their kind to the human population just before he died, which left Elan scrambling to protect the rights of Between all over the world. His family had owned San Amaro, an island off the coast of Southern California, and the United States annexed the land as a sovereign nation for the half-animal shifters.

Kira thought Elan had done a better job for their race than his father, Phillip, ever had. Good riddance to the old bastard.

The hot smell of Max swirled through the air, scattering her thoughts. She automatically moved in that direction. It was like a Lorelei, that scent. Calling to her, tempting her, taunting her. Her heartbeat quickened, blood throbbing in her veins as her body readied itself for what she had in mind. Yes. All she needed now was Max.

"Damn it, Adam. Why can't you just—" The sentence ended in a frustrated growl as she rounded a corner of the building. Pulling to a stop, she nodded to the two men standing there. Barrett Granger and Adam Lee.

"What's up, Doc?" Adam was the Between doctor on San Amaro. He was probably the most beautiful man she'd ever seen . . . tall and muscular, but with darkly exotic Asian features. Barrett was about as opposite in looks as possible. He was massive, with pale peridot eyes and wheat blond hair. Neither of them could come anywhere near the attractiveness of Max, but objectively, they were both better looking.

The anger and sexual tension between the two men was a palpable thing, but there was no backpedaling now, and since both men were Between, they'd have sensed her approach a mile off.

"Nothing's up, Kira. Thank you for asking." The doctor's voice was as mellow as always, but a muscle twitched in his cheek.

Barrett gave her a crisp nod. He'd be taking over as second in command of the King's Guard, and she knew he was solid, but this was an interesting twist. His jaw clenched as he met her gaze. "Seaton."

"Granger." Her feet crunched on the gravel path as she made to skirt around them. A lover's quarrel wasn't something she wanted to involve herself with. She had other plans for the evening.

Max's laughter jerked her around, and she watched him step through an open door, drawing Elan's pretty secretary Genesee outside with him. He was flirting, as usual.

A noise that was pure jealousy rent the air, and it wasn't just Kira who made it. She glanced at the men beside her and saw Adam's gaze locked on Genesee while Barrett reacted to Adam's response.

There was a mess even more tangled than hers. She'd thought she'd had it bad wanting her boss, but at least there wasn't a triangle of pain in her life. And Max wasn't her boss anymore, was he? Not as of Rhiannon's return. He was the head of the King's Guard and she was in charge of the Queen's Guard. That feral smile twisted Kira's lips again. Now all she had to do was get rid of Genesee and everything would be perfect.

Watching Max's long, lean body move as he prowled the pathway around the palace did nothing to cool her off. She couldn't look away, her body heating with every step he took toward her. His dark hair ruffled in the breeze, his amber eyes glinting in the light cast from lampposts. His white teeth flashed when he smiled, and her heart rate bumped up a notch. Her nipples tightened and she felt her skin sensitize.

She didn't bother glancing away from Max when she spoke. "Adam, why don't you make sure Genesee gets home safely?"

"Good idea," he replied, overriding the woman's weak protestations.

"I'll walk with you." Barrett shot Kira a nasty glare, which she ignored. "I'm headed that direction anyway."

His expression dared them to contradict him. No one did. And no one pointed out that his quarters were in the opposite direction of Genesee's house. The trio moved away in frigid silence.

That left Kira alone with Max, just as she'd intended.

He arched his eyebrows, a flirtatious grin playing over his full lips. "Well, now that you have me all to yourself, what will you do with me?"

Anything she wanted.

The fox within her writhed with the need to mate, to fuck, to burn off the craving that she'd had to keep in check for so many years. But the fetters were off now. Her father would be horrified at her desire to fraternize with her betters, but she pushed the thought away. Max being the king's brother wouldn't change tonight. She'd worry about that later.

She startled when a leonine roar shattered the quiet night, her hand going reflexively to the weapon holstered at the small of her back. Max crossed his arms, his smile widening with mockery. "Jumpy, aren't we? Sounds like the lion king is having a nice reunion."

As if she cared. She shrugged and fought the urge to drag him to the ground. "Your brother always enjoys himself with Rhiannon. Maybe that's why he's marrying her."

His grin fell away and his gaze sharpened, zeroing in on her face. "Are you okay with all this?"

She blinked, her mind unable to process the rapid change. "Why wouldn't I be?"

Then realization hit. Oh. Right. Max thought she had a jones for Elan, and she hadn't corrected that misconception for him over the years. She might even have done a few things to encourage it. The more incentive he had had to keep his distance, the safer it had been for her.

Despite being the ranking officer in the King's Guard, Max was still a freaking *prince*, and Kira's father had been his father's butler. She might have played with Max and Elan as a child, but her father and theirs had made it very clear she would never be the equal of a Delacourt. She was a servant's kid, and her father had expected her to be a servant as well. He'd been pissed as hell that she'd gone off to be a cop. Then again, she'd become a public servant and then returned to San Amaro to serve the king. She might do it with a gun instead of a serving tray, but a servant was a servant. Too bad her father hadn't lived to see his wish come true.

Max had ditched all the trappings of royalty and joined the Marines when he turned eighteen, but when he'd come back to command the Guard after his brother's coronation, he'd still had to deal with being a prince. Which had made him not only royalty, but her superior officer.

Off-limits on every possible level.

Until today.

An impatient growl spilled from his throat. "Damn it, Kira. You have to talk to someone about this, and who else do you have? Genesee is Elan's assistant and Rhiannon is his *fiancée*. Who does that leave?"

"Barrett? Or maybe Adam?"

Max's growl turned into a sound of feral jealousy, and Kira fought a grin. She liked him possessive—far more than she should. He jerked a thumb at his chest. "You'll talk to *me*."

"You're not my boss anymore, Max." She folded her arms over her chest, and his gaze dropped to her breasts. Excellent. "I don't have to follow your orders."

His eyes narrowed as they refocused on her face. "I have never held that over you, and you know it."

"I know." She sighed and dropped her arms. This was definitely *not* how she'd planned for the night to go. And standing around to listen to more of his brother's sexual antics wouldn't get things back on track. Spinning on her heel, she started down the path toward her small bungalow. He'd follow her. He was far too tenacious not to.

His boots crunched on the gravel as he fell into step beside her. Years of working together and decades of being friends made the silence between them companionable. Or as companionable as it could be when the fox inside her reared its animalistic head to demand she touch and take. Her breathing sped, drawing that intoxicating male scent into her lungs. Her skin prickled with the body heat he gave off. She wanted more. She'd wanted more since she was barely old enough to be interested in boys, but the three years between their ages had been insurmountable then. That, and the fact that her father wouldn't have stood for her consorting with a prince. He was out of her league, and no one had ever let her forget it. But for one night, she'd break the rules. She had to see what it was like. Just this once.

The warm glow of her porch light came into view, and Max followed her up to the wide veranda. Before she reached the door, he wrapped his long fingers around her bicep and pulled her around to face him. He waved his free hand between them, his expression uncharacteristically earnest. "All bullshit aside, Kira, you can talk to me about this. We're friends and I'm here if you need me."

"I do need you." The words were out of her mouth before

she could call them back. She watched his golden eyes widen with startled confusion, but it was too late now. Some relentless tension that had wound tighter and tighter for years snapped within her.

Finally.

She reached out, planted her hands on his chest, and shoved. He stumbled back until he sprawled in a big wicker chair on her porch. She came down on top of him, straddling his thighs. Stiffening beneath her, his mouth fell open in utter shock. She flashed a grin, shoved her fingers in his silky hair, and hauled his face up until there was only a hairsbreadth distance between their lips. "You have no idea how much I *need* you, Max. You. Not Elan. Never Elan. Try to keep up, okay?"

Then she kissed him.

Finally, finally. Oh, Lord. *Finally*.

He groaned, his hands clamping down on her hips. She wasn't sure if it was to hold her close or to keep her from moving closer, but she didn't care. Sliding her tongue between his lips, she let the flavor of him fill her mouth. God, he tasted good. A helpless moan wrenched up from inside her. So long. She'd waited so long to touch him, taste him. Her fingers splayed over his muscular chest, slipping down until she could circle one of his nipples through his shirt. It tightened for her, and she hummed in appreciation against his lips.

A choking sound came from him. He jerked her forward until her sex came into full, hot contact with his. A few layers of cloth separated her from exactly what she wanted. She whimpered at the steely length of him pressing against her. Her hips bucked, and she twisted to get even nearer. His tongue shoved into her mouth and his claws shredded her skirt.

Time seemed to leap forward so fast it left her mind spinning, and the only thing to hold on to was Max. His claws scraped up the outside of her thighs, almost painful, but not quite. Goose bumps exploded over her skin, and her nipples hardened with the intensity of her arousal. Her tongue dueled with his, their movements rough, nipping at each other's lips with their fangs, each struggling for control of the kiss.

He made quick work of her panties, slicing through the silk before flicking her clit with the tip of one deadly talon. She bit his lower lip hard, her body jolting in response. Her pussy drenched in a hot rush, her hips driving forward in a carnal rhythm that was as natural as breathing. His claws retracted and his long fingers glided between her slick lips to tease her entrance.

But he didn't penetrate her. He just coaxed more moisture out of her until she snarled against his lips. The tension within her twisted tighter, pushing her past bearing. Her pussy fisted on nothing, once, twice. Pulling his bottom lip between her teeth, she nipped his flesh with her fangs. Shivers raced through her, and her skin felt aflame. Even his almost gentle touch was enough to have her teetering on the edge. She could *feel* orgasm shimmering just beyond her grasp.

She broke the kiss and threw her head back. He used the opportunity to suck her nipple into his hot mouth, biting her through her clothing. Her hands fisted in his hair, holding him closer. "Max! Max, I need . . ."

This? His telepathic voice was an intimate, throaty rasp. His thumb flicked over her clit, his other fingers shoved deep inside her.

It was more than enough to send her screaming over the edge. Her body froze, every muscle inside her clenching tight, and then her hips jerked frantically as wave after wave of climax exploded through her.

He released her nipple and leaned back in the chair to watch her ride out her orgasm on his thrusting fingers. The cool sea breeze on her wet flesh made her shiver. A small smile tilted up the corners of his kiss-swollen mouth. Last shudders rippled through her body before she slumped against him, gasping for breath.

Lust flushed his face, drew the flesh taut across his sharp cheekbones. "I want you."

She dropped her forehead to his, stroking her fingers down his biceps. There was no way she was stopping. She *had* to know what it was like. "Yes. Hurry."

Something hot and feral flashed in his gaze at her words. His fangs bared when he smiled. She grinned back, grabbed the bottom of his shirt, and wrenched it out of the waistband of his pants. He lifted his arms to allow her to yank the garment over his head. Then her hands were on his naked chest.

A muscle in his jaw twitched, but he let her touch him all she wanted. Claws scoring into the arms of the chair, his grip went white-knuckled as she petted his flesh. He choked when she pinched his small, brown nipples. His golden gaze burned into her while he panted. A quick burst of power filled her, and her heart hammered as renewed passion ratcheted up inside her.

She skimmed her fingertips down the sculpted planes of his torso. Well-defined pecs led to the ridges of his abs. His stomach sucked in when she circled his navel, and a chuckle burst out of him.

"Ticklish? Really?" Devilish delight filled her and she wiggled her fingers threateningly just over his skin.

He snorted. "Really. Quit teasing, Kira. I'm dying here. I need you."

Those words from his mouth made her insides seize in shock. Her breath caught and she swallowed hard. Something sweet bloomed in her chest, and she crushed it, locked it tight into the deepest corner of her soul. No. This was *physical* need, nothing more. She didn't want more. He was way out of her league.

Letting the air out of her lungs, she reached for his belt.

Jerking the leather from the buckle, she opened it and his fly in rapid succession. She was taking this insanity for a spin before it wore off and reality returned. It would sooner or later.

He shoved his hips up to meet her touch when she reached into his pants. He groaned, his chest bellowing with each rough breath. *Please, Kira.*

The soft skin over his hard shaft was irresistible. She stroked her fingers down the underside of his cock, pulling him free of his pants. Wrapping her hand around his dick, she pumped him fast and leaned forward to suck his earlobe into her mouth.

The sounds he made in response to her touch sent wetness pulsing into her sex. His big body jolted when she bit down on his ear, and a snarl ripped loose from his throat. She could all but hear the last tethers on his control snapping.

He let go of the chair and grabbed her hips, yanking her forward until their sexes aligned. She pushed down as he shoved upward, and they both groaned as he filled her to the limit.

Oh, God. If she hadn't been so damp, it might have hurt. He was so large. She clamped her hands on his shoulders, her pussy flexing around his cock as she worked to accommodate his girth. He rocked himself against her, and the angle was perfect.

Rolling her hips with each movement he made, she increased her pleasure. His rich scent was all she could smell, his bare skin on hers was all she could feel, his low groans and the creak of the chair beneath them were all she could hear. Everything within her focused on this moment. With him.

His palm pressed to the middle of her back, arching her until he could suck on her nipple again. The fabric of her clothes frustrated her, but not enough to stop in order to get rid of the offending garments. Her hips rose and fell, her pussy stretched by his long cock. This was what she wanted, what she needed. Everything else was irrelevant.

Sinking his teeth into her soft flesh made her cry out in stunned ecstasy. Their movements became less fluid, more frantic. The drive to orgasm took over and they thrust and ground their bodies together in that one unstoppable urge.

Kira, I—

Anything he said was lost in the implosion that rocked her body. Her walls clenched tight on his cock, milking the length of him as she came harder than she ever had in her life. The intensity of it shook her, and every thrust of his dick inside her sent her spinning into oblivion once more. When it was over, her mind was blank and her body limp. She collapsed against his chest, and he cradled her close, the tenderness as shattering as everything else they'd done together that night.

A sense of unreality flooded her and she closed her eyes tight. Oh, God. It had been so good. Everything she'd ever fantasized about and more.

What the hell had she *done?*

2

What the hell had he *done?*

It had been so good. Everything he'd ever fantasized about and more.

Thank God the wedding had gone off without a hitch, and Kira was in charge of security, because Max couldn't get his head in the game to save his life, let alone anyone else's. It was perhaps the only time he'd been grateful that his position as the king's brother took him away from his duties in the King's Guard.

Guests swirled around him, laughing and dancing. A small orchestra played, and he offered a reflexive smile to a passing diplomat. She was attractive, a woman he would normally have pursued for an evening of pleasure, but tonight he didn't give her a second glance. His gaze was drawn like a magnet to Kira. He swallowed hard. He'd imagined being with her for so long, but he'd never dreamed it would actually happen. Until last night, he'd thought Kira wanted *Elan,* not him. Not Max.

Sure, he'd flirted, he'd fantasized. Kira was beautiful, intelligent, and dangerous. Irresistible temptation. But he'd thought he was the only one tempted. They'd known each other their entire lives, and their relationship was as much rivalry as friendship. Even as children, he'd loved to make her react. He'd tug on her pigtails and she'd kick his shins.

It was Elan she got along with, Elan she'd come back to the island for. Not Max.

And last night had shattered everything he thought he knew about them. It scared him more than anything had in years. Not since the last woman he'd—

No. He slammed the door on that memory. Even the thought of comparing Kira to—

Stop. He shut down all emotion the way he had to any time he worked, buried it deep where it couldn't touch him. If sickness pooled in his belly, curdling into something painful enough to bring him to his knees, he ignored it.

He dragged in a deep breath, his heightened wolf senses filtering through the explosion of scents in the room. Humans, Between, perfume, sweat, sex, food, flowers. Taking it all in, he let his gaze rove the crowd, looking for problems. That was what he did, what he was. His job.

You're not on duty, little brother. Try to relax. Elan's hand clapped down on his shoulder, his mental voice holding only the mildest of rebukes.

I'm always on duty.

This is Kira's job tonight.

He knew, and it wasn't that he didn't trust her and his hand-picked people to do their jobs, but the extra risk of these kinds of events made him antsy that he couldn't be the one running things. Usually. When he could focus for more than two seconds on something other than the mind-blowing lay he'd had the night before. He shrugged his brother's hand away and shook his head. *You hate these kinds of shindigs, too.*

It's my wedding. I'm making an exception.

Congratulations, Elan. You deserve every good thing that

comes your way. And I'm not just saying that to practice for the toast later.

Shut up, Max! Elan's laughter rippled over the crowd, and bone-deep contentment radiated from the older man. Max refused to acknowledge the stab of envy that ripped through him. Elan and Rhiannon deserved their happiness—they'd had a rough road getting to it. Max had had his chance at that kind of happiness a long time before, and he'd blown it. There were no second shots for people who'd screwed up as badly as he had.

Still, his gaze went automatically to Kira, his hand tightening on the champagne flute in his hand.

She was beautiful. That was all he could think as he watched her move around the room with that controlled efficiency of hers.

Just looking at her turned him on.

Kira moved closer to his new sister-in-law, leaning in to hear what Rhiannon had to say. After a moment, both women burst into laughter. Most people's gazes would have been drawn to Rhiannon, with her brilliant red-gold hair and rippling, infectious giggle, but Max couldn't take his eyes off Kira. She was like contained fire, her bright eyes dancing in amusement, her dark auburn hair catching the light overhead when her head tilted back in a throaty chuckle.

He smiled and didn't look away even when Elan nudged his arm to get his attention. His brother's gaze followed his and he snorted. "They make quite the picture, don't they?"

"Yeah, they really do." Max took a deep draw of the expensive champagne.

"You should do something about that yen you have for her, little brother."

For once in his life, Max remained silent.

Elan waited a long beat, then shook his head. "Come on. I want to ask my wife to dance."

"You don't need me for that." The protest was more pro

forma than anything else, because Max followed along obedi-
ently enough. Of course. He hadn't spoken to Kira since that
morning, when they'd woken up in her bed together. A new
threat against the queen had come in and last-minute wedding
details had sucked them both into their duties. He'd been at a
run most of the day. It hadn't stopped him from thinking about
how Kira looked tousled from sleep, lips swollen from his
kisses. He swallowed a curse as his cock reacted to the crystal-
clear memory.

"I'm more than ready to escape for the honeymoon, but you
just can't pry Rhiannon away from a party." Elan maneuvered
them through the crowd with the skill of a practiced politician.

"A few more hours, some royal ceremonial fun, and you'll
be free." Max pitched his voice low, knowing the crowd would
drown out his voice even from the sensitive ears of a Between.
"Then the sexfest can begin."

Max and Kira would also be along for the sexfest, serving as
security for the royal couple. Isolated in a cabin for two weeks
with a woman who'd gone up in flames in his arms. *That*
thought made his cock harden to the point of pain. He was usually more than ready to get out after a one-night stand, but it
was *Kira*. She was his friend, his colleague. Someone he respected. Someone who was already under his skin, which was
somewhere he never let his lovers get. He'd learned that lesson
the hard way.

Shit.

This was a complete disaster. What had he been thinking?
What was she going to expect from him? With most women, he
wouldn't even have to wonder. With Kira, he didn't have a clue.
Like him, she wasn't one to have long-lasting relationships,
which was his only consolation. He hated the gut-grinding sensation that accompanied the thought that she was just using
him for sex. That should have been the perfect solution. They'd
had an itch to scratch; it was scratched. End of story.

For the first time in damn near forever, that wasn't enough. He wanted more. Just a little. He could handle that, couldn't he? It wasn't as if he could take back the night before, so what could a few more nights hurt?

He rolled his eyes at the justifications. He was in such deep shit.

All he could do now was damage control.

Elan whisked Rhiannon away for a waltz, leaving Max gawping at Kira in silence. The first thing that blurted out of his mouth made him wince. "This ends when the honeymoon is over."

"Fine." Her chin lifted, her eyes flashing dangerously. "Everyone knows you're the love 'em and leave 'em type, Delacourt. Did you really think I assumed it'd be different for me?"

He tried to reel his tongue back in and clean up the usual mess his mouth made. "I just . . . I wouldn't . . ."

"Your Highness," she said coolly, using the princely title he hated. His hackles rose, but before he could reply, she flapped her hand to encompass the royal military uniform he wore. "You couldn't pay me to live in your pomp and ceremony world. I'll take the servants' entrance over the red carpet any day."

Well, it was good to see that some things never changed. He was still pulling her pigtails and she was still kicking his shins.

"Jesus, Max." Rhiannon peered out of the French doors off Elan's office suite. A small army of men and women readied several helicopters for flight. "Is it really necessary to bring everyone in the Guard on the honeymoon?"

"Yes." The answer shot from both Kira's and Max's mouths at the same time. Max glanced over and met her eyes, knowing she was thinking about the recent threats against his brother's and sister-in-law's lives.

"I already lost this argument." Elan's lips twitched in a wry smile, and he forked his fingers through his mane of gold hair. The disheveled locks made him look the part of the lion-shifter. The only lion-shifter among all the Between people, which was why he was king.

Max could only be thankful he wasn't the lion. He'd never craved that kind of power, much to his father's disappointment. If his father had had his way, Max would have been as invested in politics as he had always been, as Elan had always been. That wasn't Max and it never would be—it had taken finding a place for himself in the Marines, a place he finally flourished, to figure that out. Kira had once mocked him that the only things he took seriously were security and sex . . . and maybe just security.

She hadn't been far off.

Of course, his father would say that Max was suited to a military life. It was the only useful thing a born killer could do. His mother had died giving birth to him. As a boy, he'd even killed a man who tried to assassinate his father. And those were the least of his crimes. Covering up the dark side of his nature with the carefree playboy prince had always served Max well.

Sir, we're ready for them. Barrett's voice filled his mind. His new executive officer. It was discomfiting after years of having Kira as his right hand.

His senses vibrated with pure carnal awareness as she brushed past him and joined Rhiannon at the door. Flicking her short hair away from her face, she glanced back at him and jerked her chin down to indicate they were good to go with escorting the royal couple to the helos. With all the wedding guests and extra hired help still on the island, security was even tighter than usual. It would be easier than ever for some nutjob to do something homicidally stupid. The king and queen went nowhere without an escort.

"Let's get this show on the road, ladies and gents." Max grinned and swept his arm toward the exit with a formal bow.

He straightened and shrugged tight shoulders. He couldn't wait to get out of this room. He hated it. Elan had redecorated the office when he had taken the throne, but Max would always remember the years of disappointed lectures, browbeatings, and angry fights that made every moment in the room a misery for him as a youth. He could still see the faded marks his claws had made on the desk during a vicious beating his father had doled out. Max couldn't even recall what he'd done to deserve that particular punishment. He pushed away the unpleasant memories as he always did and focused on the task at hand.

Kira took point in the group of Guards that surrounded the king and queen, while Max brought up the rear. Ignoring the rough *thwap* of the helo's blades slicing through the air, he scanned the crowd of curious guests who came to watch them take off, noting no one out of place. Good. The Guards worked like the well-oiled machines they were, and in moments Max and Kira were in the helicopter with Elan and Rhiannon. The rest of the Guards would fill the other helos.

Kira studiously avoided his gaze on the flight to the palatial mountain cabin the Delacourt family owned. Max's great-grandfather had amassed quite a fortune before he'd become the Between king, and later generations of the family had kept up the entrepreneurial bent—something else Max's father had tried to push him into. If he couldn't be useful in politics, then he could at least do his duty to his family name and excel at business. Max snorted. His father had excelled at disappointment. Elan had had it worse, though. The old man had seen Elan as a competitor, and Max had always suspected some part of their father had known his elder son would make a far better ruler than he had the ability to be.

Max caught his brother passing Rhiannon a look, and he suspected the two were speaking telepathically. When his sister-in-law's gaze flicked between him and Kira, he knew what the topic of conversation was. Right. He sighed.

The fox-shifter had said very little to him since he'd put his foot in it at the reception, and apparently the chill had been noticed. He had his doubts that their affair would continue at all, let alone for the extent of the honeymoon, and he had no one to blame except himself and his big mouth. Give him a military operation and he did fine. Put him in a personal situation and he said the wrong thing every time. One would think he'd have learned to keep his trap shut, but not so much.

He drew in a breath and Kira's heady feminine scent punched through him. Lust rode him with a viciousness that shouldn't have surprised him, but the night before had only sharpened his craving for her. Damn his verbal ineptitude. The frustration ripping through him did nothing to cage the feral wolf-shifter within him that wanted to claim her.

The pilot raised his voice to be heard over the helo's blades. "Sixty seconds to landing."

They banked left and took a sweeping turn over forested peaks before the massive cabin and its collection of outbuildings came into view. The Delacourts owned most of the mountain, and Max had Guards crawling all over every inch of it. He wasn't taking any chances.

"Oh, it's so beautiful," Rhiannon crowed with delight as they swooped closer, and Max couldn't help but grin. Her enthusiasm for anything and everything made her a lot of fun, and he knew his uptight brother needed some of that to loosen him up. Before Rhiannon, Elan had been steadily working himself into the ground in a futile attempt to make up for their father's selfish suicidal death.

Such a waste of life, both their father's and Elan's with his workaholic penance.

"Wait until you see the lake. We can go skinny-dipping." Elan winked at his new wife and she chortled in wicked glee.

Kira groaned. "Oh, Jesus. Just make sure it's on a shift where I'm *not* working."

"What do you have against skinny-dipping?" Rhiannon turned those wide green eyes on the fox-shifter.

"Not a thing as long as it's me and some hot guy swimming around in the buff." Kira flicked her short hair away from her face. "I don't, however, have any desire to watch the queen boinking her husband."

Elan arched one regal eyebrow. "Did you just refer to us having sex as *boinking*? We are most seriously displeased."

"And that was the royal *We*." Max leaned forward to open the door as they bumped down on the landing pad.

"Exactly. I have to learn that one." Rhiannon stuck her nose in the air. "*We* are most *seriously* displeased, peon."

Something about that made the smile fall from Kira's face, but Elan cracked up. He reached out an arm, looped it around Rhiannon's neck, and hauled her close for a quick kiss. "You're not supposed to *say* peon."

"Yeah, it's just implied." Max winked at them, hopped out, and led the way into the cabin. He'd have to find out what was wrong with Kira later—there was work to do now.

The team of Guards he'd sent ahead to secure the cabin and put in place a few extra security measures was waiting for them. Everything appeared to be fine, and a deep drag of air revealed no unfamiliar scents. Guards, family, nearby wildlife. Good.

They'd be on American soil for the next two weeks, in human territory, and while as a race humans were much weaker than Between, they also vastly outnumbered the shifters on the planet. His brother's position as the Between king made him a target for people who feared the magic of their species. Their father had announced the existence of the Between to the world over a decade ago, and ever since, Elan had been scrambling to clean up the mess. Some people didn't like how successful he'd been in making sure Betweens were treated as equals, as *humans*, even though the shifter magic in their blood made them half-animal.

One recent threat in particular made Max's hackles rise. The death threats and marriage proposals the king's staff fielded almost daily weren't what bothered him. There'd been a human whose letters had become increasingly violent, and the last one had been written in blood. Max didn't know who the human was, but the scent on the paper and envelopes had been the same.

Just that morning, a wedding "gift" had arrived for Rhiannon—white roses dipped in crimson blood. They'd carried the same human's smell as the letters. The acrid stench had a hint of madness to it that said this was no prank. It lit up every one of Max's instincts.

You're thinking about the human.

Kira loped up the stairs to do a sweep of the upper floor. Of course she knew what he was thinking. She knew him better than anyone except his brother. But she didn't so much as glance at him as she passed. He answered her anyway, shielding his telepathy from everyone else. *Yeah. I have a bad feeling about this one. I want us to be cautious while our men hunt this guy down.*

We will. Catch him and be cautious. Her words were firm, left no room for doubt. Just like the woman herself.

She was right. He'd make sure of it. His only family's lives were at stake. The problem was, the letters had been sent from all over California, and it was a big-ass state with a lot of people in it. It didn't help that San Amaro was part of the Channel Islands off the coast of California. It was much too close for Max's comfort.

And they were in an isolated mountain cabin. In California. For two weeks.

Fucking fabulous.

3

"Ma'am." Barrett nodded to Kira as they passed in the cabin's foyer.

Calling it a cabin was a joke. Cabins didn't have *foyers*. It was a log mansion, really.

"Granger." She dipped her chin in a nod. There were questions in the man's eyes, but he masked them quickly enough before he turned away. About what she'd seen with Adam and him, or had he noticed something about Max and her? She'd still had his scent on her when the bloody rose delivery had dragged her out of bed to investigate. People had taken note of the way she smelled, she was sure. A Between wouldn't be able to help it. Barrett didn't ask her anything, thankfully. He jogged up the stairs to take over for Max while Kira waited for her own replacement.

She was more than ready to escape to her room. Unlike the rest of the security staff, Max and she were sleeping in the main house instead of one of the equally plush outbuildings.

Part of her wished she were out with the rest of the Guards. The pheromones in the house were thick enough to cut with a knife. Laughter floated over the balcony from the royal suite, along with the occasional moan and scream. Being Between meant there weren't a lot of secrets about what was going on. Kira could hear far more than the average human. She did her best to block out the sounds and smells of sex and concentrate on her job, but the animal within her writhed at the less-than-subtle call to mating.

Then Max's scent mixed with that of lust, and sweat broke out across Kira's forehead.

Shit.

Her replacement arrived and she barely managed a few pleasantries before she all but fled to her room and shut the door.

Her teeth ground together, her fangs elongating. Max's demand that they only get it on for the duration of the honeymoon stung. It wasn't as if she'd expected anything long-term. Hell, she didn't *do* long-term. It complicated things, and she was always going to have to put her job before anything else. Emergencies cropped up, dangerous situations happened, things that others might find morally questionable were just part of her normal day. Most men didn't understand that, but she was damn good at what she did, and she wasn't going to apologize for it.

Still, she didn't put an expiration date on her affairs. They lasted as long as they were good, and then they ended. Max's deadline pissed her off. She hadn't planned on more than a night with him, but they'd both enjoyed themselves, and they didn't work directly with each other anymore, so what was his problem?

She snorted. If she didn't know him so well, she might think it had something to do with the disparity in their social positions. But Max and Elan had never treated her the way their father had, the way her father had always warned her they would.

No, with Max, it was more likely that he'd get bored before the two weeks were up. When it came to women, the man had the attention span of a gnat with ADHD. He hadn't been that way when they were younger, but he'd apparently picked up the any-port-in-a-storm habit in the Marines.

So. She had to decide what to do. Tell him to kiss her ass and call it a one-night stand. Or she could take him up on the next two weeks. Her pride chafed at both options. She might not do long-term, but she wasn't usually a one-night wonder either. A foxlike growl emerged from her throat. She was honest enough to admit what stuck in her craw most was that *she* wasn't the one getting to end things. She wasn't the one calling the shots.

But one phone call to Max's room and she could have him again. For the next two weeks. Fire exploded in her belly at the mere thought, her pussy drenching. Damn the chemistry they generated. Damn him for backing her into a corner.

"Damn, damn, *damn*."

Frustration burned through her. She doubted she would sleep, but the morning would come early and she needed to try. With impatient movements, she yanked off her clothes and tossed them aside before she flung herself into the wide bed. The cool mountain breeze ruffled the curtains at her window, teasing her nose with the scent of the pine, teasing her over-heating body with its chill. Her nipples tightened and she had to clench her legs together and clench her jaw to keep from groaning. She was dying to have a man's hands on her skin. She was dying to have *Max's* hands on her skin. Again. One night hadn't been nearly enough to quench her need.

"Fuck," she hissed. Punching her pillow into a different shape, she tried to squirm into a more comfortable position. It was no use, and she knew it. The only position she wanted included a man between her thighs. One phone call and she could have that.

The thought was potent, addictive. Max could put his hands on her. She could have him if she wanted him, even for a little while.

His hands could be sliding over her skin instead of the damp mountain air. He could warm her to a boiling point, make her arch like a fox in heat, make her writhe and scream and forget everything but the feel of him moving over her and in her.

Her frustration peaked, battered at her already tenuous control. Bunching her fingers in the sheets beneath her just made her claws punch holes in the fabric. She squirmed, but the movement increased her agony. All she could imagine was Max and her, with nothing between them but skin.

"Fuck," she sighed again, and gave in.

Closing her eyes, she allowed the picture of him to form. It came to her, so sharp and clear that her breath caught. Dark hair that ruffled in the lazy wind, pale gold eyes that gleamed with bright laughter and dark lust. Lightness and shadow. It was one of the reasons she found him so fascinating.

She ran her hand down her stomach, wishing it were his hand, his fingers that dipped into the notch of her thighs and toyed with her clit. The tight bundle of nerves hardened and bloomed, and she could imagine the light rasp of calluses on his fingertips.

A shudder rippled through her body and she let herself go to the fantasy. The dream Max drew lazy circles around her clit, teasing her until she thought she'd die, but it was too good to rush, so she moaned and let him play with her. Pressing her legs flat to the mattress, she opened herself for more of his touch and lifted her hips in offering.

He chuckled, the sound floating through her mind, wisping like smoke. Moving her hand, she shoved her fingers deep inside her sex. She gasped, her hips bucking hard to meet the sensuous touch. The lips of her pussy were slick with juices, the inner walls squeezing and releasing around those plunging digits.

"Oh, God," she groaned between gritted fangs.

In her mind, she watched Max grin wickedly, his fangs flashing. There was a glimmer of silver to his skin, the sign of shifting for a Between. The red wolf couldn't hide his feral side when he felt passionately about something, and she loved the wildness. She wanted it for herself, in her bed, all night long.

He rubbed his thumb across her clit, and she arched into the caress. Heat burst through her and tingles rippled over her skin. His free hand reached for her nipple, plucking and twisting the tight tip. Biting her lip, she strangled a sound of utter need. She barely noticed when her fangs scraped at her skin, the coppery tang of blood slipping over her tongue. All the while, his fingers built a steady, maddening rhythm in her pussy, pushing her higher and higher.

She was soaking wet, her sex tightening on his fingers. Every movement, every breath, intensified her reaction. Her muscles shook in anticipation of orgasm.

More. That was all she could think. More, more, *more*. Even then, it wasn't enough. It wasn't real. But it was all she would allow herself, so she focused on the daydream and pushed reality away for just a few more seconds, working herself with her fingers, just as the Max in her fantasy was doing.

He licked his lips, watching her react to him. His eyes burned to molten gold, the feel of his gaze moving over her body increasing her need. Her breathing sped to rapid pants, and sweat slid in rivulets down her skin. A gust of cold wind brushed over her damp flesh, raising goose bumps and making her shiver. He chuckled, and his fingers curled upward until he rubbed her g-spot. A low snarl broke from her and the sensations catapulted her past the point of no return. Her pussy spasmed and she undulated on the sheets, the smooth fabric rough against her skin.

"I want you inside me." The words seemed to echo in the empty room around her, the desire so deep it couldn't be kept in.

He shook his head, his smile full of sin as he stroked her just right and sent her spinning into oblivion once more. Her sex gripped the fingers thrusting within her, shudders racking her.

"Max!" The fantasy exploded into a million pieces, and her dream man dissipated, leaving her gasping and alone.

Until she opened her eyes and saw the real Max standing at the foot of her bed.

Max had never been so hot in his life. Seeing Kira writhe and scream his name, knowing the sexiest woman alive was fantasizing about him, made his cock harder than steel. He wanted to join her in that wide bed and make her fantasies real, but he'd been frozen in place watching her.

"Kira . . ." His voice was little more than a rasp.

"What are you doing here?" She removed her hand from her sex and closed her legs, hiding those sleek lips from him, but she did nothing else to cover herself. Not a hint of embarrassment or anger showed on her face.

He swallowed, barely able to pull his gaze away from her pale curves. His hands shook with the need to touch, so he fisted his fingers to stop himself. "I picked the lock. I could smell your arousal. I had to come to you."

"And what will you do now that you're here?" Her tongue flicked out to lick her lower lip, but her gaze didn't waver from his face.

He choked on the need to claim every inch of her over and over again until he burned out this clawing lust. He'd wanted her before he'd had her, but now? God, it ripped into his insides. "I want to take you. Hard."

Her eyes closed and her head fell back. Dragging in a deep breath lifted her pert breasts. She sighed and shook her head, but her muscles relaxed as if a decision had been made. "Fine. If all you want is a couple of weeks . . . let's not waste a single second of it."

Was that all he wanted? Hell, no. But that was all he could allow himself. With her, he was on shaky ground. Too much more, and he'd find himself hip-deep in pain he'd sworn he'd never feel again. Light and easy was all he was good for when it came to women. It was better for all concerned. But Kira wasn't a light woman, and she'd never be easy. She was hard-nosed, stubborn, ferociously protective of those she cared for. She was complex, with depths he'd never be able to explore.

Holding out her hand, she crooked a single finger. "Come here, Max."

And that was all it took. He abandoned his reservations to go to her. Two weeks. He'd revel in it for every moment they had together, just as she'd said. A few steps and he was beside her, sliding across the sheets and dragging her into his arms. The feel of her silky skin gliding against his made him snarl in need. His cock throbbed painfully, the wolf within him insisting on what it had wanted the moment he'd come into the room and seen her.

She jerked at his clothes, growling in frustration when they didn't come off fast enough to suit her. He wanted her hands on his skin. "Use your claws."

"You won't be able to wear them out of here."

"So?" That was enough talking. He slammed his mouth over hers, shoving his tongue between her lips. She bit him, and he jolted. Heat flooded his gut, boiling beneath his flesh. He pushed his fingers into her short, satiny hair, holding her in place for his possession.

A shudder passed through him when he felt the tips of her claws running down his torso as she sliced through his shirt. He skated his palms down her back and cupped her ass, pulling her in to grind himself into the juncture of her thighs. She spread her legs for him, wrapping them tight around his flanks and lifting herself into the thrust of his hips. He groaned, feeling the heat of her through his slacks. So fucking good. It was all he could think, and he wasn't even inside her yet. This was the most amazing thing he'd ever experienced. Even more amazing than . . . He quelled the thought, withdrawing from it and from Kira.

He shouldn't be doing this. Alarms sounded in his head, warning him that he was far too close to an edge he didn't want to fall over.

Kira let him pull back and used the distance between them to wrestle his pants open. One slim hand slid inside and caught him. His brain malfunctioned when she began to pump him in the tight ring of her fingers.

"God, Kira." He groaned, arching himself into her touch. The pad of her thumb rubbed the underside of his cock, and he sucked in a breath. "That feels fucking incredible."

She hummed, her eyes glinting with laughter as she bent forward to suck his dick into her mouth. *And how does this feel, Max?*

"Holy shit," he choked.

She hummed again, and he damn near came. His fingers fisted in her hair, pressing her closer, bucking his hips to drive deeper between her lips. She flicked her tongue over his shaft and her fangs scraped oh-so-lightly against the head.

It was more than his control could take. If he didn't stop her now, the party would be over before it started.

He jackknifed upward, toppling her onto her back. Husky laughter spilled from her before he shoved her thighs wide and flat to the mattress. Bending forward, he sucked hard on her clit, nipping at it with his teeth. Her low moan rose into a thin scream. The muscles in her legs jerked, but he held her in place, dipping down to thrust his tongue into her soaking channel.

"Max!" She squirmed, scrabbling for a grip on his shoulders.

Her claws dug in sharply, and he growled against her clit at the pain. *"Max!"*

Her moisture flooded his tongue, and he drank down her musky flavor. His cock ached as it chafed against the soft sheets. He needed to be inside her. Now. He couldn't wait.

Drawing away from her sex, he blew a cool stream of air over the slick, swollen lips. She shuddered, a sound of pure need whistling from her. "Inside me, Max. *Now.*"

She didn't have to tell him twice. Crawling up the bed, he settled between her thighs and probed her entrance with his cock. Her wetness made him grit his teeth, and he felt his fully extended fangs scrape his lips. God, it felt good. Everything with Kira was good. Fighting with her, fucking her. He groaned and slid deep into her pussy.

Her knees came up to clasp his hips, her hands dragging him down for a demanding, greedy kiss. They bit at each other, as animal as they were human, hungry for more. Her taste was sweet and tart at once, so like the woman herself. He couldn't get enough of it, of her.

Their bodies moved together, skin slapping, sweat gathering and slipping down their overheating flesh. The mattress squeaked beneath them, and the scent of hot sex floated around them. The carnality of it called to the wolf within him, and both man and beast relished the moment.

He buried his dick deep inside her, over and over until he thought he might die, and knew he'd go out a contented man if he did. Grinding his pelvis against her hard little clit, he pushed her as fast as possible toward orgasm. He didn't know how much longer he could hold out, and he wanted her with him, wanted to feel that clench of inner flesh around his cock, wanted to taste the satisfaction in her kiss.

Max! Her telepathic voice held the sharp edge of pending ecstasy, and her channel clamped down on his shaft. She clawed at his back, bit at his lips. Her urgency only drove him onward.

Faster, harder, deeper. He pushed them both beyond their limits, beyond anything he'd known before. And she was right there with him, the fox in her as feral as the wolf in him.

He released her mouth from the kiss, licked a path down to the base of her throat, and sank his fangs into the sensitive tendon there.

"Oh, yes . . . yes, Max!" Her pussy fisted on his thrusting cock, her slim body shaking as orgasm took her under.

He unleashed the fetters on his control and pounded into her sex. The need to come was all that mattered, and he took her like a man possessed. Satisfaction loomed, and he threw himself toward it. His body bowed and shudders racked him as he jetted into her pussy. The intensity of it was just as good as the night before. Better, drawing everything from him in waves of blinding ecstasy. The heat of it should have set his skin on fire.

He collapsed on top of her, and her arms wrapped tight around his neck, holding him close while their bodies cooled and their heart rates slowed to normal. "Jesus, this is the most perfect thing I've ever felt, Kira."

Her laugh was a soft sound. "Let's not make this more than it is. This is two weeks of a good time, Your Highness. I'm a servant, you're a prince."

That jostled some awareness to his brain. He didn't like the way that sounded at all, though some of it was his own fault. But not all of it. "I've never thought of you that way."

"Your father did." She yawned, settling more comfortably beneath him.

He snorted. "My father was an asshole, which every Between is well aware of."

"Yep."

"So why would you listen to him?" He frowned down at her and she arched her eyebrows at him.

She stretched her arms over her head, and her response was

flippant. "Because he was my king and I was living on his island?"

"Well, he's not anymore. And you're not even living on the Delacourt island anymore—it's just the Between island, and you're a Between. It's your island." Some of this came from his father, but some of it came from hers. That was a can of worms he'd rather not open, though. Or reopen, rather. They'd argued about this before. Then again, there wasn't much they hadn't debated over the years. The woman was fiercely protective of those she loved, and that included her dead parent. He admired that about her, but he thought she brushed over some of the more archaic notions of social class the elder Seaton had clung to.

"I'm still a servant to the king." Her words slowed, slurred as her eyes fluttered closed for a moment.

"So am I, prince or not."

Her mouth opened, then closed, but nothing came out.

"Look at that. Kira Seaton rendered speechless."

She sputtered a laugh. "Shut up, Max!"

"Sure, I'll shut up." Grinning down at her, he dropped a kiss on her soft mouth. She sighed and her lips moved under his, her tongue playing with his. It felt good to kiss her, to tease her into laughter, to just be with her like this. He left her mouth and buried his face in the crook of her neck, drinking in her scent. They lay there for a long time, wrapped together in silence. His muscles loosened and he could feel sleep beckoning. This was perfect. He couldn't hold the thought back, though he knew he should.

Max . . . Her mind breathed his name before she relaxed, utterly spent.

He sensed the moment she dropped into slumber, a soft sigh on her lips that belied the tough exterior.

"Kira." He said it even though he knew she wouldn't hear him. Kira. That was the last thought he had before unconsciousness dragged him into oblivion. Just her name, and a wish that this could go on forever.

Those alarms pulsed to life again in the back of his mind, but he was too content to pay heed. Sleep took him, and his dreams were sweet.

And filled with Kira.

4

"Oh, my God!" The horror that rang in Rhiannon's voice brought Kira to full alert. She bolted up and out of bed, jerking on a set of workout clothes that were on top of her dresser as she careened out of the room.

Her nose twitched; she could smell the stench of blood in the air. That alone was enough to send her pelting down the stairs. Max was right behind her in wolf form, taking steps two at a time, his nails scrabbling against the wood floor. He leaped over the banister, passing her as they both skidded down the hallway toward the kitchen.

Elan had Rhiannon in his arms, shielding her from something or someone, and Kira could scent the ripeness of the other woman's fear. A chill rippled down her spine as the iron stink of blood intensified.

"What happened?" She swept the room with a glance, and one of the cooks met her gaze for a moment before bursting into tears.

"I'm sorry! It looked the same. I'm so sorry!" The woman covered her face and sobbed.

Max moved around the knot of people, froze, and his telepathic voice hit everyone's mind as he swore ripely.

Stepping over to stand beside him, Kira had to fight to control her gag reflex. She squatted next to him, one hand burying in the fur at the ruff of his neck.

Someone had cut off a lion's head and put it in a meat delivery box—the same company they used to deliver all foodstuffs to this cabin. From the outside, the container looked normal, so that explained the cook's reaction.

I smell him. Max's mental voice was rough, his fur bristling with his anger. This dangerous side of him only came out when he worked, when his people were threatened. It sent a chill down the spine to see him this way, his rage a palpable, killing force. A few Guards took a step back. *He wants to prove he knows where we are, that he can still get to the king.*

Message received. Loud and clear.

Kira forced herself to get a grip on her own anger, to retract her fangs. She wanted to track down and destroy anyone who'd dare threaten her people. *There can't be that many ways to get a hold of a lion's head. That's one way to trace him.*

Yes. The predatory craving for the hunt rang in his telepathic tone.

Pulling in a deep breath that only reeked of death and decay, she swallowed her rising gorge and pivoted on her haunches to look at Elan. "Why don't you and Rhiannon retire to your room? The Guard will take care of this."

She nodded to a few of the security staff, who came forward to escort the couple out. Elan's amber gaze glittered dangerously, and his fangs flashed when he spoke. "No one is supposed to be able to come near us here. What if there'd been a bomb in that container?"

"We'll find out what happened." She straightened slowly, something in his tone reminding her of his father at his most wrathful. "You'll get a full report."

"You bet your ass I will," he snarled. "This should *never* have happened. I expect you to keep my wife safe. If you can't do that, I'll find someone who can."

Kira felt her expression freeze in place. An echo of her dad's voice sounded in her head, telling her never to let any emotion show on her face. They can't take what they don't know you have, so never give anything away. He'd warned her this moment would come—that her friendship with the Delacourts lasted only as far and as long as she was useful to them.

She offered Elan a formal curtsy—the kind she would have given his father. Servant to monarch. "I understand, Your Majesty."

Her stomach churned as Elan led Rhiannon away. The drawn paleness of the woman's face and her silence spoke volumes.

He's just worried for Rhiannon, Kira. Max's voice was a quiet rumble in her head, his anger banked for the moment, and she snapped her chin down in a sharp nod, refusing to meet his eyes.

"I'll speak to the delivery company and the cook, see how the boxes got switched."

I'll speak to the Guard who was supposed to check all deliveries before they were brought to the house. This was not the cook's job. Max's molten anger had frozen to an ice-cold rage, and any smart person would understand that was where the true danger lay. That Guard's slip was likely to cost him his job today, and he'd be lucky if he got off that easily.

"Great. Let's get to work, then." Kira turned to walk out of the room, and she could feel his gaze boring into her back. The hulking form of Barrett filled the kitchen door, a large handgun cradled in his palm. He stepped aside to let her by, and she didn't meet his piercing gaze either. "Granger, take the cook to the sitting room and calm her down. I'll meet you there in fifteen minutes."

"Of course."

The need to vomit didn't dissipate when she got away from the stink of congealed blood. Never in all the years that she'd known him had Elan treated her that way—it was why she'd been willing to come back in the first place, because she'd thought he never would. Max and Elan were different from their despicable father, King Phillip.

But maybe she was wrong. Maybe her dad was right. It was in the worst times that you saw the real person under the masks they showed the world. She shook her head. It didn't matter. She'd think about what this meant when she was by herself tonight—she had a job to do now.

Hours later, she stood alone with Barrett in the sitting room. Everyone who could be questioned, coerced, or grilled had been, and they were no closer to figuring out who this stalker was than they had been before. The containers had been switched at the warehouse. How, the company couldn't explain. Anger sizzled in her veins—at this asshole human stalker, at Elan's behavior, at herself for not having any answers, at the whole damn world. She wanted to put her fist through something until these ugly feelings burned away.

"I hate this," Barrett hissed. Silver glimmered at the corners of his eyes for a moment, the feral feline in him fighting for control.

"I hear you."

"I should be out hunting this guy." He snorted. "I should be back on San Amaro keeping some woman from poaching on—"

It was the most open comment the other man had ever made, but Kira couldn't help but defend a woman she cared about. "Genesee isn't poaching on Adam."

"She doesn't have to, you can say it. I know the score." He rubbed a hand over the back of his neck. "Are you going to say anything about this?"

There was the crux of his problem, what he'd wanted to ask her since she'd seen him with Adam the other night. She met his gaze and gave him the blunt truth. "What you do with your private time is none of my business unless it affects the Guard."

"It doesn't." A muscle jumped in his square jaw. "Hell, I don't even care if people know. I am what I am. Adam is what he is, and he's not embarrassed about it either, but he doesn't want Genesee to think he's . . . unavailable . . . if she ever gets her head out of her uptight ass."

Kira sputtered a laugh, the first since she'd bolted out of bed that morning. "She's a little tense at times, yeah, but she's still my friend."

And a friend her father would approve of, one who was her equal, who wouldn't turn on her because she was beneath her. She'd always thought her dad overly paranoid because Phillip Delacourt was an especially heinous dickhead. She'd also suspected his distrust of others had something to do with her mother leaving. Kira had vague childhood memories of her mom, but her dad had refused to speak of her after she was gone. All Kira knew about her was that she was from a wealthy American family and had met her father when she was vacationing in London. She'd also died penniless four years after she'd left them. Anything else was a mystery, and Kira only knew that much because she'd done a background check after she'd joined the LAPD.

Kira had assumed her father's classist attitude stemmed from whatever had happened with his marriage, and that attitude had only been exaggerated by being Phillip's servant. After today, she wasn't so sure, and the uncertainty hurt so much it burned.

"I know Genesee's your friend. I don't have anything against *her*, really." Barrett shook his head, his gaze rueful when it met hers. "Shit. What a mess."

"On all counts." And she knew he was talking as much

about her problems as anything else. He'd smelled Max on her. Of course he had. Max wouldn't have made the man his executive officer if he were an idiot.

This whole situation was a clusterfuck. Elan going off on her, her affair with Max, Barrett's affair with Adam, Adam's yen for Genesee, and on top of all that, some crazed human after the Between king. A headache bloomed behind Kira's eyes.

"There's no way to get out of my mess with Adam, and we're already doing everything we can about the human." Barrett's pale green eyes pinned her in place with the unwavering stare only a cat could manage. "So, what are you going to do about your mess with Max?"

She didn't know. Everything had started spinning out of whack the moment she gave in to the urge to touch the wolf, and she didn't know if it would ever go back to normal.

She didn't know anything anymore, and she *hated* that.

Max found Kira in the gym, her face set in concentration as she kicked the shit out of a punching bag. He leaned his shoulder against the doorjamb and watched her in silence. The anger and frustration came off her in waves even a human could sense. Underneath that, he felt the hurt.

He winced, uncertain how to deal with Elan saying the wrong thing. Normally that was Max's area of expertise. He took a breath and tried to smile. "Think we can talk Rhiannon into a yoga lesson? You look like you could use some relaxation."

"I'm not interested in bending myself into a pretzel, thanks." Kira took a hard swing at the punching bag, and her knuckles popped on impact. She grunted and hit it again. "This is very relaxing."

"Right." He pushed away from the door and sauntered into the room. The woman looked like she was going to explode.

She was pissed at a king and there wasn't a damn thing she could do about it. It was the story of his childhood. He drew even with her, planting himself well within her reach. If she needed someone to take out her fury on, he'd take whatever she could dish out. He'd unleashed his own ire on the irresponsible Guard who'd let an unexamined package enter the cabin, so it was only fair she got to do the same. "You do look relaxed, sweetcheeks. Yep, cool as a cucumber. I'm sure Elan would be really impressed."

Wordlessly, she pivoted and caught him hard in the jaw with an uppercut.

His head snapped back and he staggered a few steps, pain shooting straight to his brain. He shook it off, rolled his shoulders, and settled into a fighting stance. Offering her a grin he knew showed his wolfish side, he gestured her forward with a mocking flick of his fingers. "Okay, let's play. C'mon, foxy. Give it to me."

"I'll give it to you, all right," she muttered and advanced on him.

He moved to keep her in front of him as she circled him. Her lithe body was displayed to perfection in her tight pants and sports bra. The creamy skin was sheened with sweat, just as it had been the night before when he'd sunk his cock deep inside her.

Bad thoughts to be having when he'd taunted a dangerous woman into lashing out at him. She swung for him, and his hand snapped out to deflect in pure reflex, saving him from a broken nose. A quick shift to wolf form would heal him, but it would hurt like a bitch until he did. And he doubted she'd pause the fight to give him the opportunity to shift.

"Damn it." She snarled at him, her fangs bared, and she slashed at him with her claws.

"I thought you were going to give it to me, foxy. Don't be shy, now." It was the wrong thing to say. Or the right thing, if he was hoping to piss her off more. He blocked her again, his movement making her stumble into him, her curves plastered to his front. Sweat beaded on his forehead, but not from the physical exertion.

They hit and kicked each other, landing glancing blows, neither able to gain the advantage. His heart rate skyrocketed, his breathing beginning to bellow in and out both from having his hands on her bare skin and from the grappling that brought them into full-body contact. God, but he wanted her. He spun her, shoving her away from him so she tripped and hit her knees.

A nimble leap brought her back to her feet. She whipped back around, her eyes blazed with the challenge, her fangs showing when she licked her lips.

He damn near groaned at the sight. This was a bad idea. He was going to get his ass kicked if he didn't get a grip on his raging lust. As if he'd ever been able to do that with her. His cock was rock hard and uncomfortable as hell under the circumstances. She charged him, her fist catching him in the belly while he blocked her other hand.

"All right, enough." He wrapped an arm around her waist and dragged her to the ground. Kicking out, she managed to flip them both until she was on top, her legs straddling his waist.

It was then that she finally noticed his erection because she froze above him, her fist half-cocked to punch him.

"Shit." She snapped her fingers around his wrists and pinned them on either side of his head. Then she kissed him.

The sweet taste of her only made him burn. He shoved his tongue into her mouth the way he wanted to shove his dick into the hot depths of her pussy. Hard and fast. He angled his head, lifting it to deepen the kiss. Any contact he could get, he'd take.

She rode him, working herself on him through their clothing. He groaned and bucked his hips beneath her, grinding his cock into the juncture of her thighs. A moan bubbled out of her and she pressed herself into him with swift urgency. The sting of her claws digging into his wrists did nothing to quell his lust—the slight pain only added to the pleasure. Every sensation ripped through him. The female scent of her dampness, the feel of her softness rubbing against his harder body, the mewling sounds she made as they moved together.

Their tongues twined, and the kiss was an animalistic thing of lips and tongues and fangs. They bit at each other, each wanting a feral claiming of the other.

He dropped his head back to the mat. "I want you naked, Kira. I want my cock inside your tight little pussy."

"Yes. God, yes." She released her grip on his arms and he wasted no time reaching out to jerk her top over her head. Her small breasts spilled free, the shell pink nipples already tightening. She lay flat against him, raising her ass slightly so they could both work her pants off. His fingers curved over her buttocks, prying them apart so he could dip between them.

She shuddered when he probed at the tiny rosette of her anus. The aroma of her wetness increased, a heady aphrodisiac that made his brain short-circuit. He slipped his fingers down into her pussy, working them deep. Her hips undulated, following his lead with a whimper that drove him wild.

"Nooo," she moaned when he dragged his fingers out of her sex. Using her juices to ease his way, he pressed two digits into the tight ring of her anus. She jolted as he twisted his hand and scissored his fingers to widen her for entry.

"I'm going to fuck you here." His voice was so guttural, he barely recognized the sound.

Yes. Her mental voice was soft, and her claws dug into his shoulders, but she gave a decisive nod.

Pushing her, he rolled her off him and onto her hands and knees. Dampness gleamed on the lips of her pussy. An irresistible temptation, just as everything had been with her since the moment she'd kissed him two days ago. He bent forward, flicked his tongue over her swollen clit, and sucked those sleek lips.

She moaned, her moisture flowing into his mouth. He lapped up the cream, hoping he was making her as crazy as she made him. Leaning back, he abandoned her pussy for the darker pleasures that awaited him. He ripped open his pants with one hand while he used the fingers of his other hand to press for entrance into her ass. Trailing wetness from her sex to her anus, he made slow circles on her flesh until he could slide three digits easily in and out of her rear passage.

"Now, Max."

"Don't say I never do anything for you." He withdrew his hand and patted her buttock. "Such a pretty little ass."

She snorted out a laugh. "You always harass me, Delacourt. Shut your mouth for once and *hurry up.*"

Taking his cock in his fist, he rubbed the head up and down her slit. "Shut my mouth before I put my foot in it, is that right?"

"Yep." She glanced over her shoulder, her eyes sparkling with repressed laughter.

"Well, that's fair." They both cracked up, but their amusement was cut short when he pressed his dick into her anus. The initial resistance of her muscles made him grit his teeth as he bore down on her. She snarled, silver shimmering on her skin as she wrestled with her fox for control. He knew the feeling.

Small thrusts of his hips pushed his cock inch by inch into her ass. God, she was tight. He wasn't sure she could take all of him. He shuddered, and beads of sweat slid down his face and chest. "Do you want more, Kira?"

"Yes, more," she groaned.

She dropped lower, her cheek pressing to the mat and her back arching to allow him deeper. He took all the access she gave him, driving his cock into her until his balls pressed against her slick flesh.

The animal noises she made pushed him past the edge of madness, calling to the most feral part of the wolf within. Shoving her hips back, she urged him onward. He thrust slowly at first, but quickly picked up speed and force. Their skin slapped together, the sound echoing through the gym. The smell of sex permeated the air, and he loved that it was his scent layering with hers. Possession dug its claws into his soul, but he was too far gone to notice or care. All he wanted was her. His hands slid up and down her back, and he could feel the way goose bumps broke over her skin. His strokes grew rougher, less controlled. Faster. Wilder. He battled with the need to come, and reached around her slim body to toy with her clit.

"I'm coming, Max. I'm coming!"

He could feel it. The deep contractions made her inner muscles clench and release on his cock, the tight passage squeezing him almost past bearing. The fetters on his restraint snapped abruptly and he hammered into her ass until their cries of completion mingled in the room. His come spurted into her, heat rippling over his limbs with each wave of orgasm that slammed into him.

"Are you okay?" he croaked. His heart still pounded so loudly, he could barely hear anything else.

"Um. I think so. Yeah." She collapsed beneath him, and they both groaned as he slid out of her. Shivering and sighing, a slight grin curled her lips. The sight made something sweet and warm squeeze his chest, and it felt far too amazing. Far too much like something he could never deserve. She hummed softly. "I'm good."

Well, that made one of them. Heaving himself to the side, he managed not to crash down on top of her. He flung an arm over his eyes. Shit. As he had every other time he'd given into the need to touch her, he asked himself what the hell he was doing.

Sex was one thing, but this was already too deep for his liking. Most women never saw all of him. They never saw the rougher edges. The man who'd killed and the guilt and emotional fallout that often came with that. They saw the mask—the easy charmer. Kira knew the darker sides of him, the secrets. Most of them, anyway. What had he been thinking to even dream that he could have a simple affair with her? She was his friend, and now she was his lover. This wasn't a quick fuck. It was more.

And that thought alone was enough to freeze the blood in his veins.

5

"Kira."

She froze in the hallway outside Elan and Rhiannon's suite. It had been two days since the kitchen incident, and she'd buried herself in tracking down who had switched the delivery, allowing other Guards to protect the king and queen. Cowardice, she knew, but she just didn't want to face it. There was a lot she didn't want to face lately. Everything had gotten so mixed up, and she wasn't sure what to do about it.

Pulling in a deep breath, she smoothed her expression, turned to look at Elan, and straightened to soldierly attention. "Yes, sire?"

A pained look crossed his leonine features. "Don't do that."

"Sire?" She arched her brows, her posture not relaxing for a moment. Her dad would have been proud, and she didn't know if that was a good thing or not.

"Don't treat me like my father."

Her mouth worked for a moment before she could get words out. "I'm not sure what to say."

"Come in, please." He stepped back and held the door open

for her to pass through. Rhiannon perched on a chair in the sitting room. The woman practically vibrated in place, but she seemed determined to let Elan have his say without interference.

He gestured eloquently with his hands, drawing her attention away from his wife. "I was a jackass and I'm sorry. You know I don't think it's right to treat people the way my father did. I was completely in the wrong and I have no excuses. I'm sorry."

Kira's lips twisted and her eyes dropped to the carpet. She shouldn't say anything, just accept his apology at face value and walk away. Her dad would have told her to reveal nothing, to give the king nothing, to deny that she had any feelings at all. Her job was to serve, and that was all. If a powerful person knew you cared, they could use that against you. They could take what you weren't willing to give. When her father had worked for King Phillip, she would have agreed. Now she had to take a chance that her friendship wasn't misplaced. If it was, she'd rather know now so she could decide what to do from here. Her palms felt slick with cold sweat and her belly knotted tight. She swallowed hard, the words squeezing past a throat that didn't want to work. "It hurt. What you said."

She felt Elan flinch. "I know. I make no excuses for myself. I was wrong. I hope you know how much I value you, how much Rhiannon and I value your friendship."

"Thank you." The air deflated in her lungs. Elan wasn't like his father, she *knew* that, but . . . God, everything was spinning out of whack lately.

His gaze cut to his wife and softened. Rhiannon shot to her feet and moved forward to slip her hand into his. "I'm the one who should thank you for everything you've done for me."

Kira nodded, but said nothing more.

"I hope you can forgive me." His amber eyes, only a shade or two darker than Max's, reflected his remorse.

"And me." Rhiannon lined herself up beside the king. "I should have kicked him on the spot. I was still pretty shaken up."

Kira tried to form her face into a tight smile and knew she failed. "You both were. I understand."

"But we were still jerks. Elan for what he said, and me for what I didn't. What happened wasn't your fault, and we know that you and Max are doing the best you can to keep us safe. You're the best at what you do, and we know that, too."

She pulled in a shaky breath. "Thank you."

"You're welcome." Rhiannon's gaze was frank when she looked at Kira. "Now tell me why you've gotten distant lately. And don't say it was Elan having his dorkfest. It started before that. I thought we were friends."

Kira folded her hands behind her back and tried not to appear uncomfortable. "We were."

"We are."

But, in the end, she now worked for Rhiannon. They weren't on equal footing anymore.

"It started in little ways, at first," the queen continued. "But now, all you talk to me about is Guard stuff. I talked about being in Portland and being Between and planning the wedding, and you put everything in terms of safety and security. You let Genesee be my maid of honor without so much as a protest. In fact, you bowed out completely."

"Max was already the best man. Someone had to be in charge of the Guard."

"And Barrett couldn't do it?" Rhiannon shook her head. "No, you've backed off and I want to know why."

"She's trying to get some professional distance." Elan sighed. "You'd have to have met Seaton to understand."

He was right. It was a slap in the face to realize it. God, she hadn't even *seen* it until they pointed it out. How much had she taken her consummate servant parent's words and actions to heart? Was that what she really believed, that she had to have distance with the royal family in order to serve them? That didn't seem to be the case with Max, or she wouldn't be sleeping with him, and it would mean losing Rhiannon as a close friend.

"I have met Seaton. Kira Seaton." Rhiannon's gesture encompassed Kira from head to toe.

"He means my dad." She shrugged the tension out of her shoulders and forced herself to relax her stiff pose. "He was the butler at the palace."

"Why didn't I know that?"

"You never asked."

Rhiannon's green eyes narrowed. "You wouldn't have answered if I had."

"True." An unapologetic grin curved Kira's lips, and she let it widen when Rhiannon's eyes narrowed further.

She huffed and jammed her fists down on her hips. "Well, knock it off. You're one of my best friends and I don't give a damn if I'm queen or not. That doesn't change a thing. There are going to be enough people acting weirdly because I married the lion king without adding my friends to the list. None of that professional distance crap."

"Yes, Your Majesty."

"Kira!"

"Sorry, you were spewing orders like a queen." Kira tilted her head. "I call it like I see it."

Rhiannon opened her mouth for a moment, then snapped it shut. Her expression went from annoyed to speculative in under a second, which Kira knew from experience meant the other woman was about to do something unpredictable. Rhiannon didn't disappoint. She grinned. "Well, fine. If we're calling it like we see it, then we should talk about how you're finally getting busy with Max. About damn time."

"It's temporary."

Her mouth opened and Kira could tell she was going to say something sarcastic, but then their eyes met and the queen's face sobered. "That's too bad."

Discomfort wound through Kira, and her shoulders twitched in a shrug. "It's fine. I'm fine. We're fine."

Rhiannon pushed back her long red hair. "Yeah, that's really convincing."

"I think the lady protests too much." Elan slung an arm around his wife's waist and drew her close, but he pinned Kira in place with his gaze.

Kira pulled a sour face. "Hasn't anyone ever told you to mind your own business?"

"You have, many times." He grinned, and for a moment, he looked so much like Max, it startled her. "I just didn't listen."

She snorted. "Jerk."

He lifted his hands to concede the point, still smiling. "I'm a king, Kira. I'm automatically concerned with all my citizens, especially those I count as friends or family. Or both."

"You consider me family?" Her world took another spin. This roller coaster of emotions was going to make her motion sick. He considered her *family?* The king? Yes, he wasn't Phillip, but this was way beyond not being a snobby ass.

"Yes. Though I'd prefer if you put Max out of his misery and made it more official than that."

"Ha. Max doesn't want to marry me." For some inexplicable reason, tears pricked at her eyes even as she said the words. What the hell was wrong with her?

Elan's tone was careful, and tinged with an edge of what might have been sadness. "Max has his reasons for being . . . cautious about commitment, but I'd hoped he'd move past them with you."

A short knock sounded on the door, and Max's scent

reached her. He strode through the door without waiting for an acknowledgment. "Sorry to interrupt, but I need Kira."

"Of course." Rhiannon's hands made graceful arcs in the air. "Don't let us keep you."

"Thanks, sweetheart." Max winked at her, wrapped his fingers around Kira's bicep, and drew her out of the room. He led her across the hall to his room and shut the door firmly behind them.

Kira sighed and sagged against the wall, pulling away from him. "Thanks for the rescue."

A wry grin curled his full lips. "I heard them talking to you, and I guessed you could use a hand."

"Yeah. That was . . . rough."

"Weird to have a king apologize to you, huh? I hope you got it in writing." He chuckled. "Make big brother twist for a few days before you forgive him. He deserves it."

She strangled a laugh. "You're bad."

"So my father told me. And since I have you in my room and we're both off duty . . ."

She stepped into his embrace easily, willingly. For once she didn't have the energy to fight her craving for him. She didn't even want to. She was tired of fighting, of questioning herself, of doubting everything she knew about everyone she knew.

His arms locked tight around her, pulling her close until her face was buried in his chest and she could inhale the rich, masculine scent that was uniquely Max. "There's something I don't understand."

"Mmm?" She flattened her palms against his strong back.

"I always thought you came back because you wanted Elan—"

"Haven't we been over this?" A spurt of irritation threatened to quash her mellow mood.

His big hand moved up and down her back, rubbing the

tautness out of her muscles. "Okay, but you didn't come back for me, because you returned first. Not for Seaton, because he was already dead. So, why did you come back? What was in it for you?"

"There are a lot of reasons." The response was automatic, but she paused and made herself give the questions more thought than normal. She blinked for a moment, her conversation with Elan and Rhiannon meshing with this one. Why *had* she come back? She'd had a good life in L.A. Her career with the police department had been on a fast track. Was it just because she felt as if she should fulfill her father's wishes for her? Was she born to be a servant? Was that who and what she thought she was? Did she think it was beneath her to serve? As Max had pointed out, he served the king, too, prince or not.

He jostled her a little. "And those reasons are?"

"Elan was my . . . friend. He was going to need help. I could help." That much was true. Her father would balk at calling the king her friend, but she shoved that away. Elan hadn't been lying when he said he considered her family.

"Other people could have helped."

She worked her hands under the bottom of his shirt, pressing her fingertips to his warm, resilient flesh. "People like you?"

"Yeah, like me." He huffed out a breath.

Shaking her head, she smiled a little. "We are so alike. We both had to leave to feel . . . worthy." God, it made her ache to say that. As much as she'd loved her father, and as much as he'd loved her, his worldview meant she was never as good as her friends. The Seatons were always less than the Delacourts, no exceptions. Everyone had their place and their purpose. And Max's upbringing had been worse. She seriously doubted Phillip was capable of loving anyone.

"Yeah. I know what you mean." Max's tone turned contemplative, which was a side of him he allowed few to see. "The Marines gave me a sense of self and worth that I'd never have gotten if I'd stayed on the island."

Burying her face deeper into Max's chest, she sighed. "But there's no place like home. Living among humans meant lying about what you were. Even now, there's enough prejudice against Betweens that it's safer to lie."

"San Amaro is home, more so now than it ever was when Father was king. It's good not to have his judgment hanging over my head every day."

It was good not to have her own father's judgments hanging over her head, too, and the thought made her feel disloyal. She tensed, but Max's arms tightened around her, offering her nothing but comfort and understanding. Everything else fell away, and there was only him, only her, and only this moment. Yes. That was perfect, that was exactly what she needed. Somehow he had known before she had.

Her body loosened, warmed. It was going to be so hard to walk away from this. Max understood parts of her that she didn't even want to acknowledge in herself. He made her smile, he made her think, he made her *feel*. His body against hers was divine, and began to have predictable effects on her hormones. Even as she felt her arousal build in slow increments, her skin tingling, her nipples tightening, her sex dampening, she let herself lean into him, reveling in the feel of his hands stroking up and down her back in slow, soothing circles. Soon it wouldn't be enough for her. Soon she'd need more and more until they were naked and all but feral in each other's arms. She wanted that, but not yet. Not now. Now she needed just *this*.

Curling his fingers around the nape of her neck, he massaged any lingering tension away. He nuzzled his nose into her temple, and she sighed.

His low voice rumbled in her ear. "Wanna do it?"

Snorting out a laugh, she drew back to give him an incredulous look. "You really never say the right thing, you know that, don't you?"

"It's part of my charm." His hands slid down to bracket her hips, pulling her close so she couldn't miss the evidence of his arousal. "Women find it irresistible."

"Uh-huh." She ran taloned fingertips up his chest until the deadly points rested against his jugular. "Is that what you tell yourself?"

He froze when her claws scored his flesh. He didn't breathe, didn't swallow, his golden gaze locked on her face. *I think we're good together. That's what I tell myself, all joking aside.*

Okay, so every now and then you say the right thing. She rolled her eyes, trailing her talons down to flick open the buttons on his shirt.

He unfastened her pants and slipped his hand in to rub his knuckles over the sensitive skin of her belly. "Don't worry. I promise not to make a habit of it."

A chuckle bubbled out of her, and he grinned down at her.

"I like the sound of your laughter. You do it more when we're alone together now."

She blinked up at him, replaying the last few days in her mind. He was right. He'd always been the first to get her to laugh . . . and to make her temper flare, but the effect had been exaggerated since they'd begun sleeping together. They'd had nights where they'd spent hours just . . . playing. Laughing and teasing.

He really was perfect for her.

The thought shocked her more than even Elan's suggestion that they should marry. That was his opinion, but this was *hers.*

And there wasn't a damn thing she could do about it. Because unlike Elan, she knew Max didn't want anything past the two-week honeymoon. But Elan knew something she didn't . . . he'd said Max had his reasons, and sheer gut instinct told her it had to do with the years he was in the Marines. He'd come back different, but she'd always assumed it was just cutting loose from his father's influence. Now she wasn't so sure. She'd have to think about it more, consider what Elan had meant. Her brows drew together and she bit her lip, stepping back from the situation to look at it objectively.

Max's fingers dipped below the edge of her panties, making her breath catch. "Do I have your attention, Ms. Seaton?"

His other hand came up to palm her breast, tweaking the tip. The air whooshed out of her lungs at the strength of feeling. He used one claw to circle her areola, and her nipple puckered tight. She shuddered and licked her lips. "Yeah, you have my attention."

"God, you're beautiful." He leaned in and ran his tongue over her lips, just as she had done. "And you taste like sugar."

"Mmm." She hummed in her throat and opened her mouth to invite him in. The fox in her was too curious not to wonder what he'd do next, and she wanted more. All of him. Everything. She just couldn't have it. Her heart twisted, but she tucked the pain away and enjoyed what she could have. This. Here. Now.

He flicked his tongue over her teeth before slipping it in to twine with hers. The taste of him was just right, hot and male and all Max.

Dropping her hands to his waist, she slid them down to cup his erection, stroking him through his pants. He jerked and then arched into her grip. "God, Kira. This is amazing. You're amazing."

"Why, thank you." She offered up a wicked little smile, and his eyes gleamed with amusement down at her. She laughed, and it felt good. Light and free. So unlike her. But she liked it. She liked how she was when she was with him. The prince. Her Max. She shook her head, but her smile widened.

She stroked his cock through his pants, and he pushed his hips into her, working himself through her fingers. Harsh groans spilled from his mouth, and her body reacted to his passion. Her sex grew unbearably damp, and she squeezed her thighs together to savor the ache. It was so good with him. Her breathing sped and her heart hammered in her chest, her blood coursing lava-hot through her veins.

Excitement shivered over her skin while he continued to toy with her nipple. He favored the other breast with the same treatment, and she moaned. "This is good."

"It's only going to get better."

Until it ended, he meant.

She shoved that thought away brutally. No. She wouldn't let that ruin the time she had left. If this was all she'd ever get from a man who fit her so seamlessly, then she wasn't going to waste it whining about what she couldn't have.

Tightening her fingers around his dick, she pumped him harder. She watched his lids drop to half-mast and a little grin curl his lips. It made her heart stop, and an answering smile formed on her lips of its own volition.

She loved him. God, how she loved him. She'd run away from it for so long, but that hadn't stopped it. Giving in to the physical craving for him had unlocked everything else, sent it spilling out until she could no longer deny any of it. She wanted him, she loved him, she loved who she was when she was with him. Lighter, more optimistic. And he understood her enough to handle the darker sides of her, too. He understood because he was just like her in so many ways.

Rising on tiptoe, she brushed his lips with hers, but continued to caress his thick sex. He drove his hand into her hair, holding her in place while he ravaged her mouth. She kissed him back, needing more of him. All of him. Everything she could get. Squirming, she worked her fingers around to unbuckle his belt and unfasten his pants. Then he was in her hands, his cock hard and pulsing.

A growl rumbled out of him, the sound of a volcano erupting. Silver flickered around his arms, the sign of incipient change telling her just how close he was from losing control. She grinned, loving how she could push him over the edge. He set her away from him, his hands urgent as he yanked off their clothing. He had them both naked in moments. Spinning her around, he pressed her face against the wall.

She braced her palms on the hard surface and moaned when his muscular form came into full contact with her back. His hands slipped up her ribs to cup her breasts, his claws flicking her nipples. A broken cry jerked from her, the sound edged in need. "Max, I want you inside me. Now, now, *now!*"

The lupine growl that rumbled from him reverberated against her back. His hands abandoned her breasts and dropped to grip her hips tight. His talons bit deep into her flesh as he jerked her ass toward him. Yes. God, yes. She spread her feet, supporting herself for the impact of his entry.

Arching her back to open herself further, she glanced over her shoulder to meet his eyes and demand he give her what she craved. They both groaned when he slid home within her. She could *feel* every inch of him, he filled her so perfectly. The rhythm he set for them was swift and almost rough, calling to the feral woman inside her. Yes. Yes, it was just what she needed.

Wrapping his arms around her again, he moved one hand up to continue fondling her breasts, teasing her nipples until she knew she'd come just from that if he didn't stop. Then his other hand moved down to cover her mound, slipping into the damp folds to rub the stretched lips of her pussy. It only emphasized how full she was, how deep and hard his strokes were. Tingles broke over every inch of her skin, and she bit back a scream. *Yes, Max. Just like that. More, please, more!*

"I'll give you more, sweetheart." He used the hot juices to trail a slippery path up to her clit. He pressed down on that sensitive spot and let his thrusts drive her forward for increased stimulation.

"Oh, God." Her face pressed to the wall, their frantic movements scraping her cheek against the rough surface. The discomfort wasn't enough to stop her. She needed this, needed him. Love squeezed her insides so tight, she ached with it. Rocking her hips into his thrusts, she took everything he could give her.

Orgasm exploded through her, gripping her deep inside and spreading outward until her entire body shook. He groaned, his hips faltering in their rhythm before he slammed deep and came with her. His fluids pumped into her pussy, and each spurt made her inner muscles clench around him. It was so right, the way they moved together, the way they fit.

Shudders racked them both, sweat sliding down their skin, sticking their bodies together. His breath cooled the moisture on her flesh when he dropped his forehead to her shoulder. He didn't loosen his hold on her, didn't pull out of her. His semi-hard cock still worked her in infinitesimal thrusts.

He seemed as reluctant as she to end the interlude, and she knew it was a figment of her imagination, but she clung to it because she had nothing else. Time was running out, and there wasn't a damn thing she could do about it. She laid her arms over his and wrapped her fingers around his wrists, holding on for dear life.

The physical was all she had to cling to, and it was bitterly ironic that a week ago she'd told herself that was all she really wanted from him.

She was such a fool.

Max had already had her three times that night, and he already wanted her again. They curled together naked on the couch in his room, her back to his front, as they laughed over some ridiculous old black-and-white comedy on TV. He'd never have imagined that Kira would be so open in a sexual relationship, and suddenly he was fiercely jealous of any man who'd ever seen this side of her. It was ludicrous, but that didn't change a thing. He wanted all of this for himself. He just couldn't have it. He couldn't even *want* to have it.

She snagged the remote off the coffee table and snapped off the television when the movie ended. Rolling onto her back beside him, she smiled slowly, lifting her hand to trace a fingertip over his eyebrow, down the bridge of his nose, and across his bottom lip. "You're quiet."

Shaking his head, he forced himself to grin and keep his tone light. "Just thinking. You know how dangerous that can be."

He expected her to laugh, but she didn't. Instead, her expression intensified. She opened her mouth to speak, but didn't. She glanced away and glanced back, meeting his gaze squarely. "There was a woman while you were in the Marines, wasn't there?"

Every muscle in his body went rigid. He couldn't help it. It was as if she'd prodded a fatal, slow-leaking wound and ripped it wide open. It was all he could do not to leap off the couch and run from the simple question. "Are we really talking about my other women while we're naked together?"

That steady gaze didn't waver. "I'm not talking about all the man-whoring you've done, Max. I'm talking about serious relationships."

"I don't do those." The pain spread through him, the sickness and guilt enough to drop him if he weren't lying down.

"But you did once, didn't you?" Her hand cupped his jaw, refusing to let him look away. "There was a woman, and she was important to you. You loved her."

He flinched from her stare. "It was a long time ago. It doesn't matter. What even made you ask about this?"

"Something Elan said got me thinking." Her breasts rose

and fell as she drew in a deep breath. He let himself be distracted by the sight. Any excuse to not think about what she was asking him. But the next questions hit him like a fist to the solar plexus. "What happened? Did she cheat on you or dump you for another guy?"

"*No.*" His gaze flew to her face and he knew horror shone in his expression. Clenching his fingers, he tried to hide that his hands were shaking. "Michelle would never have done that. Not to anyone."

"So . . . this Michelle was loyal, and you loved her. Why aren't you still with her?" Kira's voice was low, and nothing about her tone accused or demanded an answer, which made it harder to deny her.

He blew out a breath and gritted his teeth. "Because she died, damn it."

"I'm sorry." Her thumb glided over his cheekbone, the simple gesture gutting him. He didn't deserve her sympathy. He tried to shut down the utter craving he had for her understanding.

"It was a long time ago. It—"

"Don't say it doesn't matter." Her fingers tightened on his jaw. "It does matter."

"Yeah. It does matter. She mattered. A lot." He closed his eyes and turned his head away. Kira was the last person in the world he wanted to talk to about this. Or was she? Perhaps she deserved to know. Perhaps it would push her away and keep him from doing something stupid, like asking her to stay with him, to keep this amazing thing they had going for as long as possible. Forever. But forever hadn't lasted long before, had it? He swallowed and told the bald truth. "I loved her and she died."

"How?"

His stomach heaved and he pinched his eyes shut tighter, unable to look at Kira while he told her about the other woman who'd meant the world to him. So long ago. He'd been so young, so cocksure, so damn foolish. He shook his head and snorted. "It was stupid. We had some leave time and we went up to Yosemite to climb Half Dome. She was a Marine, too, and she knew what she was doing, so it was just us, cutting loose and doing something fun. It wasn't supposed to be dangerous. She was right behind me and she just . . . slipped. She was there one second and then she was gone." He pressed his fingers to his burning eyelids. "It was just . . . stupid. She shouldn't have died. If she'd been Between, she *wouldn't* have died. The fall would have hurt her, but it wouldn't have killed her."

"You wish you had made her Between."

"Yes. No." He dropped his hand to meet her gaze. "Hell, I don't know. I've gone over it in my mind a million times, and I wish she'd been Between so she'd have lived, but . . . we weren't in a place yet where I could tell her the truth, where I could even consider changing her."

Her fingers stroked down his jaw, his neck, and his shoulder. Her touch was soothing, her expression understanding. She should be pushing him away; instead she cuddled closer. "The potential was there, though."

"Yeah. The potential was there." He sighed, and the sound was weary. He should have known the truth wouldn't scare her. Not Kira. They had that in common, the two women he'd loved. The thought should have terrified him, but it didn't. He ached from the inside out. "I'll always wonder what might have happened with us if she'd survived."

"I'm sorry."

"Me too."

"It wasn't your fault, you know." She pressed a kiss to his jaw.

He shook his head, unwilling to absolve himself so easily. "I should have been watching her. I should have taken better care of her."

An impatient noise escaped from his little fox. "She was a trained Marine, you said. You couldn't have known what would happen."

"We were goofing off. I was being irresponsible. She died."

Irresponsible. The word his father had used to describe him more times than he could ever count. Irresponsible, the disappointment, the son who would never behave like a real prince, who didn't want to take a hand in ruling his people. Useless. Except when it came to making sure people ended up dead.

As much as his father had always been at loggerheads with Elan, at least they'd understood each other. They hadn't agreed on how affairs should be run, but they both wanted to have their fingers in the pie, they both wanted to be running the show. Not Max. Max was the one whose only talent was as an enforcer, a thug, a weapon.

"You're not irresponsible."

He shrugged, letting his hand drift in circles over her flat belly. "I'm good at my job."

"That's not all you're good at."

A snort erupted from him. "Yeah, sex. I'm good at that. I've had a lot of practice." Favoring her with a slow smile, he moved his hand down to slip into the soft hair between her legs. "But one can never be too skilled, right?"

She gave him a look that said she wasn't going to let him off the hook. "You're a great friend, Max. You're an amazing brother. You're a good boss. You're not a great prince, but you don't need to be. That doesn't make you irresponsible."

Bending over her, he licked each of her nipples in turn. "I never say the right thing."

The shiver that passed through her made him grunt in pleasure. He loved her reactions. She began to writhe as he pressed his fingers into her sex. "But you *do* the right thing, and you make up for it when you realize you've put your foot in your mouth again."

"Again."

"Yeah, again. So what?" She parted her legs and lifted her hips for him to tease her sex. He rubbed his thumb over her clit, and her legs jolted, her knees rising to clasp around his forearm. She licked her lips, her auburn brows drawing together as she struggled to focus. "How long are you going to let your dad's bullshit color your view of yourself? You told Elan to knock that off, so why can't you take your own advice?"

He paused in his movements. "Because . . ."

"Because you don't think he was wrong about you." She nudged his arm with her upraised knee.

His finger began stroking up and down her slit, drawing her moisture from her core to her clitoris. "No, I don't." He spoke slowly, unable to deny that his father's view of him had helped cement his own. "I was fourteen the first time I killed a man."

"I remember. You saved your father from being assassinated." Knees clamping on his arm, she stopped him again. Her hand bracketed his chin so he had to look at her. Whatever she saw in his gaze made her shake her head and snort in disgust. "Only King Phillip could make having two strong, capable sons a *bad* thing. You know what his problem was? He was jealous of you both. You're better men than he could ever be, and deep down he knew it."

A wry grin touched his lips. Hardly. "Elan maybe, not me."

"Yes, Max. *You.*" She poked his chest, scowling up at him. "You have the strength to do what needs doing, no matter what it costs you personally, in order to *protect* what matters most to you. You're not a murderer. You don't kill indiscriminately."

"A tool to be used. A thug."

The fox growled. "Those are your father's words. Not mine. Not Elan's. Not anyone who knows you."

"I killed my mother." God, that hurt to say. He didn't think he'd ever voiced it out loud. His father had, many times. After he'd stopped the assassin in his teens and especially after he'd joined the Marines.

"What?" The utter shock on Kira's face made him wince. "Oh, my God. That is such bullshit. That is so like your father. Think about it, Max. You were an infant. She died in childbirth. It was a tragic accident. And your girlfriend's death was a tragic accident. There is nothing you could have done to save either woman. Don't let Phillip's endless crap twist you up so much that you can't separate *his* issues from *your* job or from your mom's and Michelle's *accidental* deaths."

He stared at her silently for long moments as he let that sink in. He swallowed, but still said nothing. Shit. She was right. He'd let Michelle's death justify everything his father had ever said about him while he was growing up. But he knew his father thrived on controlling everything and everyone around him—Max had easily seen how his father's selfishness had hurt Elan and had, in fact, led to his father's suicide. Only a lion got to be king, and when he'd forced the Between into human awareness, he'd stopped shifting into a lion. Elan had become the lion, the king. His father couldn't handle it, and the shame had made him take his own life. What an ass. And Max had based his understanding of his own worth on that. But how could his father's opinion not matter to a young boy?

None of that brought Michelle back, or assuaged his guilt at her death. Had there been anything he could have done? He didn't know. He'd never know. Even then, he couldn't change it.

"You're a good man, Max. Better than your father ever managed to be. Work and sex aren't the only things you excel at, and anyone who knows you would agree with me." Kira stroked a fingertip over his lower lip. "I get that we all have masks we show the world, but you're not a carefree princeling and you're not a stone-cold killer. The truth isn't that simple, but it's there if people bother to look." She pulled his head down and brushed her lips over his. "I see you."

Wrapping one arm around her, he jerked her under him and stopped the painful conversation in the most enjoyable way he knew. She opened her lips for his tongue, kissing him just as fiercely as he kissed her. Her passion always rose to match his, and when it came to her, he was insatiable.

Forcing his thigh between hers, he shoved her legs wide and mounted her. Hands clutching at his back, he felt the bite of her talons into his skin. He growled, the wolf ripping loose the way he rarely allowed with other women. But this was Kira. Kira, who knew all his secrets. Kira, who understood every part of him, good and bad. Kira, who'd never turn away from the darkness that lived inside him because of all the things his profession made him do. She had the same relentless need to defend and protect.

It was no wonder he loved her.

His chest tightened with emotion until he could barely breathe, and still he kissed her. He couldn't stop—he needed her now. He'd never get his fill of her, and he didn't want to. He poured everything he could never say into the kiss, mating his mouth to hers. She whimpered against his lips, her claws raking down his sides and her legs cinching around his waist to urge him onward.

Not yet. Not yet. He needed more. He needed this to last for as long as possible.

Slipping his fingers into the short silken strands of her hair, he pulled her head back so he could lick and suck his way down her long neck. His fangs nipped at the spot at the base of her throat that he knew made her squirm.

"I want you, Max." She moaned when he dug his fangs in deeper. "Max!"

Her cry of his name echoed in his head, her demand as much mental as verbal. He couldn't resist her. Reaching between them, he grasped his cock and guided himself to the slick opening of her pussy. She rubbed herself against him in shameless abandon, her nipples sliding against his chest and her sex dampening the head of his cock.

Driving partway into her, he withdrew and she moaned a protest. He pushed back in, deeper this time, and pulled back, thrusting still deeper every time until he was hilted inside her. She clung to him, and he reveled in the feel of her. Her satin skin, her inner moisture that welcomed him. He sealed himself against her, grinding his pelvis into her clit.

"Yes! Oh, my God!" Her back bowed and her claws raked down his flesh. He winced at the sting, a growl soughing from his throat. Her heels dug into the backs of his thighs. "Harder. *Faster*. I need . . . I'm going to . . ."

Damn, but the woman got to him. He laughed and gave her exactly what she wanted. Bracing his hands on either side of her, he rose above her and used the extra leverage to fuck her hard. Ecstasy rocketed through his system as he let loose. Ramming deep into her pussy with every thrust, he took them both to the very edge in moments.

"This is so fucking good." Sweat slipped down his back, and he moved faster and faster, anything to keep this sensation going. Gazing down at her, he could see her eyes losing focus, a faint silver light glowing beneath her skin as her cries grew louder. He pounded into her, knowing he wouldn't last, knowing nothing this perfect could ever last. The scent of her passion was one he'd never forget, locked into his memory for all the days of his life. Seeing her like this was as close to heaven as a man like him would ever get. Her sex pulsed around his dick once, and he could sense how close she was. "Come for me, Kira."

Her muscles locked tight on him, her pussy flexing in waves around his cock as she climaxed. The feral side of his nature wanted to take, to claim. The wolf wanted to be in command.

Silver swirled around the arms he had bracketing her body, and he felt change riding him as he rode her. He fought it, raced it, and flung himself toward orgasm.

He threw his head back, a howl ripping free as he jetted hard inside her. He hadn't come that close to shifting during sex since he was a teen. It would have been embarrassing, but he was too spent to care. She'd wrung everything from him, and he collapsed on top of her. He felt her arms come around him, and something deep within him loosened and gave way.

"Kira, I . . ." He paused, not certain how to say what he wanted to say, not even certain *what* he wanted to say.

"Yeah?" Her voice was smoky with sleep, her limbs falling open and away from him as her breathing deepened into that of slumber.

He'd never know now what he would have said. An affectionate smile formed on his mouth as he stroked her hair away from her face. For a long while, he just watched her sleep. His chest squeezed tight, and it was the most amazing moment of his life. Unlike the last time he'd fallen in love, this time he didn't take it for granted. Nothing lasted forever, so now he was old enough and mature enough to appreciate it.

He'd just never thought he'd fall again. He hadn't wanted it, had run from any inkling of it since Michelle had died, but with Kira, it had built so gradually that he hadn't noticed until it was too late. The woman owned his soul now.

Whether he ever got up the courage to tell her was another matter entirely.

Saying it somehow made it more real, made it undeniable that he could lose Kira as easily as he had lost Michelle. But there had been sides of him Michelle had never seen because she'd been human. For better or for worse, part of his relationship with her had always been a lie. Not with Kira. As she'd said, she saw him. She saw through the masks he wore for the world. She knew him for what he really was, just the way he knew her. The prospect of having her, *really* having her and admitting that to lose her was to lose a part of himself, was more than he could handle.

Maybe someday he could get to a place where he believed it could last, where love was something safe to feel. Maybe. Someday.

But not yet.

6

Everything was still up in the air.

Kira's insides churned as she escorted Rhiannon and Elan out to the waiting helicopter. Max kept pace beside her, close enough that she could feel the heat of his skin, but the distance between them was painful. They didn't look at each other, didn't speak, didn't share thoughts.

It was over, just as they'd promised each other. This morning was the last time she'd wake up in his bed.

The pain of it shredded her, and there wasn't a thing she could do about it. Except put on that professional mask her father had valued so highly and get on with her life.

But, God, it hurt. She didn't know if it would ever stop hurting.

Movement flickered at the corner of her vision. It was just a subtle flash of light from a distance hillside, but every instinct inside her screamed.

She didn't stop, didn't think. She simply reacted, launching herself forward to knock Rhiannon to the ground and shield the other woman with her body. The breath rushed out of her lungs when they hit the ground hard, and pain exploded from her side and shot straight to her brain. The sound of gunfire roared, Max howled in lupine rage, and in a twist of silver light, the huge red wolf was in pursuit of the gunman.

"Move, Rhiannon!" Hauling them both into a crouch, Kira hustled Rhiannon toward the helo.

More shots rang out, and huge holes ripped into the side of the helicopter. Fifty-caliber bullets and someone who knew how to use a long-range rifle.

Fuck.

One look was all it took for Kira to know that bird wasn't getting off the ground any time soon, despite the spinning propellers. Pushing Rhiannon around to the front, she scuttled under the nose of the helo to take cover on the far side. Elan, thankfully, was one step behind them.

The pilot bailed out of the cockpit and hit the pavement beside them just as the huge window exploded and rained glass down on them.

"Oh, my God. You're bleeding, Kira. You're bleeding." Wildness flashed in Rhiannon's eyes, and she panted for breath.

Kira ignored her, barking at the pilot. "How fast can you get one of the other helos off the ground? The king and queen need to be evacuated *now!*"

The man pointed. "That one's prepped and ready, I just need to get to it."

A bullet slammed into the propeller above them and the sound of rending metal sent chills down Kira's spine. A quick upward glance confirmed that the thing was going to snap any second. "We're going have to make a run for it."

Elan and Rhiannon both made sounds of protest. Rhiannon shook her head, her hair whipping into her face. "No, Kira. You're—"

"No time to argue, Majesties. Let's move out!" Wrapping her hand around Rhiannon's bicep, Kira dragged her into a run.

A whistling crash told her the propeller had given way. *Keep your heads down!*

She sent the telepathic thought as widely as possible, hoping all her Guards remained safe. Bullets slammed into the pavement as they sprinted forward, spraying debris that sliced into her flesh. Her heart hammered and pain ricocheted through her with every pounding footstep. Three yards to go, two, one. Their pilot clambered into the cockpit with another pilot who was already there. Kira ducked below the spinning propeller and stuffed Rhiannon into the back. Elan crawled inside with them and shoved the door closed.

"Take off, now!" Kira followed the order with a mental command, hitting the pilots on every possible level. They jerked in their seats, but obeyed her as all Guards had been trained to do. In moments, they were in the air, winging away from the cabin.

Rhiannon knelt on the floor in front of her, tugging at Kira's clothes.

"What the hell are you doing?" Kira grabbed for the other woman's hands, trying to direct her into the next seat. Her grip didn't seem to be as tight as it should, and her voice sounded weak, but she pushed that away. It didn't matter. "Get up here and put your seat belt on."

"You're bleeding," Rhiannon snarled. She wrenched the bottom of Kira's wet shirt up.

It was only then that the agony hit her, a cry jerking out of her at Rhiannon's rough treatment. Kira gritted her teeth and rode out the pain. "Shit."

"Sorry." There wasn't a shred of remorse in Rhiannon's voice. Elan knelt beside her, a first aid kit in his hands. Kira blinked. When had Elan moved? She hadn't noticed anything.

"Get us to a hospital!" Desperation and terror made Rhiannon's voice a brittle slice of noise.

One of the pilots responded, but Kira couldn't focus on

what he said. Time became fluid, slipping past her. The pain was a living, writhing thing, branding her side, radiating up to her skull. Her thoughts hazed around the edges, and part of her recognized that there was a lot of blood pooling on the floor of the helicopter. Too much blood.

Elan glanced up and met her gaze. "Can you shift?"

"No." Her lips were numb, stiff as she slurred the word. Her heart thudded slowly in her chest, every beat weakening her as blood pumped from her body.

"Shift? Why would she shift?" Rhiannon's voice cracked as she pressed a thick white bandage to Kira's side. It soaked through with crimson in moments. "She has a bullet in her!"

The king knew what his wife didn't yet. She was a new Between—she hadn't seen shifting save a person's life. If Kira could change forms, the split second where her body was neither human nor animal, but pure energy, would heal her of all wounds.

It was far too late for that.

She didn't even have time to be afraid. She had a single moment for regret. She wished she'd told Max she loved him, wished that she let slip the mask she'd worn for more years than she had realized. It was a foolish, asinine, pointless wish. Max wasn't even here. She was going to die without ever seeing him again. It made her angry, so enraged to have lost any chance at real happiness, but the tiny spurt of emotion exhausted her. Tears burned her lids, hopelessness crashing down around her.

"Max." Looking at Elan, she tried to will her lips to move, her mind to send the telepathic thought. His big hand closed over hers, and the heat seared her cold flesh. "Tell Max . . ."

Her voice failed, the last of her strength deserting her no matter how she fought against it.

Elan shook his head fiercely, his amber eyes locked with hers, and as her vision blurred, he almost seemed to glow with his ferocity. "You can tell him yourself, damn it. I refuse to let you die."

Too late. Too late for any more foolish wishes.

Then there was nothing. The agony stopped, the shudder of the helo going at top speed, the sound of Rhiannon's sobbing, the rumble of Elan's voice. It drifted away like mist on the San Amaro coast. And all she knew was . . . nothing.

He'd ripped the man's throat out, left him gawping like a landed fish as the life drained out of him. Max had tracked the fleeing human through the mountains, his wolf senses more alive that they'd ever been before. He doubted the man had ever heard him coming, doubted he'd had any idea that death was so close. Max had shown no mercy and no remorse.

He had, without a doubt, lived up to his father's low expectations for him. He was nothing but a killer. And he hadn't even managed to use that to protect the people he loved.

God, he loved her. Even now, hours later, all he could see when he closed his eyes was the blood splattering across the landing pad. All he could smell was the coppery scent of it. Her blood. Kira.

A shudder rippled through him and he buried his face in his hands. He sat, like so many others, and waited to see if she would survive. Elan had gotten her to this hospital alive. Max didn't know how, but he was grateful for even the hope of seeing her smile again.

The human doctors had taken her into surgery, pulling the bullet fragments out, pumping fresh blood into her veins. Max and the Guards had arrived at the same time as the Between doctor, Adam Lee.

And now they waited to see if a miracle could happen.

Rhiannon huddled in Elan's arms in the chairs across from Max. His brother watched him, concern in his eyes, but Max was glad no one tried to talk to him. Barrett and a few other

Guards paced back and forth down the sterile hallway, something that Max would normally be doing, but he couldn't move, couldn't think, couldn't breathe.

Fear twisted like a coiling snake within him, a living evil that was ready to strike. Ready to kill what was left of his soul.

His stomach heaved, and he swallowed the acrid bile that burned the back of his throat.

"Adam."

Max's head came up at the single word from Barrett. He rose to his feet, his gaze locking on the doctor coming down the hall toward them. The man looked haggard, his face ashen, his eyes bloodshot. He looked like someone who'd fought a war. And lost.

No. Please, God, no. He couldn't survive this again. Not again. Not Kira. Ice froze the blood in Max's veins and he swayed on his feet. The world tilted in front of him and a roaring filled his ears even though he *needed* to hear what the doctor had to say. His life depended on it.

He caught his hands on his knees before he slammed face first into the linoleum. The next thing he knew, Elan was on one side and Barrett on the other, each pushing him back into the chair and shoving his head between his knees.

"Are you all right?" Adam's quiet voice sounded right in front of him, and Max looked up to meet the man's dark eyes.

"I don't know. Am I?" Because God knew, he'd never be all right again if Kira hadn't survived. And he'd been too gutless to tell her he loved her. His heart stopped as he waited for the other man to speak.

The doctor crouched in front of him, his serious expression breaking into a smile of pure triumph. "It was rough, but she pulled through."

A joyful cry spilled from Rhiannon and echoed through the small cluster of Guards. Max just dropped his head between his knees and laced his fingers through his hair. *Thank you.*

He sent the telepathic thought out, and he wasn't even sure to whom. His brother for getting Kira here in time, Adam for doing what the human doctors couldn't, God for not taking her away. Gratitude flooded him, making his heart thud painfully in his chest. Moisture burned his lids, and he sucked in a deep, calming breath.

Elan's hand squeezed his shoulder in support. "When can we see her?"

"She's sleeping right now, but give her an hour or so and she should be just fine."

"And we can take her back to San Amaro then?" Rhiannon flopped onto the floor next to Adam in a very unqueenly manner. "She's fine, just like that?"

"Just like that. It took a lot of energy transfer to get her to shift forms, but she did, and now she's fine. Exhausted, but fine."

"*You're* exhausted." Barrett spoke up for the first time, his fingers digging into Adam's shoulder.

Adam met the blond man's gaze for long moments, and Max could almost sense the telepathy flowing back and forth between them. Finally, Adam simply nodded. "Yes. I'm exhausted."

"Let's get some coffee. The shit they have in the cafeteria shouldn't kill you, and it's caffeinated." Barrett stood and offered his hand.

Adam grabbed the Guard's forearm and allowed himself to be hauled to his feet. He glanced back at Max before he walked away. "Give her an hour and she's all yours."

The words snapped something inside Max's head. She wasn't all his, and she never would be. For all the reasons that hadn't changed and never would. Guilt went crashing through him, and along with it, a sense of inadequacy unlike anything he'd ever known. Not even his father had brought him so low. He had done nothing to save her. Elan had. Adam had.

Max had been good for nothing.

Except killing the shooter.

Because that was all he was good for.

"Energy transfer." Rhiannon refolded her legs, wiggling around as though she could find a comfortable position on the cold tile floor. "Maybe it's because I haven't even had a whole year being Between, but the idea of transferring your energy to someone else is just so . . . weird to me. Still. Maybe it always will be." She met Max's eyes. "That's what Elan did to keep her alive until we could land here."

"Don't try it yourself, baby." Elan's voice deepened to a low growl. "It takes training and skill you don't have. You could drain yourself of energy until *you* couldn't shift to a solid form."

She shivered. "I don't want to try it. But I would if I had to. If there was no one who knew how and you or Max or Kira or Genesee were dying . . . you can bet your ass I'd try."

He opened his mouth as if he were going to argue, but then sighed. "I know you would."

The sparkle of good humor in Rhiannon's gaze made Elan grin and shake his head. She rose gracefully to her feet and dusted her pants off. "While we're waiting, I'm going to run down to get some of that battery-acid coffee. You guys want me to bring you back some?"

"Yeah, bring some for both of us." Elan's hand squeezed the back of Max's neck, and he nodded to a couple of Guards to go with his wife. "Thanks, baby."

She bent forward and pressed a quick kiss to his lips. "No problem. Back soon."

The moment she'd gone, Elan's fingers tightened on Max's nape. "What are you thinking? It's not like you to be silent."

Max snorted and pulled away from his brother's grip. "I'm not always a loudmouth."

"I never said you were." The older man's words were quiet

and measured. "I know you, Max. I know all your secrets and you know mine. So, I have to wonder why you're getting defensive when all I asked was what's on your mind."

The truth burst out of him, a dam rupturing deep within. "I'm not good enough for her."

"What? What's this?" Elan reared back, then hissed. "Since when have you let something that stupid crawl into your head?"

"Since always."

"And always started . . . when, exactly?"

"Shit, Elan." Max shoved his fingers through his hair. "You know when."

"Father."

"Yeah." He let his arm drop and sighed, feeling more defeated than he ever had in his life. "She deserves better. She deserves . . . Hell, I don't know. *You.* A king. Whatever she wants."

His brother made a disgusted noise. "Kira wouldn't be a queen if you paid her. She'd hate every second of it, and she and I have never felt that way about each other. She's like my sister—she sees me like a brother."

"I know that." Now, anyway. A couple of weeks ago, he'd have argued differently.

"So, what's the problem? She doesn't want a king. After Seaton was done with her, she probably thinks she isn't worthy of one anyway. It's *above her place.*" Elan's voice took on a remarkably accurate Seaton-like English accent. "And even that was bullshit. She's good enough for whomever she wants and so are you. You want each other. It's done. It was done years ago, but the two of you are stubborn asses."

"You're one to speak, brother."

He snorted. "Yeah, well. I didn't say I wasn't stubborn, I said you were."

"I'm a killer." Max swallowed past the huge lump that stuck in his throat. "She deserves better."

Settling back in his chair, Elan hitched his ankle onto his knee. "You've killed people before, yes. A few times because I ordered it. Does that make me worse for asking my little brother to do my dirty work for me?"

"You're a good man. A *great* man."

"I feel the same way about you, Max. You left San Amaro and made a life for yourself that was just your own. I just took on the family's issues. Business and government." He gestured down at himself, at his expensive clothing. "None of this is mine—I wasn't the first and I won't be the last. I admire the hell out of you for breaking out and making your own way."

Max stared blankly at his brother, unable to take in everything he'd said. Max was the screwup. Always had been, always would be. The thug. The weapon.

This was one thing he'd never talked about with Elan. A part of him hadn't wanted confirmation that his older brother—his only real family—agreed with their father's assessment. He wouldn't be as cruel about it, but he also wouldn't lie. And Max hadn't wanted the truth.

He swallowed hard. "She could have died. Like Michelle."

"Yes, she could have." His brother pulled in a slow breath, and when his spoke, his tone was considering. "What happens to us in life leaves scars. For Between, those scars are just inside. It doesn't mean they aren't there just because the magic heals the outer marks. What happened with Michelle, how we grew up with Father, leaving home to make your way among humans, coming back and cleaning up the messes of our entire race . . . all of those things left their marks on your soul, Max. It doesn't make you a better or worse person than anyone else. We *all* have those marks. We do the best we can from one day to the next. That's all we can do, isn't it?"

"Yeah." A huge weight crumbled away from Max. The relief was staggering. He'd had been carrying it around for so long he hadn't even noticed it until it was gone. Elan was right. Kira was right. He'd used his father's opinion of him to color everything around him. He'd let that keep him from getting over Michelle's death. It had taken learning to love again to see it.

Elan crossed his arms over his broad chest. "So, is the best you can do running from a living, breathing woman who loves you?"

"No." The best he could do was love her back, hold on tight, and pray he could keep her safe. Though she'd kick his ass for thinking he needed to protect her. He grinned for the first time in what felt like forever.

Kira opened her eyes to a familiar face. "What's up, Doc?"

Her voice was scratchy and weak to her ears, and she realized she was ferociously thirsty. Dead people didn't feel anything, and she felt like shit warmed over, so she was definitely *not* dead.

Adam groaned. "You really need to find a more original line."

A plastic cup with a straw appeared in front of her, and she latched on to suck down the cool ambrosia. The water flooded her mouth and moistened her parched throat. She drained the glass before she sank back against the pillows, shaking but replete. "I feel like someone took a baseball bat to me."

"Getting shot and almost bleeding out will do that to you." His voice was weary, and she looked at him more carefully. He looked like she felt.

"You helped me to shift."

He nodded, picked up her medical chart, and started reading it. "Yeah. Elan got you here alive, the human doctors got the bullet out and managed to stop the bleeding, and I got you to shift. If any one of those things hadn't happened, we'd be attending your funeral this week."

The air seeped out of her lungs. "I was pretty sure you would be. I . . . really didn't think I was going to wake up again."

It was almost disorienting to find she *was* alive. There'd been no question in her mind that she was done. Show over. Time for white light and angels singing.

"Welcome back, then." Adam's smile was as calm and reassuring as ever, though there was some tension around his mouth that she'd bet wasn't due to doctoring her up. Barrett. It had to be.

As if on cue, the big cat-shifter knocked softly and poked his head in her door. He flinched when he saw Adam, but a grin lit his face when he looked at her. "Hey, Kira. There are some people who want to see you."

Adam set down her chart, crossed his arms, and pointedly did not look at the other man. "Are you up for visitors?"

"You two need to work this business out." She glanced between the two men.

Barrett rolled his eyes. "Okay, pot. I'll go see if the kettle wants to see you."

"He probably doesn't." She glanced down at the blanket covering her legs, plucking at a loose thread. Barrett hadn't heard her—or he'd ignored her—because he'd already gone to get Max.

"It's rough, this love thing." Adam sighed. "And I ended up with a double dose."

"I'm sorry. For the double whammy you got and for butting in." She pushed back the blanket and slid her legs over the side of the bed. "I want to shift again before I see anyone. Then I won't feel like roadkill."

"I'll help." Adam braced her while she stood, his arms beginning to glimmer with silver light.

"Are you sure you're up for this?"

He simply nodded in his reassuring way. She closed her eyes and leaned against him, letting his energy spin through her to boost her own flagging reserves. The heat of magic burned within her, sputtering and then flaring to brilliant life.

She flashed into fox form, stretching her front paws into the new shape, twitching her tail. No pain, not even a twinge of discomfort. *Nice.*

Are you ready to shift back to human form or do you want to stay an animal for a while? The doctor's telepathic voice came from the sun bear before her. The wicked curl of his claws scraped against the linoleum when he moved in the small room.

She cocked her head, considering. It would be too easy to face Max as a fox, because what she felt and what she needed to tell him was about very human emotion. No more running, no more hiding, no more lying to herself about what was in her heart. That would be the coward's way out. *I'll go human, but I think I can do it by myself this time.*

I'm here if you need me. The bear grunted and eased back as much as possible to give her some space.

She pulled in a deep breath and shut her eyes, drawing up the energy inside her. The silver glow filtered through her eyelids as she felt herself swirling into pure magic. She had the briefest moment to wonder if she had enough energy to make the change, but then she was already reforming into a solid shape. When she looked again, she was human.

"Kira?" Rhiannon's voice echoed outside the door.

Adam, also in human form and already clothed, handed her a set of sweats and turned around to let her dress while he went to open the door for the queen.

Kira shrugged into her top just as the royal couple strode into the room. She rose to her feet and felt . . . good. Rock steady. As if nothing had ever happened. Sometimes, it was good to be Between.

Elan and Rhiannon both hugged her, told her how relieved they were. The queen shoved her red curls over her shoulder. "Though I swear if you ever do anything like that again, I'll shoot you myself."

Arching an eyebrow, Kira looked down her nose at the other woman. "Taking a bullet for you is part of my job. Suck it up."

Rhiannon huffed. "Fine. Be that way."

"I will." Then she hugged her friend tight and ignored the fact that her father would be horrified at the familiarity with her employer. So what? If she was going to put her life on the line for the woman, it was better that it was someone she actually liked. She realized just how much she'd fallen back into the pattern of her father's mind-set when she'd returned to San Amaro. As much as she'd adored the man, she didn't agree with him. She was as good as anyone else. It wasn't about who was destined to be servant and who was destined to be master. If she wanted to quit, she could. She made those decisions for herself, not fate. But she loved what she did. It fulfilled her, and it was important to her to make a difference for her people. It was important to her to keep those she cared for safe. Even if it meant she'd take another bullet for one of them. That was the kind of person she was—regardless of anyone's social class—and she was content with that.

"We're going to get our transport in order." Elan put his arm around his wife's shoulder. "I don't know about you, but I'm ready to get back home."

"More than ready." Kira pulled herself up onto the side of the bed while everyone disappeared.

They were all letting Max have some alone time with her, which was nice, but if he hadn't trampled everyone on his way to see her, that really only meant one thing. She could smell him nearby, could practically *feel* his guilt wafting toward her. A sigh spilled past her lips. She knew the shooting would bring up some terrible memories for him. It was the hardest part of all this. She knew him. She understood him. She understood what made him who he was, but that also meant she knew why he needed to stop punishing himself for things he couldn't change.

I know you're there, Max. Come in or leave.

Which do you want me to do?

She closed her eyes. It hurt that he had to ask, that he didn't know. Her mental voice was terser than she intended when she replied. *Come here.*

His scent drew closer, and then his big body filled the doorway, blocking the light beyond. "The shooter's dead. I killed him."

"Good." She spoke bluntly, and that seemed to ease some of the tension vibrating through him. "Who was he?"

"We don't know yet. Barrett has our people looking into it, dealing with local authorities, figuring out how the hell a human got on our property." He sighed, his expression haggard and wary.

"You look like hell."

She expected a sarcastic reply, but instead his throat worked for a long moment, he swallowed hard, and it almost looked as if he might cry. "You look beautiful."

Damn. She had to glance away or *she* was going to start tearing up. But she held her hand out, and his warm fingers immediately engulfed hers. He set his free hand beside her hip and buried his face in the crook of her neck. The naked need in that gesture staggered her. Moisture burned her eyes as she wrapped her arms tight around him. She dragged in a steadying breath. "I'm all right."

"You were right beside me . . . and then you were gone." The ragged edge to his voice, the echo of words he'd spoken about Michelle, made pain shaft inside her.

She ran her palm up and down his back. "I'm not her. I'm Between. I survived."

He nodded and squeezed her tight, all but lifting her off the bed. "Logically, I know that."

"But it brought everything with Michelle back."

"Yeah."

"I'm sorry." Was his upset really for her, or was it just that she'd dredged up old memories? They were friends and colleagues and he'd be upset for those reasons alone, but that wasn't enough for her. Not anymore.

His embrace loosened and he braced his hands on either side of her hips. His gaze met hers, open and honest. No masks to hide behind. "I don't know how I can do this, Kira."

Her chest tightened until she couldn't draw breath. A harsh laugh spilled out of her. Well, that took care of that, didn't it? Did it really matter what she wanted or how she felt if he walked away? She pushed out of his arms and stood, heading for the bathroom door before what was left of her dignity completely deserted her. "I'm going to grab a shower before we leave for San Amaro." She paused and glanced back. "Look, I get it. You don't have to pretend you wanted more than sex. We were friends before and that's what we're back to. It's fine."

"Let me finish. Please." Two strides and he caught her elbow. "I don't know how I could live if I lost you now, but it'd be a lot worse to watch you find someone with the guts to hold on to you." He swallowed hard. "I love you."

All the blood drained out of her face, and she swayed. "Wh-what?"

"I love you. I've always loved you. As a friend when we were kids, and now as a lot more. I've wanted you for years, which I was pretty open about, but . . . that's not everything." His grip tightened and he met her gaze dead on. "I love you. As in, the kind of love that means marriage and kids and whatever you want. I'm in, I'm yours. If that's what you want, too."

"I . . . I honestly never expected you to. I thought . . . Hell, I don't know what I thought." Her legs gave out and she slumped against the bathroom door frame. "Oh, my God."

A muscle in his jaw twitched. "Is this a no?"

"No! Are you insane?"

He barked out a laugh. "Sometimes it feels that way when I'm around you."

"Are you sure?" Her heart thudded against her ribs, the shock still thrumming through her. Love was one thing, even staying together, but marriage? To Max? She hadn't even let herself go there in her mind. Hell, not even in her wildest dreams. Not really. She realized that was part of her father's training, thinking she wasn't good enough for a prince to actually marry. Time to put that kind of logic away. That wasn't her. She wanted a different life than her father had planned for her. She stared up at Max. "I mean, are you *sure* this is what you want? Because if you change your mind . . ."

"I'm sure." He took her face in his hands and let her see everything he felt. "Marry me, Kira. Look, I know you'd hate the princess part of this, but I'll do anything I can to make it easy on you. I know I've got a lot of shit to sort out in my head about my dad and my last girlfriend and, hell, everything, but I promise I will. All of this is probably a raw deal for you, but no matter how badly I screw up, I'll always keep trying until I get it right, and I'll try to keep you laughing enough that you don't notice you could have done better."

As if she could do better than her own prince charming. "Okay."

He chuckled, pulled her to him for a quick kiss. "Okay, you'll marry me . . . because you love me?"

"Yeah. Because I'm crazy in love with you." She twined her arms around his neck and pressed herself against him. "Kiss me again."

He kissed her, hot and hard. His tongue filled her mouth, his hands sliding over her until he cupped her ass and drew her up on tiptoe. Passion bloomed within her, heating her from the inside out. She twisted against him, the soft material of her sweatshirt rubbing over her nipples and making them tighten to stiff points. His hard body, hard arms, hard cock overwhelmed her, made her wet. She could feel everything and nothing. Their clothes kept her from stroking her wolf the way she wanted.

The tension soon became unbearable. Her sex was soaked, clenching on emptiness. Her skin burned with the need for his touch. She'd become addicted to it in the last weeks. When she jerked away from the kiss, it made him growl and he nipped at her exposed throat. She choked on a laugh. "I still want that shower."

His fangs scraped the tender spot where neck and shoulder met. "I'll join you."

"*Yesss.*" She all but purred the word.

"Mmm, you sound like a cat, my fox." He flicked his tongue over the flesh he'd just bitten.

She shuddered and pulled back, yanking at the bottom edge of her sweatshirt. Tossing it aside, she shoved down her pants and watched Max whip into a whirlwind of light and energy. His clothes fell to the floor and he reformed in his human shape, naked, hard, and ready. His cock curved to just below his navel, the head glistening with a single bead of pre-cum that trailed down the long shaft. The rough spiral pattern that marked him as Between gleamed silver on the muscular slab of his lower abdomen.

She turned and walked into the shower stall, flipping on the water. He came up behind her, his finger stroking down the line of her spine, swirling into the small of her back to trace her Between mark. "I've always loved that this was here."

Glancing back, her heart tripped at the soft smile that kicked up the corners of his lips. God, she adored him. Clearing her suddenly tight throat, she grinned back. "Yeah, it was so kind of Mother Nature to land me with a permanent tramp stamp. Bitch."

A chuckle bubbled out of him, just as she'd intended, but he bent forward and slid his tongue around the edge of her mark. His fangs scored her flesh, and she shivered, reflexively arching away from the hot, sharp touch.

His arm snapped around her waist, reeling her back in. He nipped at the upper curve of her ass. Her breath hissed between her teeth, and heat shimmered through her body, dampening her core even more and pinching her nipples tighter.

She gasped when he straightened and spun her under the pounding rush of hot water. Backing her up against the slick wall, he lifted her off her feet. She wrapped her arms around his neck and her legs around his waist. They both groaned as every inch of them came into contact. "Kira, I need you. Now."

"Take me. Now." Yes, she wanted him to take. She wanted to give him everything. The last barriers of her upbringing fell away, and she gave in to the life she wanted for herself.

She tilted her hips in offering, and he plunged his dick hilt-deep in one swift thrust. Crying out, she arched hard, which only drove him deeper. He rode her against the wall, and the water made their bodies slide together. The beads of moisture trailing down her skin just added to the ecstasy streaking through her body. She wouldn't last long. Already, she could feel orgasm building within her, the muscles in her pussy clenching and releasing in time with his stroking cock.

Her claws dug into his shoulders, and she closed her eyes and buried her face in his neck, drinking in his scent as he fucked her hard. Hot water pounded over her flesh, sent her hair streaming into her face. Too many sensations demanded her attention. Her breath sobbed out, and her body slapped against the slick wall behind her. The water glued their fronts together, increasing the wet friction, and her thighs burned with the strain of moving faster and faster. Gravity would have kept him inside her, but she couldn't wait. Lust and love spurred her onward.

Orgasm broke within her, and stars burst behind her eyelids. The stunning force of it left her gasping. She should be used to how powerful sex was with him, but she wasn't. It would always be better with him than it could be with anyone else. She loved him. And he loved her. Her prince. Her Max.

Her pussy clamped tight on his cock, milking his shaft in rhythmic waves. Still he ground himself into her, and every time he entered her, another wave of climax crashed through her.

She threw her head back against the wall, her mouth opening in a silent scream, her fangs punching through her gums. *Max! Max, please!*

A helpless groan echoed in the room, and he drove deep one last time before his come flooded her pussy. "I love you, Kira."

"I love you, Max."

Shuddering, he dropped his head to kiss the side of her neck. His arms tightened around her and compressed her ribs, squeezing the breath out of her. "God, how I love you."

And that was all she needed. They brought out the best in each other, and she'd never known anyone who accepted her, valued her, just as she was. Except Max. She knew what had happened in the last day would continue to affect them, but it wouldn't conquer them. They wouldn't let it. No matter what happened, they were strong enough to face it.

Together.

THE RIGHT NUMBER

LYNN LaFLEUR

1

Jamieson Edward Millington liked things orderly. He insisted on his house being neat, his vehicles clean, and his desk uncluttered.

Today, his desk looked as if an office supply warehouse had exploded on top of it.

Jay threw his pen on top of a tall stack of papers and blew out a sharp puff of breath. His cousin—the vice president of development at JEMATAR—had gone on vacation ten days ago and left Jay with several possibilities for investment property acquisitions. Jay trusted his cousin's instincts implicitly. If Troy recommended something to purchase, it would be profitable in the long run.

With all the work he already had to do on the upcoming release of JEMATAR's latest computer and new operating system, Jay had no room to add anything else to his list. He wished Troy had had the time to finish his investigations before he left for vacation. It hadn't been the best of times, business-wise, for Troy to leave, but he'd made his vacation plans months ago. He couldn't change them without paying penalties and extra fees. Besides, there wasn't ever a good time for Troy to leave. If there were forty-eight hours in the day, both Jay and Troy would stay busy constantly.

Shaking his head, Jay tried to marshal his thoughts back to the ream of paper on his desk. He knew he had only a short amount of time to act before the San Francisco properties were snatched up by someone else. Picking up his pen once more, he tackled the next pile of spreadsheets and copies of website pages on his desk.

The more he looked, the less he liked what he saw. Jay wondered if he should check property outside of San Francisco. There were definitely places in the U.S. that would be cheaper than the Bay Area.

Jay called up his Web browser and began checking real estate sites in the Midwest. He had no idea how much time passed before a property south of Dallas caught his attention. Good location, reasonable price, low taxes. As much as that area was growing, it would be a great investment for the future.

His attention still focused on his computer screen, Jay picked up the telephone receiver and punched in the number for the real estate company.

"Hello?" a soft feminine voice said.

Instant erection. One word from the woman on the other end of the line and his cock hardened. That had never happened to him. The wolf inside him snapped to attention. "Uh, hello. Have I reached Big D Properties?"

"I'm sorry, you have the wrong number."

If possible, his cock grew even harder. He tugged on the fly of his pants, trying to give his shaft more room. Her voice sounded so sexy, with a hint of a Texas drawl that made his heartbeat speed up and his inner wolf pace in impatience. It wanted her *now*. "Isn't this 972-555-9443?"

"No, it's not."

He glanced at the phone's display to verify the number, not

remembering until that moment that his telephone had died yesterday. This phone, a substitute until his could be replaced, didn't have a display window. "Then what number did I dial?"

She remained silent for several seconds. When she spoke again, he thought he heard amusement in her voice. "My mother always told me never to give out my phone number to someone I don't know."

Jay leaned back in his chair and smiled. He liked this game, despite his aching cock. "Oh, come on. I'm a nice guy, I swear."

"Isn't that what Ted Bundy said?"

Not only did she have a beautiful voice, she had a sense of humor, too. His wolf panted. "Okay, don't give me your number. But if this isn't Big D Properties, who is this?"

"Uh-uh, that won't work either."

"Are you always this suspicious?"

"Do you always flirt with strange women on the telephone?"

Good question, and one he had no problem answering honestly. "Only when they have an incredible voice."

"So do you," she said softly.

Her compliment sent a shaft of desire straight to his dick. He groaned, his wolf howled. Just listening to this woman's voice on the telephone made him feel like a randy teenager.

He couldn't let her go.

"If you won't tell me your name or number, how am I supposed to call you again?"

"You aren't. This was a wrong number, remember?"

"I don't think so. I think it was very much the right number."

She turned silent, but Jay sensed she wanted to keep talking. "Tell me about yourself."

"I can't. I have to go. I have an appointment."

He didn't want to let her go. Jay knew it was crazy, but he didn't want to sever the connection between them. He had no idea with whom he spoke, only that she was somewhere in the Dallas area, almost two thousand miles away from him. The distance didn't matter. He'd reached *her*.

His mate.

"I understand the importance of appointments. Please give me your number so I can call you later."

"I don't think so. Good-bye."

"No, wait!"

The soft click over the line told Jay she'd hung up. "Damn it," he muttered. He clutched the receiver, debating whether or not to press the Redial button. At least the older phone had one of those.

She said she had an appointment, but perhaps she hadn't left yet.

He replaced the receiver in its cradle and tugged on the fly of his pants again. The part of his anatomy with a mind of its own wasn't relaxing one bit. Nor did he think it would until he found her.

He *had* to find her.

A soft rap on his open office door made Jay look up. Troy sauntered into the room as Jay's phone rang.

His cousin's arrival destroyed his chance to use the Redial button.

Jay answered his call while Troy crossed the floor. His cousin stood six feet tall with a slim, athletic build. His icy green eyes and dark good looks turned women's heads and made lust light up their eyes. Today, he looked like hell. His long brown hair lay tousled about his head. His face bore a three-day stubble. A wrinkled white T-shirt and baggy jeans covered his frame.

Anyone who saw him now would never believe the high level of intelligence that existed behind those bloodshot eyes.

"Hey, cuz," Troy said after Jay hung up.

"Hey, yourself. When did you get back?"

"About fifteen minutes ago." Troy flopped down in one of the three leather chairs before Jay's mahogany desk. "I just wanted to check in before I go home and crash."

"I gather by your . . . casual appearance that you had a good time."

A wicked smile crossed Troy's lips. "Oh, yeah. You should've gone with me, man. Sun, surf, booze, and babes. I fucked until I thought my dick would fall off. I won't be able to walk upright for at least a week." His smile widened. "It was worth every second of misery."

Jay chuckled. "I'm glad you had a good time. Have you seen your mom yet?"

Troy winced. "I need a long, hot shower to wash off the evidence before I face my mother."

"Then I suggest you leave pretty quick, 'cause she's due back in about fifteen minutes."

"I'm outta here." Troy jumped up from his chair. "I'll be in early tomorrow," he said while striding toward the door. "I know you have a dozen questions for me."

"Make that *two* dozen. Plus I have something to tell you."

His cousin stopped at the door and looked at Jay over his shoulder. "Something important?"

"Yeah."

Troy closed Jay's office door, wandered back over to the chair where he'd sat earlier, and flopped down again. "Talk."

Jay wasn't sure where to start. His cousin would probably think he was crazy if he said he believed he'd found his mate over the telephone. "I've been researching the property descriptions you left for me."

"Anything you like?"

"Yeah, there are some possibilities. But after I researched a few of the local ones, I thought about checking property outside the Bay Area."

Troy frowned. "Why?"

"Maybe it would be a good idea to invest in a different state, maybe someplace in the middle of the country, like . . . Dallas."

"Why Dallas?" Troy asked, his frown deepening.

"Because it's a perfect location. It's right in the middle of the country, with a large interstate system. Plus there are still some great deals there."

"And it has bugs big enough to carry you off. Don't forget that little fact. Not to mention the heat and humidity in the summer. I went there for a convention in July a couple of years ago, remember? Thought I was gonna melt." He rested one ankle on the opposite knee. "What's going on, cuz? What's the real reason you're thinking of Dallas?"

Jay should've known he couldn't fool Troy for one second. His cousin knew him too well. "My mate is there."

Troy arched one dark eyebrow. "Your mate is there. And you know this . . . how?"

"I spoke with her on the phone a few minutes ago."

"I think you'd better start at the beginning."

The skepticism in Troy's eyes didn't surprise Jay. Jay had trouble believing what had happened, and he had experienced it. "I called Big D Properties in Dallas to check on a listing. Except I misdialed and got her instead of the broker. As soon as I heard her voice, I knew. She's my mate. I have no doubt about that."

When his cousin still looked skeptical, Jay huffed out a sigh. "My wolf reacted, Troy. Immediately. I'm talking instant hard-on."

"You think just because you got a hard-on, this gal is your mate? Hell, I walked around with a hard-on all the time on vacation."

"Wolves are sexual creatures. We both know that. We crave sex almost constantly. But this was different, Troy. I've never felt this way in my life."

"So what are you going to do?"

"I'm going to find her."

"How? You said you dialed a wrong number. You don't even know for sure you called Dallas."

"I dialed area code 972. That's Dallas."

"You might've dialed 971 or 973, or even an area code that starts with an eight."

"She had a Texas accent. She's in Dallas."

Leaning forward, Troy braced his elbows on his knees. "I don't like this. You know we've had a problem with hackers trying to break through our firewall over the past several months. She could be one of those hackers and flirted with you on the telephone to get past your guard."

"How the hell could she have done that? *I* called *her*, remember?"

"Maybe she got into our phone system so any number you dialed would go straight to her."

Jay thought Troy had been watching too many sci-fi shows. "That's ridiculous. How would she get into our phone system?"

"There's a way to do anything if someone wants it badly enough." He leaned back in his chair again. "She might even be from a rival pack. Have Mom check your outgoing calls and find out exactly which number you dialed."

Jay hadn't thought of that. His assistant and aunt, April, would hunt down the number he had accidentally called. She wouldn't give up until she found it. "That's a great idea. I'll have her do that when she gets back from lunch."

Troy rose and headed for the door again. "As soon as she finds out who you called, I'll start my investigation of your mysterious caller."

"You won't find anything bad," Jay called out to Troy's retreating back.

Once his cousin left, Jay swiveled his chair around to look out the window. The last wisps of fog were slowly dissipating from the San Francisco Bay. He loved this area, he truly did. He'd love it more with his mate by his side.

Jay was a year older than Troy, but Troy had always been overprotective and taken care of Jay. He assumed the same thing applied here with wanting to check out the woman Jay had accidentally called. If it made Troy feel better, Jay wouldn't interfere with any investigation. After all, he was confident his mate had nothing to hide.

Unavailable.

Veronica St. James stared at that word in the call list on her cell phone. It had come up in her phone's display yesterday afternoon when *he* called. Since she refused to answer a call from someone who hid their number, she'd almost ignored it. Something inside told her to answer it, that it was important.

That feeling had been right.

The moment she heard his voice, her wolf had come to life. Even now, just thinking about that sexy voice over her phone made her wolf whimper to be let free, to run and find its mate . . . to lie with him, spread her legs, and take his cock deep inside her pussy.

She couldn't do that when she had no idea where he lived.

Her brother could find out. As head of St. James Security, Clint could find ways into computers or anything to do with electronics. Her youngest brother, Dean, was only nineteen, but already knew almost as much as Clint.

Roni was still trying to decide whether or not to ask Clint to help her as she stepped inside the twelve-story office building that housed St. James Security. What started out as Clint's idea had exploded into one of the most successful computer security firms in the United States. Clint, Dean, and their other brother, Vince, did most of the work in the office. Roni and her two sisters, Mackenzie and Samantha, flew all over the country, selling their service to businesses. It gave her the chance to travel and meet some very interesting people.

She followed the latest hit from Maroon 5 to Dean's work area. He looked up long enough to smile and wave before he turned his attention back to his computer screen. She gave his shoulder a loving squeeze as she passed him on the way to Clint's office.

Her brother was on the phone, as usual. Roni crossed the floor to the small kitchenette and took a bottle of water from the minifridge. Sinking into the chair by Clint's desk, she removed her phone from her pocket. The word *Unavailable* in her call list jumped out at her again. So close, yet unable to touch him.

"You okay, sis?"

Completely absorbed in thinking about the man on the other end of this phone number, she hadn't heard Clint end his conversation. Roni pressed the Home button to clear the call list. "Sure. I'm great." She motioned toward the multibutton phone on his desk. "Someone important?"

"Maybe a new client. Parks Bank."

Clint had been trying to get the contract for Parks Bank's security for months. His persistence had apparently paid off. The company had banks up and down the West Coast. Rumors flew around that they would soon expand into the Midwest and the East Coast. Their contract would be huge for St. James Security. Roni smiled. "That's great."

"I'm still trying to set up an appointment for you, Mac, or Sam to fly out to Oakland to talk to the head honcho. That's where their main office is located. It would probably be sometime next week."

"Sam's going to Miami next week, remember?"

"Yeah, that's right. Okay, so you and Mac can flip for it."

"I'll tell Mac I'll take it."

"Deal." Clint pointed to the cell phone in her hand. "Expecting a call?"

"No. Why?"

"You've been caressing your phone ever since you got here."

Her brother was much too observant. Roni frowned to cover her embarrassment. "I'm not 'caressing' my phone. I'm just holding it."

"Uh-huh." He picked up a file folder from his desk and handed it to her. "Your itinerary for the day. All the appointments are in Fort Worth."

"Thanks. I'll check in with you later."

Once back in her car, Roni opened the folder and checked the itinerary. It would be a full day . . . much too full to hang around here while her brother tried to find out the identity of *Unavailable*.

She unlocked her phone and looked at the call list again. She'd been so shocked by her intense feelings yesterday that she'd gotten off the phone as quickly as possible. As soon as she'd disconnected the call, she wished she hadn't. Her wolf knew *he* was the one.

Now if she could only find him.

2

Roni's cell phone rang shortly before nine that evening. Before she looked at the display, her wolf told her it was him.

A 415 area code appeared on her screen. The San Francisco area. Disappointment gripped her heart at the realization he lived two thousand miles away from her. She'd suspected from his accent that he wasn't in Texas. Seeing that area code confirmed it.

Another ring urged her to answer her phone. She pressed the button to accept the call. "Hello?"

"Hi."

Clutching the phone tighter to her ear, Roni sank into her favorite recliner. "You're a determined man, aren't you?"

"Yes, when it's something I want."

"And you've decided you want me?"

"Very much. I meant to call you this time, so it isn't a wrong number."

Roni wasn't sure of that, since they lived so far apart. A long-distance relationship rarely worked in the human world. It would be impossible in the pack world.

"I'm Jay."

"Veronica, but everyone calls me Roni."

"Roni," he said, his voice low and husky. "I like that."

She curled her legs beside her. Her heart thudded heavily in her chest, her breathing became fast and shallow. Her body prepared itself to take him, simply from the few words he spoke to her.

Roni's wolf demanded sex often, so she frequently took lovers . . . sometimes full humans, sometimes wolf shapeshifters from other packs. She always had sex in her human form. Having sex as a wolf with a wolf would be the ultimate surrender, the acknowledgment that he was her mate. She hadn't met the man who would capture her heart, her soul.

At least, she hadn't met him in person.

"Tell me about yourself," Jay said. "I know by your phone number that you live in Dallas."

"Highland Park. You live in the Bay Area?"

"Yeah. I wish . . ."

He stopped. Roni knew what he wished—that they lived closer. She wished the same thing.

"What do you do for a living?" he asked.

"I work in the family business."

"So do I. My cousin and I started our business eight years ago."

"What kind of business?"

"Computers. Software. All that nerd stuff."

Roni chuckled. She liked his sense of humor. "Isn't it a law for everyone who lives in the Bay Area to work with computers?"

"Damn near." She heard ice cubes clink against a glass. "You have an incredible voice."

Roni placed a hand over her jumping stomach. The sexy tone to his voice sent desire zinging to her clit. "You realize we live two thousand miles apart."

"You realize there are airplanes."

"Jay, that's crazy. We don't even know each other, and you're talking about one of us flying two thousand miles?"

"So we'll get to know each other first, over the phone. I'll call you every night and we'll talk."

"What if I don't want you to call me again?"

"Don't you?"

She couldn't say no, not when she didn't mean it.

He sighed heavily. "You probably think I'm a perverted stalker."

"No, of course not," she said quickly to reassure him.

"Good. Because I'm not. I felt something the first time I heard your voice, Roni. I want to explore that something and see where it leads."

He made it sound easy, uncomplicated. Living so many miles apart was far from uncomplicated, especially if he was a wolf, as she suspected.

"I'll let you go for tonight, but I'll call again tomorrow evening. If you decide you don't want me to call after that, I'll respect your wishes. Okay?"

"Okay."

"Dream of me."

He disconnected the call. Powering off her cell, she laid it on the end table beside the chair. She suspected dreaming of him wouldn't be a problem at all.

Jay glanced at his watch for what he figured had to be the thirtieth time so far today. Time had never moved so slowly for him. He had hours and hours of work to do, but he wanted to push all that aside and call Roni. Since it wasn't even lunchtime yet, he had a long time to wait.

God, he wanted to hear her voice again.

Forcing his attention back to work, Jay looked at Troy

seated across the conference table. "What's going on with the O.S.?" he asked.

Troy raised one hand and tilted it back and forth. "Still a few things I'm not happy with."

"I want it perfect before we release it."

"It will be, cuz, don't worry. JEMATAR's new O.S. will be the best, easiest to use, most stable operating system ever invented."

"How much longer to work out the bugs?"

"I don't want to rush it, Jay."

"I don't want to rush it either, but I'd like to start shipping it with our new computers in August."

"So I have three months to make sure everything is perfect." Troy shrugged. "No problem."

Jay believed his cousin. He knew Troy would work day and night to be sure their operating system would do everything they had envisioned.

A movement in his office's doorway drew Jay's attention. His assistant and aunt entered the room, looking lovely and professional as always. Without hesitating, she strode directly to Troy and kissed the top of his head.

He grinned at her. "Hi, Mom."

"Don't 'hi, Mom' me," she admonished in her soft English accent. "Why didn't you tell me you were back?" April asked her son as she slipped into the chair next to him.

"You weren't at your desk when I got here."

"And what's wrong with a phone call? I know you got back yesterday."

Jay covered his mouth with one hand to hide his grin. His aunt could make Troy feel like a naughty little boy when she arched an eyebrow at him.

"I, uh, had to unpack and . . . stuff."

"You had to get rid of all the evidence of too much drinking and sex."

Jay chuckled while Troy squirmed in his chair. "Geez, Mom."

"You went to the Bahamas. You think I don't know what you did?"

Troy threw Jay a "help me" look. Jay leaned back in his chair, thoroughly enjoying his cousin's discomfort.

"You can make up for it by coming to dinner tonight," April said.

Troy smiled, then leaned toward his mother and kissed her cheek. "Sure. How's seven-thirty?"

"That's fine." She turned her head toward Jay. "You, too?"

Normally, Jay would accept the invitation in a second. Since his father and stepmother lived in England, April and Troy were the only family he had close to him. But if he went to his aunt's house for dinner, he wouldn't be able to call Roni. "Not tonight, April. I have some projects I want to finish."

She frowned. "You *always* have some projects you want to finish. There's more to life than work, Jay." She shifted in her chair to face him. "I know you see me every day, but this is work. I'm your assistant here. There are times when I'd like to be your aunt."

Guilt tickled at his conscience, but he wouldn't let it change his mind. He had to talk to Roni tonight. "You're *always* my aunt. I'll come for dinner soon, I promise." He gestured at the huge pile of papers on the table, even though the reason for his rejection had nothing to do with his work. "Give me a chance to get through some of this first, all right?"

"What can I do to help you?"

"Nothing yet, but hold that thought."

She looked from Jay to Troy and back again. "I suppose you two still have things to discuss, so I'll get back to my own work."

"See you later, Mom."

Once April left, Troy faced his cousin again. "Anything else we need to go over before I head back to the dungeon?"

Jay chuckled at his cousin's nickname for the computer lab. "I think I'm good for now."

"Okay." Troy stood and headed for the door. Halfway across the floor, he stopped and looked at Jay again. "I haven't had the chance to investigate that phone number yet."

"No rush."

"I *will* do it, Jay, as soon as I'm through tweaking the O.S. This wrong number thing doesn't feel right."

Arguing wouldn't do any good, so Jay decided to go along with Troy. Besides, his cousin wouldn't find anything suspicious about Roni. "Whatever you think is best."

As soon as Troy left, Jay glanced at his watch again. Almost noon. That meant almost two o'clock in Dallas. She'd be through with lunch by now and back to work. He didn't know what she did for a living, only that she worked for the family business.

She could work as a circus clown and he wouldn't care.

He couldn't wait any longer. He needed to hear her voice *now*.

Although he had a private office, the walls were made of glass and Jay left his door open so his employees could talk to him at any time. Except now. He didn't want anyone to interrupt his conversation with Roni. He also didn't want anyone to see the hard-on he had no doubt he'd get when he heard her voice.

Jay grabbed his jacket and left his office, pausing at April's desk long enough to tell her he had an errand to run. He exited the building by the back door and crossed the parking lot to his car. Once inside the private space, he removed the cell phone from his jacket pocket. The cell clipped to his belt was for business. This phone was the one he used strictly for family and close friends.

He located Roni in his favorites and placed the call. Two rings later, her soft voice came over the line.

"You're early."

Jay swallowed hard as his cock responded. His wolf paced and growled, eager to be with its mate. "I didn't know I was on a schedule."

"You aren't. But you said you'd call tonight."

"I couldn't wait any longer to hear your voice."

He thought he heard her whimper. His wolf paced faster.

"Am I interrupting something?"

"No. I just pulled into my garage. I'm working from home today, but had to make a fast trip to the grocery store. I was almost out of Dr Pepper."

Jay liked learning these little tidbits about her. "You're a Dr Pepper fan?"

"More like addict."

"Regular or diet?"

"Regular. I hate diet anything."

Which meant that she could be very overweight. Jay didn't care. He only cared that she made him feel alive.

He heard a car door slam and the rustle of plastic bags. "Should I let you go?"

"No, don't. Unless you need to go."

It pleased him that she so obviously wanted to keep him on the phone. "I don't need to do anything but talk to you."

More rustling, then the sound of a door closing. "Sorry. I'm in the house now. Let me put these bags on the counter and I'll be free to talk."

He had time to adjust the hard-on in his briefs before she came back on the line. "Okay, all done."

"Did you get your Dr Pepper?"

"Right here in my other hand."

Jay laughed. Everything she said delighted him. "So instead of flowers and jewelry, I can woo you with carbonated beverages?"

"Are you wooing me, Jay?"

"Damn right."

She remained silent for several seconds, long enough that he wondered if he'd lost the connection, before she spoke again. "Are you at lunch?"

"Not yet."

"Where are you?"

"In my car. I wanted privacy to call you."

He was sure he heard her whimper this time. His wolf paced faster, growled deeper. His cock jerked. Jay pressed his hand over the hard bulge, wishing with all his might that it was Roni's hand touching him instead of his own. He imagined her on her knees before him, her tongue running up and down his hard flesh. . . .

Meetings and press conferences and deadlines would keep him at his desk almost nonstop for the rest of May. Perhaps he could breathe a little easier after that. Until then, he was tied to JEMATAR.

As if to emphasize his insane schedule, his work cell phone rang. Cursing beneath his breath, Jay looked at the display to see the name of his vice president of design.

"Roni, I have to go. I'll call you later tonight. Around nine your time, okay?"

"Okay," she said softly.

"Bye."

He reluctantly ended the call. Even though he could no longer hear her voice over the phone, he heard it in his mind. He felt her in his heart.

She was his mate. He had no doubt of that.

A beep from his work cell announcing a voice mail jerked Jay back to the present. Slipping the phone back into his pocket, he unclipped the one from his belt and listened to his VP's message.

3

Roni closed her book and laid it on the bed beside her. She refused to look at the clock. She already knew it was almost ten.

Jay hadn't called.

She told herself it was ridiculous to be upset, even while her inner wolf whimpered in disappointment. She felt in her heart that he was her mate, yet she wouldn't know for sure until they met. One look into Jay's eyes, one whiff of his scent, and any doubt would vanish.

Perhaps he'd decided pursuing a long-distance relationship would never work. What sometimes worked for humans didn't for wolves. They had to be close, had to protect each other.

Had to have sex.

She'd thought of Jay most of the day, imagined him here beside her . . . kissing her, touching her. She'd pictured his hands on her body, gliding over her slick skin. His mouth would move down her body, stopping long enough to suck both nipples before he kissed his way to her pussy.

Closing her eyes, Roni slipped her hand between her thighs. Her fingers slid across warm, wet flesh. Panties were a nuisance she'd rather be without whenever possible. She dipped into her channel, gathered up a generous amount of cream, and spread it over her clit. The nub grew larger and firmer beneath her fingertips.

"Mmmmmm."

She placed her feet flat on the bed and let her knees fall apart. Gathering more cream, she slid it all over her freshly shaved pussy. The fragrance of her juices drifted to her nose. She inhaled deeply, loving the scent of her arousal. Roni pushed two fingers into her channel to coat them with as much of her cream as she could, then licked them clean. She repeated her action again and again, unable to get enough of her taste.

She continued to rub her engorged clit with her other hand, pausing only long enough to tweak her nipples before pushing her hand back between her legs. She took herself right to the peak, then pulled her hands away from her body. An orgasm was always so much more powerful when she made herself wait.

Wanting to prolong her pleasure, she lay still for several moments. Her clit pulsed, begging for her touch.

Begging for Jay's touch.

The thought of him sent a fresh surge of desire to her pussy. Roni's hips bucked off the bed as she touched her clit again. She couldn't stop the orgasm this time, even if she wanted to. Pleasure flowed through her body, curling her toes and making stars burst behind her eyelids.

She had no idea how long she lay still, panting to get her heartbeat back to normal. Her hand still rested between her thighs. A gentle brush of her clit proved she could easily come again with only a few swipes of her fingertips.

Her cell phone rang. Roni gasped and quickly grabbed it off the nightstand. She scrambled to sit upright on the bed when she saw Jay's number.

"Hi."

"Hey, I'm sorry I'm late. I was in a meeting and it went way longer than I . . ." He stopped. Several seconds passed, then she heard a low growl over the phone. "You just came."

His deep, gravelly tone—so unlike his usual smooth voice—sent goose bumps scattering across her skin. "How do you know that?"

"I can feel it. *Fuck!*"

He groaned loud and long, as if in pain. Except Roni knew he didn't feel any pain. She could sense his desire, the same way he sensed hers.

"Are you alone?" he asked, his voice still deep and gravelly.

"Yes."

"Did you use your hand or a toy?"

She hesitated answering such a personal question. They hadn't even met in person yet. Her hesitation quickly evaporated. She already felt closer to Jay than any man in her life. She would honestly answer any question he asked. "My hand."

Another groan, another deep growl. "I wish I could be there to watch."

"If you were here, would you only watch?"

"At first, yes. I'd love to see you pleasuring yourself. But I wouldn't be satisfied with just looking for long. I'd have to touch your body, to suck your nipples. I'd spread your legs and lick all over your sweet pussy. God, I want to taste you."

The mental vision his words caused made her womb clench in need. She wanted to taste him, too . . . to run her tongue down his neck, over his chest. She wanted to swipe the tip across his nipples before she ventured farther down his body. She wanted to bury her nose in his groin, inhale that musky male scent that would be uniquely his.

Then . . .

"Make yourself come again," he urged, his voice soft and pleading. "I want to listen."

While she had no doubt she could quickly bring herself to

another orgasm, she didn't want to without him. "Come with me."

He chuckled. "Hell, I'm already halfway there and I haven't even touched my cock."

"Are you hard?" she purred.

"Like a rock."

Her womb clenched again. She wished he were with her right now, pumping into her channel in long, slow, deep strokes.

She slipped her hand between her thighs again.

"Are you touching yourself?" he asked.

If Roni didn't know better, she would swear he had a camera set up in her bedroom. He seemed to know everything she did. "Yes."

"Where? Tell me *exactly* what you're doing."

"I'm circling my clit with one fingertip."

"I'll bet you're really, really wet."

"Yes, I am."

"Okay, you are officially killing me."

Roni laughed, delighted that he could tease when they were both so turned on. "What are *you* doing now? Exactly."

"Fisting my cock."

"Slow or fast?"

"Slow. I won't speed up until you do."

"Do you want me to speed up?"

"I want you to come, whatever it takes for you to do that."

Roni added a second fingertip and rubbed her clit faster. "I'm close. Really, really close."

"That's what I want. Come for me, Roni."

He'd barely said her name when the pleasure shot through her body again, the orgasm even more powerful than her first one. Roni collapsed on the bed, heart pounding, skin slick with sweat. She thought she heard a grunt from Jay, but the roar in her ears kept her from being sure.

"Holy shit," he muttered.

Unsure what to say after sharing something so personal with Jay, Roni pushed her damp hair back from her face and waited for him to speak again.

"You okay?" he asked softly.

"Yes."

"Are you sorry I listened to you come?"

"No. It was very hot. I just . . . I've never had phone sex."

"Neither have I." His voice turned deeper. "But I doubt if it'll be the last time."

"You think this will become a habit?"

"I'm going to call you every evening. We'll see what happens then."

"Jay, this is insane."

"Yeah, it is. That's what makes it so exciting."

He disconnected the call. Roni stared at her phone while little pulses of sensation tickled her clit. She couldn't believe she and Jay had had phone sex. Or that she'd enjoyed it so much. Already, she looked forward to the next time.

He lived somewhere in the Bay Area. Clint planned to set up an appointment with Parks Bank in Oakland. If everything went as her brother hoped, Roni would fly to the West Coast in the next week or two. She could arrange to meet Jay in person.

Her wolf happily panted at that thought.

She made a mental note to ask Clint tomorrow if he'd finalized things with Parks Bank yet. She also put a visit to her favorite lingerie shop at the top of her to-do list. Roni wanted to be ready to see Jay when Clint gave her the go-ahead for the trip.

"Push it all the way inside you," Jay urged. He couldn't see what Roni was doing, but he could encourage her over the phone, the same as he'd done every evening for almost two weeks.

Her soft sigh indicated she'd obeyed him. Jay squeezed his cock, trying to hold off the orgasm that was so close. "Did you do it?"

"Yes."

"Turn it on."

Roni's moan grabbed Jay's balls. He could picture her in his mind, holding the base of the vibrator while it caressed the inside of her pussy. He wanted to be inside her, not some piece of plastic.

For the last twelve nights, he'd called Roni shortly after seven. Each time they talked, his hunger for her grew. His wolf fought to get out, to get close to its mate.

Neither of them had said the words, but Jay knew a wolf lived inside Roni, the same as it did him. He could feel that desire, that need to mate, even from two thousand miles away. Now, two days away from the full moon, the wolf paced restlessly inside him, demanding to claim Roni.

Jay knew many women willing to spend an evening with him. He'd accepted their offer of sex because his wolf craved it. Ever since the first time he'd talked to Roni, the thought of being with another woman churned his stomach. He hadn't been with her in person, yet their phone sex bound him to her just as strongly as if they'd touched flesh to flesh.

Her soft whimpers dragged his attention back to her. He wished he could see her. He'd almost asked her to send pictures of herself, then decided he'd rather wait to see her for the first time when they met. Looks didn't matter anyway. He wanted her for *her*, not that she had brown hair or red or blond. Whether she was a tall, slim woman or short and chubby, he'd feel the same way about her. She hadn't asked him for pictures either, so assumed she felt the same as he.

They had to meet. Jay didn't know how much longer he could contain his wolf.

Roni's breathing became heavier. Jay pumped his cock harder, knowing she would come soon.

"Oh, God, Jay, it feels so good."

"Tell me what you're doing."

"I'm fucking myself with the vibrator."

That mental image was much too specific for Jay to hold back his orgasm any longer. His cock jerked in his hand. He groaned as his cum splattered on his stomach and chest.

A keening cry came over the phone when Roni reached her climax. Jay plucked a couple of tissues from the box on his nightstand and wiped off his cum while he gave her a few moments to recuperate.

Roni's cry turned into a long moan . . . a very pleasurable moan. "What are you doing now?" he asked.

"Licking my cream from the vibrator."

Just like that, his cock was hard again. He couldn't stand this any longer, and neither could his wolf. It growled and clawed to get out, to possess its mate. "I have to be with you, Roni. No more phone sex. I want to touch you for real."

"I want that, too."

He thought about his insane work schedule. The release of JEMATAR's new computers and operating system meant working practically twenty-four hours a day for him and his entire crew. He didn't care. He had a personal life, too, and it was time he lived it. "I'm going to clear my schedule and come see you this weekend."

"Wait, Jay. You may not have to do that. I may be flying out to Oakland this week on business. I was supposed to go last week, but the man I'm seeing was on vacation. I should find out tomorrow, Tuesday at the latest, if I'm going this week."

She was coming *here?* If it was possible for a wolf to do a happy dance, his did.

"Call me as soon as you know for sure, no matter what time it is. If you can't come here, I'll come to you."

"Okay."

"Dream of me."

"I always do."

He pressed the button on his phone to end the call. Still painfully aroused, he had to do something to get his mind off sex. His wolf knew the perfect solution—run.

Jay made his way to the lower level of his house and to the French doors that led to his patio. Stepping out into the cool air, he lifted his head and closed his eyes.

Power flowed through him, the power of generations of wolves. He felt no pain or discomfort . . . only a delicious shiver as his form changed from human to wolf.

He opened his eyes to peer into the night. His enhanced canine vision let him see everything as clearly as if the sun shone. With a burst of energy, he ran toward the woods that surrounded his house.

Moonlight filtered through the wispy clouds, a reminder to him that the moon would be full Tuesday night. His sexual craving would be at its peak then. That didn't matter. He had to fight that craving and not give in to the moon's pull. Sex with any woman other than Roni was unthinkable.

Jay ran until he could run no farther. Panting deeply, he slowly padded to his house. Once on his patio again, he shifted back to human form. His entire body felt weak from the long run. A shower would feel wonderful. His bed would feel even better.

Deciding the shower could wait until morning, Jay took the stairs to his bedroom on the second floor. He pulled back the covers, fell on the bed facedown, and closed his eyes.

Thoughts of Roni and what they'd shared tonight on the phone had his eyes popping open again. Jay lifted to his elbows and looked at the other side of his big bed . . . the side where Roni would soon lie. He could reach out in the night and touch her, pull her to his side, wrap his arms around her. He could slide his hard cock into her wet pussy over and over again.

His erection pulsed back to life. Not wanting to jerk off again without Roni with him, Jay tugged one of the extra pillows to his chest and closed his eyes once more.

Soon. He'd have his mate with him soon.

4

Seeing Mackenzie chatting with Clint in his office surprised Roni. She hadn't expected Mac to be back from her trip to Kansas until Wednesday. "Hey, you."

Mac turned her head and smiled when she saw Roni. "Hey, back."

Roni gave her sister a quick hug before she took the chair next to her. "I didn't think you'd be back until later this week."

"I got everything done early. Woodthorpe Investments loved everything about our security system. I had them signed up and ready to go Saturday morning."

"Mac and Vince will go back and set up Woodthorpe next week," Clint said.

"So I'm free until then." Mac crossed her legs and smiled at her brother. "What else ya got?"

"I should get a call from the vice president at Parks Bank today. Their CEO has already indicated interest in our system. I'm just waiting for a set appointment time later this week."

"Their main office is in California, right?"

Clint nodded. "Oakland."

"I'll take it."

Panic grabbed Roni's throat. This was her chance to meet Jay. She couldn't let her sister take that from her. "No! I'll go."

Mac turned her head and looked at Roni, a perplexed expression on her face. "It's okay, sis. I'll make the trip."

"You've taken two trips since my last one. I've already told Clint I'll go to Oakland."

"Roni, I don't mind—"

"*No.* I'll go, Mac."

Mac remained silent for several moments, that perplexed expression still on her face. "Okay, no problem. You can go."

"Is it settled now?" Clint asked. "I need to know for sure before I make flight and hotel reservations."

"Yes, it's settled," Roni said to her brother. "I'm going to Oakland."

"Okay. I'll call you as soon as I know for sure when you'll make the trip."

"Do I need to make any calls on clients today?"

"No. I sent Sam out this morning. You and Mac have a free day."

"Wow," Mac said. "That doesn't happen very often. I'm speechless."

Clint's eyes twinkled with amusement. "Better get out of here before I change my mind."

"I'm gone." Mac gathered up her purse and briefcase from the floor and stood. "Roni, how about a cup of coffee?"

Roni knew Mac's invitation wasn't a friendly let's-have-coffee-because-we're-sisters offer. Mac would demand to know why Roni was so set on going to Oakland. Since Roni knew her sister wouldn't let the subject rest until she knew everything, she decided she might as well confess now. "Sure."

"I'll meet you at Stacy's."

Stacy's Place had been around as long as Roni could remember. She and Mac and Sam often went there for Sunday brunch.

Generous portions and private booths meant patrons could eat and visit with each other for hours. Roni assumed Mac had picked that restaurant so she could grill Roni without witnesses.

She parked her car next to Mac's and walked into the restaurant with her sister by her side. Mac didn't say anything until the hostess had seated them in a booth along a wall of windows. She clasped her hands together on top of the table and gave Roni what she called the "big sister" look.

"Talk."

"How was Kansas?"

Mac frowned. "Flat. And that's not what I meant."

"I know."

"What's in Oakland that's so important for you to go there?"

It would probably sound crazy, but Roni had to tell her sister the truth. "My mate."

Mac blinked. "What?"

"He called me by accident two weeks ago. He was trying to call Big D Properties and got me instead."

"So how do you know this wrong number is your mate?"

"We talked for a few minutes and I knew. I don't have a doubt in my mind about that."

Mac reached across the table and covered Roni's hand with hers. "Roni, you can't know for sure from a telephone call."

Roni straightened her shoulders and lifted her chin. "You're wrong, Mac. As soon as I heard his voice, my heart started pounding and I . . ." She glanced around to be sure no one would hear her, then leaned closer to her sister. "Got wet. And I mean immediately. That's never happened to me."

"It's almost the full moon. We always get horny at this time of the month."

Roni frowned, annoyed at her sister's narrow-mindedness. "Mac, I *know*. We've talked every night on the phone and it's been incredible. I have to meet him. He lives in the Bay Area. That's why I want to go to Oakland."

Mac leaned back in the booth when the waitress arrived with their coffee. She took a cautious sip of the hot brew before speaking again. "I don't like the idea of you flying to California to hook up with some man you know nothing about."

"I know a lot about Jay. I told you, we've talked every night. I know his favorite color, favorite movie, favorite food, favorite—"

"What does he do for a living?"

"He works with computers."

Mac studied Roni long enough to make Roni want to squirm in her seat. "What?"

"I just don't want you to get your hopes up and be disappointed when you meet him and discover he isn't your mate."

"That isn't going to happen. He *is* my mate. I'm certain of it."

Jay paced the length of the conference table, over and over, while Troy droned on about motherboards and one-piece construction. He didn't care about any of that. He only wanted Roni to call and say she was coming to see him.

"Jay!"

Troy's sharp voice penetrated Jay's thoughts. He stopped pacing and looked at his cousin. "What?"

"Where are you today, man? I said your name three times before you responded."

Jay rubbed his forehead. "I'm sorry, Troy. I have a lot on my mind today."

"Full moonitis?" Troy asked, grinning.

It would work in Jay's favor to let Troy believe the restlessness was simply a by-product of a wolf's cycle. He didn't want his cousin to know that he would soon meet Roni. "Yeah."

"You got a date lined up for tomorrow night?"

"Not yet."

Troy winced. "Better get one quick or you'll wear out your hand."

The comment made Jay laugh, although there was nothing funny about a wolf's reaction to the full moon. There was no turning into a monster, as folklore reported, but a constant craving for sex. Jay had always managed the craving with the woman he dated at the time. This month, there would be no woman, no way to satisfy his wolf's need. The woman he wanted lived two thousand miles away from him.

His personal cell phone rang with the ringtone he'd assigned to Roni's number. Jay almost tripped in his hurry to get to his desk and snatch up the phone. "Hello?"

"Hi."

His body responded the way it always did at the sound of her voice. Jay turned his back so Troy wouldn't see the hard-on pressing against his fly. "Hi."

"I have news."

"Good or bad?"

"I hope you think it's good."

Jay glanced over his shoulder at Troy. "Just a sec," he said to Roni before speaking to his cousin. "I need to take this."

"Everything okay?" Troy asked, a puzzled expression on his face.

"Sure. It's a personal call."

"Oh." Troy grinned. "Setting up that date for tomorrow night?"

"Trying to."

"I won't stop you from saving your hand." He gathered up his paperwork and headed for the door. "Catch you later."

Once Troy left, Jay crossed the floor and closed the door. "Sorry about that."

"It's okay. I know you're probably at work, but you said to call as soon as I knew something about Oakland."

"And I meant that. Does your good news mean you're coming here?"

"Thursday. I'm flying out early for a three o'clock meeting. I'm free after that."

Finally, after two weeks of dreaming about Roni and nightly phone conversations with her, he would meet her in person. "How long will you be here?"

"Until Sunday. I normally would've flown back Friday, but I told my brother as long as I was so close to San Francisco, I wanted to hit some of the shops."

Thursday to Sunday. She wouldn't be with him for the full moon, but would be here soon. His wolf panted happily. "The city is a shopper's paradise. I'll take you wherever you want to go."

Her voice turned low and sultry. "I'm sure we can think of better things to do than shop."

If possible, his cock grew even longer, thicker. Oh yeah, he had all kinds of ideas of the things he and Roni could do together. "Shall I pick you up at the airport?"

"No. I'll have a rental car. I don't know how long my meeting will last. I'll check into my hotel and meet you after that."

"You won't need a hotel, Roni. I want you to stay with me."

"I want that, too, but I have to at least check in to justify the expense to my brother. I . . . told one of my sisters about you, but I haven't said anything to my brothers. I thought it would be better to meet you first before saying anything."

Jay understood that, and he agreed with her. There was no reason for families to get involved until he and Roni knew for sure they were mates.

Although he already knew in his heart.

"Do you have a pen and paper? I'll give you my address."

"Yes, I'm ready."

He spouted off his address along with the best way to get to his house. "Think you can find it?"

"I have GPS on my phone, so no problem."

"I'll be there waiting for you, no matter what time it is."

"Will I talk to you tonight?"

Jay would never give up the chance to talk to her. "I'll call you at our regular time."

"Okay. Bye."

A huge smile spreading over his face, Jay laid his phone back on his desk. Roni would be here in three days. Tomorrow would be hell on him because of the full moon, but he'd at least talk to her on the phone. The sound of her voice—and more hot phone sex—would get him through the night. The craving would taper off starting Wednesday before beginning the climb again at the new moon.

He had four weeks to worry about the full moon again. Right now, he planned to concentrate on nothing but Roni.

Clint looked up from the pile of papers on his desk when Malcolm Lander walked into his office. Annoyance spread through him that his investigator would show up at his office unannounced.

"What the fuck are you doing here?" Clint demanded.

"My job." He tossed a file folder on top of the paperwork before sprawling in one of the chairs before Clint's desk. "Don't worry. I waited until everyone left the building."

"How do you know..." Clint stopped. He'd already learned that Malcolm seemed to know things that no one else did.

He glanced at the clean-cut man sitting before him dressed in a blue button-down shirt, creased jeans, and brown boots. No one looking at Mr. Average would guess Malcolm Lander dug up dirt on people for a living. And a very healthy living, if what Clint had paid the private investigator indicated how much the man normally made per job.

Opening the folder, Clint rummaged through the photographs of the handsome, dark-haired man. "This is him?"

"That's him."

Clint peered at Malcolm. "Are you sure?"

Malcolm gave Clint a look that clearly said he shouldn't ask such stupid questions. "Of course I'm sure. I wouldn't be here if I wasn't."

Clint continued to peruse the photographs. He saw shots of Jamieson Millington getting out of a black SUV, going into an office building, pushing a cart of groceries through a parking lot. There were also shots of a large white house on the water with thick trees on either side of it.

"Those woods will easily hide me," Malcolm said. "It won't be any trouble getting a good shot. If that's what you want."

"Does the house have a garage?"

"Yeah, but half the time he parks in the driveway in front of his house."

Clint rubbed his upper lip while trying to decide the best way to handle this. The pack way—the honorable way—would be to challenge Millington to a fight as wolves. Clint hadn't felt the least bit honorable ever since Millington killed Highland Pack's Alpha two years ago. Although there was no law dictating it, as one of the pack's guards, Clint felt obligated to avenge his Alpha.

Thanks to Malcolm Lander, he could do exactly that.

"What do you want me to do?" Malcolm asked.

Clint closed the folder and handed it back to the investigator. "Kill him."

5

Roni pulled her rental car to the side of the road half a mile from Jay's house. She pressed a hand to her stomach, where a thousand butterflies pinged and zinged. In only a few minutes, she would meet the man who had appeared in her dreams for two weeks, both during the day and while she slept.

The man who had fulfilled almost every sexual fantasy she'd ever had, and he hadn't even touched her yet.

Thinking about all the things she'd done while he listened on the phone sent desire shooting through her body. She shifted positions to try to ease the throbbing in her clit. The movement across the seat made her silk panties slide gently across her pussy.

Well, that didn't help.

Nothing would help until she had Jay's cock buried deep inside her.

Taking a deep breath to calm the butterflies, Roni looked at her reflection in the rearview mirror. He'd told her on the phone last night that he planned to take her out to dinner at one of his favorite restaurants. Wanting to look her best for him, she'd gone heavier than normal with her eye makeup. Diamond studs adorned her ears. She'd worn her favorite black dress, long-sleeved with a scooped neck low enough to give a generous hint of cleavage.

He'd never asked anything about her looks or body, or requested she send him a picture of herself. Although she didn't believe looks were as important as the inside of a person, she couldn't help wondering what Jay looked like. She'd wanted to request a picture so badly, but hadn't asked him because he hadn't asked her.

They would discover each other together.

After checking her side mirror for approaching traffic, Roni pulled back onto the road. A few moments later, she saw a small sign next to a paved driveway with the number of Jay's house. Thick trees kept her from seeing the house until she'd driven halfway down the driveway. She gasped when she saw the gray-trimmed white contemporary house. Two stories in height and at least five thousand square feet, it sat on a cliff overlooking the bay.

Living on the water anywhere in the Bay Area had to be expensive. Jay's job in computers and software must pay very well.

She continued up the driveway until it circled in front of the house. Roni turned off the ignition and clutched the steering wheel as her butterflies took off again. Whatever happened in the next few minutes, she knew her life would be changed forever.

Picking up her purse and wrap from the seat, she opened the door.

Jay looked at the clock on the wall. Barely three minutes had passed since the last time he looked. He'd paid more attention to time in the last two weeks than he had his whole life.

"Scowling at the clock won't make her get here any quicker."

Turning at the sound of the man's voice, Jay watched his father, Jamieson, walk toward him. He leaned on his cane, something he hadn't done earlier today. The injury from two years ago must have flared up. "Hey, Dad. Is your leg hurting?"

"A bit."

Jay knew his father didn't use the cane when his leg only hurt "a bit." He clenched his hands into fists, still angry that he hadn't been there to defend his father two years ago. "I'm glad you're here, but I know that long flight had to be tiring for you. Why don't you lie down a while?"

"I will, after I meet your mate."

He'd decided not to call his father and stepmother until after he met Roni. As soon as he knew for sure Roni was coming to see him, Jay couldn't wait to share his news. Jamieson had surprised Jay by flying over from England. As Alpha of the Millington Pack, Jamieson met all the prospective mates of his wolves. Jay respected pack law, but he hadn't planned for his father to meet Roni so soon. He didn't want her to feel uncomfortable in any way by producing a father she hadn't expected to see.

Jamieson lifted one hand, palm toward Jay. "I know what you're thinking. No, I'm not going to hang around here and intrude on your first meeting with her. But I would like to meet her before you take her to dinner."

The tension seeped out of Jay's shoulders. That he could do. "Sure. After I have a few minutes with her, I'll . . ."

He stopped and tilted his head. Thanks to his enhanced wolf hearing, he heard a car door shut. That, and the way his cock immediately hardened, proved Roni had arrived.

"Dad—"

"I heard it, too. I'll be in the family room when you're ready to introduce her."

Jay waited until his father left the foyer before he opened the front door and stepped outside. He'd heard the phrase "his heart slammed into his throat" but never truly understood it until now. A vision rounded the hood of a tan sedan. Chin-length black hair swept back from her face in gentle waves. A long-sleeved black dress slid over her voluptuous body to her knees. Black heels covered her feet, sheer black stockings ran up her legs. He had only a moment to admire her cleavage as she draped a black wrap around her arms and tossed one end over the opposite shoulder.

He longed to lick every inch of her ivory skin.

She took two steps before she lifted her head. Eyes widen-ing, she froze. Her lips parted as her gaze passed over his body. He couldn't be sure from twenty-five feet away, but he thought he saw her swallow.

Jay forgot how to talk. He had so many things he wanted to say to her, but the words simply wouldn't form. Instead, he held out one hand to her.

She walked toward him slowly, almost timidly, as if she wasn't sure he would accept her. He waited, his hand out-stretched, letting her come to him at whatever pace she chose.

The moment she laid her hand in his, fireworks erupted in-side him. His wolf growled, demanding to take its mate. *Now.*

"Come in."

Entwining their fingers together, he led her into his house. Once inside, he released her hand and cradled her face. He stared into her icy blue eyes and felt as if he were drowning. "I can't believe you're finally here." His thumbs drifted over her cheeks. "My God, you're so beautiful."

She slipped her hands inside his jacket and caressed his chest. "And you're magnificent."

It pleased him for her to think so. He'd chosen to wear a medium gray suit with a white silk pullover. He wanted com-fort, yet also wanted to look good for Roni. His father had teased him about spending more time in the bathroom than a woman.

Unable to wait any longer to taste her, Jay lowered his head until their lips touched. The soft whimper that came from Roni's throat urged him to deepen the kiss. Jay swept his tongue across her lips. They parted for him, and the tip of her tongue touched his.

Jay had never experienced such heat from a simple kiss. Sliding his fingers into her hair, he tilted her head and drove his tongue into her mouth. The bite of her fingernails into his chest proved their kiss affected her as much as him. Her tongue dueled with his as her arms snaked around his back. Jay let his hands glide across her shoulders and down her back. Cradling her ass in his palms, he lifted her until her mound cushioned his hard cock.

The long moan that came from her throat released his wolf. Jay backed Roni up to the front door. He let go of her long enough for her to jerk off his jacket before he cupped her ass again. She wrapped her arms around his neck, her legs around his waist, and devoured his mouth.

Jay could feel the heat and dampness through her panties. He could smell her arousal, that irresistible scent that urged him to bury his tongue in her pussy. With a hard tug, he could rip off her panties and fuck her until they both fell to the floor in a boneless heap.

He started to slide one hand beneath her dress, intending to do exactly that, when sanity returned. This was his mate, the woman he would share his life with. He didn't want to fuck Roni against a door. He wanted to wine and dine her first, then make love to her. Plus his father, his Alpha, waited in the family room. Respect for his Alpha dictated Jamieson meet Roni first before she and Jay sealed their relationship with sex.

He ended their kiss and buried his face against her throat. Moaning again, Roni tilted her head, offering her shoulder for his bite. Her act of a wolf's surrender made it even more difficult for him to pull away from her. He looked at her flushed cheeks, her closed eyes, her parted lips. Each puff of her breath brushed his mouth.

"Roni, we have to stop."

Slowly, she opened her eyes halfway. "Stop?" she asked, disbelief evident in her voice.

"We aren't alone in the house. My father is here."

Roni's eyes flew open. "Your *father* is here?"

Jay nodded. "He flew over from England and surprised me."

A blush blossomed in her cheeks. If possible, it made her even more beautiful.

She unwrapped her legs from around his waist. Jay held her tightly until he was sure she could stand on her own. "Jay, I can't meet your father. Not now."

"Why not?"

"Look at me." She fluffed her hair. "He'll know we . . . You know."

He couldn't help chuckling at her obvious embarrassment. "Kissed?"

Her eyes narrowed. "We did more than just kiss."

And he wanted to do a lot more than just kiss with Roni, although kissing her entire body sounded like an excellent idea. "He knows you were coming today. I'm sure he assumes we did a little petting, too."

The corners of her lips twitched with laughter. "Petting. How high school."

Jay chuckled. He could already tell life would never be dull with his mate.

He picked up her wrap and his jacket and hung both in the coat closet to the right of the front door. When he turned around to face her again, he caught her straightening her dress.

"Do I look all right?"

He pressed his hand over his erection. "Does this answer your question?"

Desire flared in her eyes. Before he said "to hell with my father" and dragged her to his bedroom, he took her hand and led her to the family room.

The moment she'd touched his hand, any doubt that Mac had put into Roni's head about Jay not being her mate completely vanished. And if his touch hadn't convinced her, his kiss would have. She'd never felt such a sharp flare of desire. Her body had immediately prepared itself for his possession. She'd been ready to tear off Jay's clothes and beg him to take her.

The mention of Jay's father squashed that idea.

Roni never expected to meet any of Jay's family so soon, and especially not when she was trying to get her head to stop spinning from Jay's kisses. She hoped she didn't make a fool of herself in front of the older gentleman.

He faced the large plate windows, looking out at the choppy waters of the bay. He stood straight and tall, his hands clasped behind his back. His hair didn't brush his collar as Jay's did, but he possessed the same dark brown hair as his son, although she could see a few strands of gray peeking through. The wolves' aging process slowed dramatically once they hit thirty. They could reproduce for decades longer than humans. Jay's father could be fifty or four times that age and she wouldn't be able to tell.

"Dad."

He turned when Jay spoke, a smile on his lips. As she suspected, she would guess him to be in his mid fifties. He was just as handsome as his son. No one could look at the two of them and not guess they were related.

He picked up a cane that leaned against the glass before he started toward them. Roni inhaled sharply as he drew closer. That scent. She'd only encountered it twice in her life, that hint of exotic spices along with the essence of wolf.

My God, he's Alpha.

She immediately lowered her head, placed her fist over her heart, and dropped into a deep curtsy. "Sire."

He touched the top of her head. "Thank you for honoring me."

She looked up into dark brown eyes exactly like Jay's. He laid his cane on the large coffee table and offered his hands to her. Roni took them, letting him pull her back to her feet.

"She's lovely, Jay," he said, smiling at Roni.

"I think so, too."

He shifted his attention to his son. "Perhaps proper introductions are in order?"

"Dad, this is Veronica St. James. Roni, my father, Jamieson Millington."

"It's a privilege to meet you, sire."

"Please call me Jamieson. There's no need for formalities here."

Something tickled the back of Roni's mind. Jamieson Millington. She should know that name, yet wasn't sure why.

"I know Jay has made dinner reservations for you two," Jamieson said. "We will speak more tomorrow."

"Are you sure you won't come with us, Dad?"

"Yes, please, come with us."

Jamieson smiled. "I appreciate the offer, but this is your night. Enjoy yourselves. I'll see you in the morning."

"*Late* in the morning," Jay said with a grin.

Heat seeped into Roni's cheeks again when Jamieson chuckled. "Let's say eleven for brunch."

"That should be about right."

"I'll let Flora know that's when we wish to eat."

"Thanks, Dad." Jay slipped his arm around Roni's waist. "We'll see you tomorrow."

Jay led her through the dining room and back to the foyer. Pale icy colors mixed with deep jewel tones and splashes of gray in the furnishings. Whoever had decorated Jay's house had leaned toward the masculine side. Different paintings and wall hangings, perhaps some candleholders, and fluffy throw pillows would add a touch of feminine to the beautiful home.

She'd been in Jay's house half an hour and she was already redecorating in her mind. That kind of thinking had to stop. Yes, they were mates and would spend the rest of their lives together, but they still had a *lot* to talk about before there would be any redecorating of any kind.

"Who's Flora?" she asked when they stopped at the coat closet.

"My housekeeper." Jay held up her wrap to help her with it. "She has her own living area and bedroom off the kitchen." He squeezed her shoulders after draping the wrap over them. "Jealous?" he whispered in her ear.

"Insanely."

"I like that." Nuzzling her neck, he slipped both arms around her waist and pulled her into his body. His arms pushed up her breasts and deepened her cleavage. "Maybe I should've had her prepare a romantic meal that we could eat in my bedroom."

Little fingers of desire crawled up her spine. "Is it too late for her to do that?"

"Unfortunately, yes. I gave her the night off. She's visiting her sister in Palo Alto." He turned her to face him. "Besides, I want to show you off. One of my best friends owns the restaurant where we're going for dinner. I want him to meet you."

She waited while Jay removed his jacket from the closet. "I'm meeting a lot of people my first time here."

"Does that bother you?"

"Don't you think we should figure out . . . us . . . before you introduce me to everyone?"

Jay took her hands and held them tightly in his. "We never talked about our heritage on the phone." He ran his thumbs over the back of her hands. "The fact that you honored my father in the pack way told me you're a wolf, the same as I am."

"Yes, I am," she whispered.

"Then you know we mate for life. We take lovers—usually a lot of them—but there's only one true mate until death. I knew, the first time I heard your voice, that you're my mate. Seeing you, touching you, has proven that to me. I believe you feel the same way."

"I do."

"We'll make love tonight, Roni." A grin tilted up one corner of his mouth. "We'll fuck a lot, too."

Roni returned his grin. "I hope so."

Squeezing her hands, he turned serious again. "But the first time we're together, it'll be lovemaking . . . as romantic as I can possibly make it. I want to start the evening at my friend's restaurant with a special dinner he's preparing for us. I didn't know for sure what time you'd be here, so he promised to save my favorite table by the fireplace for us, no matter what time we arrived."

He walked past her and picked up her small purse from the floor by the front door. Roni had forgotten she'd brought it in with her. She must have dropped it when Jay kissed her. Smiling, he held it out to her. "Ready?"

She took her purse, then his arm. "Yes." She was definitely ready for whatever the night would bring.

6

The wine made Roni a little tipsy. She giggled a lot when she was tipsy, and worried that Jay would think her silly. Instead, he smiled and laughed at her jokes and continued to add wine to her glass, as if he liked her giggling.

Jay's friend Thomas had outdone himself on their meal. He'd started them with Caesar salads and French onion soup. Their main course of rare prime rib served with whipped potatoes that contained chives and bacon, fresh broccoli with cheese sauce, and hot rolls slathered with butter had been one of the most delicious meals she'd ever eaten. Roni had been sure she couldn't eat another bite, until Thomas served a decadent chocolate soufflé. She couldn't possibly say no to chocolate.

Now, completely sated on the excellent food and wine, Roni sat back in her chair and sipped on her cup of coffee. She stared into Jay's warm gaze, content to simply be with him.

"You look sleepy," Jay said, his lips curving in a slight smile.

"Not sleepy, but satisfied. Everything was so delicious."

"I agree. Thomas is an excellent chef. He always caters my company's Christmas party."

This was the first she'd heard of Jay owning his own business. "Your company? You told me you work with computers
and software."

"I do. Have you heard of JEMATAR?"

"Of course I've heard of JEMATAR. I have two of their
computers. I love them. But you . . ." Roni stopped. That little
tickling in the back of her mind when she'd met Jay's father
made sense now. "What's your middle name?"

"Edward."

"Jay Edward Millington. The J-E-M in JEMATAR. You
own the company?"

"My cousin Troy and I do. He's the T-A-R part. And actually, my first name is Jamieson, too. My father is the senior, I'm
the junior."

She thought of Jay's house on the water. As half owner of
JEMATAR, money would never be an issue for him.

Jay's smile faded. "I'm sorry I didn't tell you sooner."

"You have no reason to be sorry. I never asked you where
you worked. If I had, would you have told me?"

"Yes, I would have. I don't want any secrets between us,
Roni."

"Neither do I."

She studied him as she sipped her coffee. The firelight from
the fireplace highlighted one side of his face, leaving the other
side in shadow. His dark brown eyes seemed almost black in
the dim light. He'd removed his jacket before their main
course. The white pullover stretched across his broad shoulders
and wide chest. The scoop neck was low enough to give her a
hint of dark chest hair. To use the words *handsome* and *sexy* as
descriptions didn't do him justice.

Roni swallowed. She grew warm, and it had nothing to do
with her coffee and the fire. Desire gripped her body again, the
need to be with Jay in every way a woman could be with a man.

He leaned forward and rested his folded arms on the table. "You're devouring me with your eyes."

"Am I?"

"Big-time. I think we should go back to my house."

"I think you're right."

He draped her wrap around her shoulders before donning his jacket. With his hand on the small of her back, he guided her toward the front of the restaurant.

"Don't we need to wait for the check?" Roni asked.

"I have an account here."

Of course he did. Jay probably had accounts all over the area. While Roni's income allowed her to live very comfortably, she wouldn't call herself wealthy. Not like Jay.

Jay didn't speak again until he sat behind the steering wheel of his car. "Does my financial situation bother you? Having money doesn't make me any different, Roni. I'm fortunate that the dream Troy and I had for a new type of computer operating system has been such a success. I shop at discount stores, just like most people do. I draw enough of a wage to support myself, but rarely take any extra. I'd rather turn JEMATAR's profits into improving our computers or back to the employees in higher wages and better benefits."

A man of principle. Roni hadn't met many of those in her life. She reached over and cradled his cheek in her palm. "You're a special man, Jay."

"I'm pleased you think so." He kissed her palm, then placed her hand on his thigh.

She left her hand where he placed it, enjoying the feel of his firm, warm flesh beneath her palm. He had powerful thighs from his wolf's running.

She waited until he'd pulled out of the restaurant's parking lot before shifting closer to the console so she could slide her hand higher up his leg. He glanced at her, but said nothing. She slid her hand almost to his knee, back up again. "Your suit is very nice."

"You're just feeling the fabric, right?"

"Of course," she said, trying not to smile.

She ventured a little higher. His breathing grew deeper, faster. Continuing her exploration, she slid her hand down to his knee and back up the inside of his thigh.

"Roni."

Ignoring his warning tone, Roni traveled all the way up his thigh to the crease where his leg met his groin. Before she could venture any farther, he laid his hand over hers to stop its movement. "That's enough."

His voice came out low and rough. It thrilled her to know how strongly her touch affected him. "Why?"

"Because we're in the middle of traffic and I don't want to cause an accident."

"You told me on the phone you dreamed of me touching you."

"I did, but wait until we get home."

Waiting didn't sound any fun at all. The moment Jay's grip relaxed, she slid her hand between his legs.

Jay bucked his hips. His cock was already hard at her first touch, but it thickened and lengthened beneath her palm. She let her fingertips dance over him, wishing nothing separated her hand from his flesh.

He pulled her hand away from him and kissed her palm. "I love your touch, but I want to be able to focus all my attention on you and not traffic."

She appreciated his thoughtfulness for the other drivers. Yet now that she had touched that hard shaft, her wolf demanded more. A *lot* more. She leaned over the console and nipped his earlobe. "I want your cock in my mouth."

The growl she heard came from deep in his throat. "We'll be home in ten minutes."

"I can't wait that long."

She laid her other hand over his fly and squeezed. When he didn't attempt to move her hand, Roni unfastened his belt and pants. She dipped her hand inside his fly and wrapped her fingers around his shaft. She silently damned the console that kept her from snuggling up to Jay's side.

"You're determined to make me have a wreck, aren't you?"

Roni noticed he complained, but he didn't pull her hand away from him. In fact, he bucked his hips again and hissed when she pulled his cock from his briefs. Long and thick and so hard, it felt like velvet-covered steel. She slid her hand all the way to the base, squeezed, returned to the head. A circle of her thumb over the slit spread the slick pre-cum.

Her mouth watered with the desire to taste him.

Unable to wait any longer, Roni leaned over and swiped her tongue across the head. He tasted delicious and smelled even better . . . that intoxicating mixture of musk and man and wolf. She licked the head again, ran her tongue down the heavy veins.

Jay groaned. "God, that's so good."

No arguing there. Roni took him in her mouth, as far as she could. Relaxing her throat, she let her lips slide all the way to his balls.

Jay took a corner a little too fast. Roni released his cock and peered up at him. His obvious rush helped to cool her ardor enough so she could tease him. "In a hurry?"

"Hell, yes. I want us naked."

Roni sat up as Jay took the turn into his driveway. He pressed the button on his rearview mirror to open the door to his wide, three-car garage. A light came on, letting her see an SUV and a small compact car also occupied the space. The SUV had been there when they left, the compact car had not.

"Flora's home." Jay quickly tucked his still-hard cock inside his briefs, fastened his pants and belt. "We'll take the main stairs in the foyer. The back stairs by the kitchen are right by her rooms. If she hears us, she'll come out to see if we need anything. And her hearing is excellent."

"I don't get to meet Flora?" she asked, pretending innocence.

Jay frowned at her while Roni drew her bottom lip between her teeth to keep from grinning. "You don't get to meet Flora when I have a hard-on."

Roni met him at the hood of the car. He took enough time to thoroughly kiss her until her desire came roaring back, then took her hand and led her inside the house.

Night-lights illuminated their way. Jay turned left at the top of the stairs and through open double doors into a large bedroom. Roni stepped into the room, her gaze immediately falling on the huge bed. Soft light flowed from the lamps on either side of the bed. The covers had been turned back to expose pale blue sheets. A red rose rested on each pillow. A silver bucket sat on the dresser, holding ice and a bottle. Two tall wineglasses sat next to the bucket.

The *snick* of the doors closing drew Roni's attention back to Jay. "I think Flora has been here."

He looked at the dresser, the bed, back at Roni. "She was so excited when I told her you were coming. Looks like she let her romantic side run free."

He remained standing at the doors, his hands behind him as if he held the door handles. "What is it?"

"You look so perfect standing there. I can't believe you're finally here."

Roni smiled. "I'm finally here. So why are you way over there?"

Jay was afraid to approach Roni, afraid the growling wolf inside him would take over. He'd promised her a romantic night. If he touched her now, after she'd had her mouth on his dick in the car, he didn't think he'd be able to stop until he fucked her, long and hard and rough.

Ordering his wolf to behave, Jay crossed to the dresser. He lifted the bottle out of the ice. "Would you like a glass of champagne?"

"Please."

She moved to stand next to him. He picked up the hand towel next to the bucket and wrapped it around the wet bottle. The cork worked free with a gentle pop. Roni held the glasses while Jay poured the sparkling liquid. After he replaced the bottle in the bucket, he held his glass up to her.

"To our first night together."

She tapped her glass against his. "To our first night together."

He held her gaze as they sipped the cold wine. A drop clung to her bottom lip. A swipe of her tongue whisked it away.

Jay somehow managed not to groan.

Roni took another sip. "It's very good."

"I think Flora just earned a raise."

"I can hardly wait to meet her. Is she wolf, too?"

"No, but she knows my family is."

She took one more sip, then set her glass on the dresser. "I believe you said something in the car about wanting us naked."

Not yet, not until he had his wolf under control. "I've cooled down some since then."

Looking into his eyes, she laid her hands on his chest. "I haven't."

She slid her arms around his neck, tugged him close enough to kiss. Jay couldn't fight her, nor did he want to. He set down his glass and wrapped his arms around her, holding her as close to his body as he could. Finally, he could run his hands over her, touch her wherever he wanted to, without worry of someone interrupting them.

His wolf howled in pleasure.

The kiss turned deeper, more frantic. Jay shifted his hips from side to side, grinding his cock against her mound. His tongue thrust into her mouth, twined around hers. The whimpers he heard from Roni's throat urged him for more, more.

She tunneled her hands beneath his shirt. Jay swallowed when she ran her fingernails down his chest and stomach. His control gone, he picked her up and carried her to the bed. Their lips met again as he laid her on top of the bedspread.

She opened her legs for him, creating a cradle for his hips. Still kissing her deeply, Jay ran one hand up her stocking-covered leg. He didn't stop at the hem of her dress, but continued to glide his hand up her leg. He stopped long enough to appreciate the smooth skin of her outer thigh above her stocking before climbing higher to her ass. Her bare ass.

"Thong?" he whispered against her mouth.

"Yes."

"Mmm, love thongs, but it has to go."

Jay rose to his knees. He slid his hands up both her legs, taking her dress with him until it pooled around her waist. Wide black lace surrounded the top of each stocking. A tiny black thong barely covered her mound. No matter how sexy the black looked against her ivory skin, he wanted nothing covering her skin at all.

He clasped the waistband of her thong. Roni lifted her butt and he gently tugged the thong past her hips. His wolf panted happily at the sight of her bare pussy.

Once he'd tossed the tiny scrap of fabric to the floor, he moved between her legs on his knees. He used his thumbs to spread the lips of her wet flesh. Her swollen clit peeked out from beneath its hood, calling to him to touch, to taste.

To possess.

Jay bent over and licked her from anus to clit. Her taste exploded on his tongue.

Delicious.

One sample not nearly enough, he licked her again and again. Roni inhaled sharply, grabbed handfuls of the bedspread in her fists. Jay watched her face as he licked her pussy. Her closed eyes and parted lips proved she enjoyed every lap of his tongue. He'd always loved oral sex, but oral sex with his mate surpassed anything he'd ever experienced. He didn't want to ever stop.

He circled her clit with the tip of his tongue, drove his tongue inside her channel, licked her anus. Concentrating on that sensitive area, he pulled Roni's cheeks as far apart as he could and rammed his tongue into her ass.

She jerked and grabbed his head. "Oh, God!"

She didn't push him away, but held his head tightly as if to keep him from moving. Jay fucked her ass with his tongue, stopping only long enough to lap at her clit for several strokes before returning to her ass. Her juices trickled from her channel, letting his tongue glide easier over her anus.

Jay stood and pulled Roni's hips right to the edge of the bed. Dropping to his knees, he pushed her legs apart and up, giving him more room at that beautiful cunt. She helped him by hooking her hands behind her knees and pulling them even farther apart.

"You like me eating your pussy, huh?"

"God, yes. More."

Happy to obey her command, Jay dragged his tongue up and down her slit. He tongue-fucked her ass again, lapped at her clit. Wanting Roni to come, he fastened his mouth over her clit and sucked.

Her legs fell on either side of his head, her back arched off the bed. A keening cry filled the room as her body trembled. Jay continued the gentle licking of her pussy until she once again lay still.

He leaned over her body, arms straight, fists by her shoulders, and waited. Her eyes finally opened, the pupils large and unfocused. She closed them again and blew out a breath that caressed his face. "You okay?" he asked.

"No. Is the top of my head still on?"

Jay chuckled. "Yep, still there."

"Wow." She opened her eyes again. "You have a *very* clever tongue." She cradled his face, caressed his cheeks with her thumbs. "Kiss me."

He did, gently, sweetly, until Roni swept her tongue across his lips. Stretching out on top of her, he kissed her with every bit of the desire still rampaging through his body. He pumped his hips, pressing his cock between her thighs with each movement.

He kissed his way to her ear, nibbled on the lobe. She must have dabbed whatever cologne she used behind her ears. It smelled like night. Wildness.

Sex.

Roni pushed her hands between their bodies. When he felt her fumbling with his belt buckle, he pulled away and rose to his knees. He stripped off his shirt and tossed it to the floor. Roni's sharp gasp froze his hands on his belt buckle.

"What's wrong?"

"Not a thing." She splayed her hands across his stomach. "You really are magnificent."

Propping herself on one elbow, Roni pushed away his hands and unfastened the belt buckle herself. She tugged his pants and briefs past his hips. His cock sprang from his clothes, full and hard. Gripping it tightly, she moved her hand up and down the length.

"Take off your clothes, Jay."

7

Roni rose to her knees and watched as Jay removed his clothing. Each bit of skin that he revealed made her clit pulse. He'd given her a mind-blowing climax with his tongue. Her body didn't care. It wanted another one, as quickly as possible . . . preferably with that scrumptious cock.

She could see the reflection of his back in the dresser mirror. She whimpered when he bent over to pull off his socks. His olive skin gave him the appearance of a tan. Everywhere.

He placed one knee on the bed and reached for the hem of her dress. "Your turn."

She lifted her arms so he could take off her dress. His gaze dipped to her breasts, barely covered by her black demi-bra. Because of her large breasts, she usually wore a bra with more support. For tonight, sexy and alluring won out over support.

Gently, almost reverently, he ran the tips of his fingers across the top of her breasts. "So beautiful," he murmured.

Reaching behind her back, Roni unhooked the bra, drew the straps down her arms. She tossed it to the floor with the rest of their clothing. She knelt before Jay wearing nothing but her stockings and heels.

He held her face and kissed her. With their lips still pressed tightly together, he slid his hands down to her breasts. Roni moaned at the feel of his hands on her sensitive flesh. She arched her back, silently asking him for a firmer touch.

His thumbs circled her aching nipples, caressing the areolae but not touching her where she needed it the most. "Feel good?"

She caught his thumbs and pressed them in the center of her nipples. "This feels better."

His chuckle sounded wicked and sexy. "I like a woman who tells me what she wants." He lifted and kneaded her breasts, causing her to moan. "How's this?"

"Wonderful."

Bending over, he drew one nipple into his mouth. Roni already knew Jay had a talented mouth from the staggering orgasm he'd given her with his tongue. He proved it again with her nipple. He stroked it with his tongue, sucked with his lips, nipped with his teeth. The entire time he loved one peak with his mouth, he caressed the other with his fingers.

Roni sank her fingers into his thick mane. Closing her eyes, she let her head fall back as she absorbed the delicious sensation of Jay's mouth on her breasts. Her body became warmer, her breathing more erratic. Another orgasm loomed. She only needed a little more. . . .

Jay fastened his mouth over her nipple and sucked hard while pinching the other one. Roni flew apart. She gripped his hair tighter and cried out in pleasure.

Before she had time to catch her breath, Jay pushed her down on the bed and covered her body with his. He kissed her with hunger, one hand covering her breast, one between her legs. He rubbed her clit as he kissed her, keeping her desire burning hotly despite her recent climax.

His mouth trailed over her jaw to her neck. "I can tell you aren't in heat now by your scent." He scraped his teeth over the pounding pulse. "Do you want me to wear a condom?"

Although wolves didn't transmit sexual diseases as humans did, Roni had always insisted her lovers wear condoms. With Jay, she didn't want anything separating them, not even a thin layer of latex. "No."

She'd barely said the word when he drove inside her. Roni dug her fingernails into Jay's shoulders, lifted her hips. He gripped her ass and began to pump . . . long, deep thrusts that filled her completely. He didn't increase his speed until she wrapped her legs around his hips. The long thrusts turned into quick, short ones, each stroke brushing her clit perfectly. She couldn't believe a third orgasm could sweep through her so soon after the other two, until it happened.

"*God!*" She clutched Jay's shoulders tighter. "Yes, oh *yes!*"

Jay jerked and released a long moan. She could feel the spasms of his cock inside her channel. His body jerked again, then stilled.

He didn't remain still longer than a few moments. Roni hadn't caught her breath yet when he clutched her tightly to him and rolled to his back.

"I'm not through." Grasping the back of her head, he gave her a hot, passionate kiss. "Ride me."

The feel of his still-hard cock inside her fanned her desire back to life. She braced her hands on his chest, lifted her hips until her folds clutched only the head. She lowered her hips, taking all of him inside her again. Staring into Jay's eyes, she repeated the process over and over while he thumbed her clit, tugged on her nipples.

"You're so beautiful." His voice came out deep, raspy. "I love it when you come."

He increased the pressure on her clit, rubbing it in little circles that caused her womb to clench. Roni caressed Jay's nipples as he caressed hers, tightened the walls of her pussy with every movement. Sweat formed on his forehead, his neck, his chest. He had to be close, as close as she to another mindless orgasm.

Jay squeezed his eyes closed and threw back his head. *"Fuck!"* His body jerked, his cock pulsed. Seeing his reaction, feeling that hard column of flesh throb inside her, pushed Roni over the edge with him.

She wilted on top of him. She didn't know whose heart beat harder—his or hers.

"It isn't nice to try to kill me the first time we make love," Jay said between pants.

"What a way to go."

Chuckling, Jay slid his hands up and down her back. "Can't think of a better way."

Roni didn't know how long they lay together, Jay gently rubbing her back, until she raised her head. His eyelids were half-closed in that I'm-completely-satisfied look. "That was amazing."

He squeezed her buttocks. "I agree." He danced his fingertips up her spine. "Would you like to shower with me?"

"Don't think I'm crazy, because I know I should be exhausted, but I'd like to run."

A pleased smile spread over his lips. "That is an excellent idea."

Roni lifted her body until his soft cock slipped from her. It was wet from a combination of her juices and his. Too tempting to resist, she bent over and licked it from his balls to the crown.

Jay groaned. "No fair. I thought you wanted to run."

"I do, but . . ." She licked him again. "I think I should finish what I started in the car, don't you?"

"You can't expect . . ." He stopped and arched his hips when she opened her mouth over the head. *"Jesus, Roni."*

Roni slid her lips down his shaft until her nose brushed his pubic hair. She could taste each of their unique flavors. The mixture was absolutely delicious.

Growing bolder as Jay hardened, Roni slipped her knees between his. She wet her forefinger with the cum from her pussy and transferred it to Jay's anus. He hissed in a sharp breath between his teeth. His cock grew larger in her mouth. She kept gathering their cum until her slick finger easily glided over his anus.

Roni took his cock all the way in her mouth, pushed her finger in his ass. His legs trembled against hers as he began to pump his hips. Each time he lifted his hips, she pressed her finger farther inside him. She cradled his tight balls with her other hand, gently rolling and squeezing them.

"I'm gonna come, Roni. Oh, yeah, I'm gonna come."

She pushed a second finger in his ass. His cock erupted, streams of cum filling her mouth. She swallowed again and again, not wanting to lose a drop.

Once she was sure she'd swallowed all of his essence, she released his cock. It lay against his thigh, soft but still large enough to take her breath. She let her gaze travel up his body, past his dark pubic hair, the flat stomach with its swirl of hair around his navel. She followed that path of hair up the center of his body, where it widened across his chest. One arm lay across his eyes. The dark hair in his armpit looked soft and silky.

She sighed. She couldn't believe someone so gorgeous now belonged to her.

Not yet. Not until she surrendered to him as a wolf. Then she and Jay would be bonded for life.

She rose from the bed long enough to remove her shoes and stockings, then lay by his side. Jay turned toward her and entwined their legs. He smiled sleepily. "Hey."

Roni smiled. "Hey."

"I think the run is out. My legs won't work now."

"I don't mind lying here in your arms."

With a tender smile, Jay wrapped one arm around her, pushed her hair back from her face. "I'm so glad I called the right number."

"It was a wrong number, remember?"

He shook his head. "Something this perfect couldn't be the result of anything wrong."

She snuggled against his chest, comforted by his warm breath against her temple. She could've fallen asleep if the need for a bathroom hadn't nagged at her. Since ignoring that wasn't an option, she reluctantly moved from Jay's embrace.

"Where are you going?"

"Bathroom."

He pointed to a white door across the room. "Through there."

As luxurious as his bedroom, Jay's private bath had a shower big enough for three people, and a huge garden tub that sat beneath a wall of windows overlooking the bay. Roni could easily imagine sitting in the tub with Jay, surrounded by candles and drinking wine while they enjoyed the view.

Wanting to be back in Jay's arms as quickly as possible, Roni took care of business and returned to the bedroom. Jay stood at the end of the bed, holding two glasses of champagne. She liked the way his gaze dipped down her body as she walked toward him. She felt no shame, no shyness, to be naked with him. He apparently felt the same, since he hadn't bothered to put on a robe.

"I thought you might want something to drink."

"Mmm, yes." She accepted one glass from him, holding his gaze while they drank. "Oh, that is so good."

"Flora has very good taste in wines. She's an amazing cook, too. She takes really good care of me."

"How long has she worked for you?"

"Going on ten years."

"And she knows you're a shapeshifter?"

Jay nodded. "Not at first. She worked for me almost a year before I confided in her. I had to be sure I could trust her not to run away screaming or spill my secret to the press."

"I gather she didn't do either."

"No. She loves to read paranormal romances and got so excited the first time I shifted in front of her. She thinks it's cool to work for a shapeshifter."

Roni chuckled and took another sip of wine. Then she realized what Jay had said. "You shifted in front of her?"

"Yeah."

"We're naked when we shift."

He tapped the end of her nose. "I stood behind the kitchen island so she wouldn't see any of my good parts."

"Oh."

Jay grinned. "Jealous?"

Yes, but she wouldn't admit that to him. "Of course not. And wipe that cocky grin off your face."

"Yes, ma'am." He drained his glass. "I think I have my second wind now. Want to try that run?"

"I'd love to, but my suitcase is in my rental car." She looked down at her nude body. "I can't walk through your house like this."

"It wouldn't bother me if you did."

She frowned at his teasing. "Jay."

He laughed, gave her a quick hug. "I've got it handled, sweetheart."

He took her glass and placed it along with his on the dresser, then crossed the floor to a door next to the bathroom. A light came on when he opened the door, exposing a large walk-in closet. He stepped inside and came out wearing a dark blue silk robe. Holding up its mate, he helped Roni slip into it.

"I bought these when you told me you were coming. I didn't think you'd want to walk naked through my house with other people here."

She tied the belt and turned to face him. The robe fit her perfectly. "Thank you. But how did you know my size?"

"I, uh, cheated. I bought the same robe in three sizes."

Roni laughed at his ingenuity. Jay grinned. "I figured I could take back the two that didn't fit you."

She tugged him closer for a kiss. "Very smart."

He took her hand, entwined their fingers. "Ready to run?"

She squeezed his hand. "Ready."

Jay watched Roni shed her robe on the patio. He took the chance to admire her perfect form in the moonlight before she closed her eyes and shifted. Instead of the incredibly sexy woman he'd been with all evening, a black wolf stood before him. She sat on her haunches and looked up at him, her pink tongue hanging out of her mouth.

"God, you're even more beautiful as a wolf."

She tilted her head and whimpered. With a sharp *yip*, she ran five feet across the patio, stopped, and looked back at him.

Jay laughed. "Okay, I get the hint. You're ready to run."

The power flowed through him as he shifted. Roni took off toward the woods that surrounded his house. Jay hurried to catch up. He ran next to her, their strides in sync, until they were deep in the woods with nothing surrounding them but trees and the sound of the night creatures.

She got ahead of him, her bushy tail high. A wolf's natural urge to dominate, to mate, gripped Jay. He ran faster until he caught up to Roni again and nipped at her shoulder. She nipped back, catching his ear. He tried to circle her, but she kept moving, dodging him, avoiding his paw when he tried to hold her in place.

He would swear there was a smile on her face.

She took off again, bounding over downed trees and through low bushes. Jay ran full out to catch her. He finally cornered her in a patch of ferns. Growling softly, he approached her. She stood with her head high, her mouth open as she panted. He pawed at the ground, then moved closer. Her position in the trees wouldn't let him get behind her the way he wanted to.

Jay moved a bit closer, released a low bark. He tensed, ready to stop her if she tried to run away. She surprised him by turning around and moving her tail to the side.

Offering her complete surrender.

He placed his paws on her back and mounted her. She spread her legs wide, taking all of his weight as he thrust into her. The knot to tie them together passed from him to her. She whimpered softly, lowered her head. He could feel the ripple of her sheath around his cock, signaling her climax. Holding the back of her neck in his teeth, he followed her over the edge.

Minutes passed while they lay bound together on the ground. Jay slowly pulled away from Roni and stood. She stood, too, and faced him. He nuzzled her neck, rubbed his muzzle against hers. She growled low in her throat, a sound of happiness and satisfaction.

Turning, she broke into a run toward Jay's house. *Race you!*

He started forward, stumbled to a stop when he clearly heard Roni's voice in his head. Legend said that once mated, wolves could talk to each other. He'd never been sure whether to believe that.

Now he did.

Wait! He took off after her. *Roni, wait.*

Her laughter rang in his mind. Reaching her side, he ran with her all the way to his patio. He shifted as she did, drew her in his arms for a long, deep kiss.

"I love you," he whispered in her ear.

"I love you, too."

He drew back enough to see her face. Her eyes reflected her declaration of love, as did the smile that curved her lips . . . lips he couldn't resist tasting again.

"Shower?" he asked after kissing her once more.

She nodded.

Scooping up their robes from a chaise lounge, Jay took Roni's hand and led her back into the house.

8

Roni gripped Jay's buttocks and threw back her head as the orgasm flowed through her body. She hadn't uncurled her toes yet from the powerful sensations when Jay flipped her to her stomach. Drawing her up to her knees, he rammed his cock into her pussy.

Just like that, her body was on fire for him again. Roni spread her knees to balance herself for Jay's hard thrusts. She had no idea how many times they'd made love the last two days, but she'd already learned some of his habits and quirks. On top of her, he was more tender and loving. When she was on top, he let her lead them on the path to orgasm at whatever speed she wanted to go. No pushing, no urging her to ride him faster. She set the pace and he followed.

His wolf came out in this position. He liked it hard and fast, almost animalistic. So did Roni. Clutching a pillow, she spread her legs even farther apart.

"Oh yeah. You like me fucking you this way, don't you?"

"I like you fucking me *any* way." She arched her back, trying to take him even deeper. "Harder."

She moaned when he reached under her and cradled her breasts, pinched her nipples. Another twist of the hard peaks sent her tumbling again. He pumped once, twice, then trembled and moaned. His warm breath brushed her nape, sending little fingers of desire up and down her spine.

Wolves were naturally sexual creatures, but Roni had never craved anyone the way she craved Jay. Even once a year when she was in heat for two weeks, the desire to fuck didn't overwhelm her the way a simple look from Jay did.

She didn't know she could love so fiercely.

Gently, he pulled out of her and helped her roll to her back. Once she'd gotten into a comfortable position, he lay on top of her and smiled. "Good morning."

"Good morning," she said, returning his smile. "Although I think it's technically afternoon."

"Details." He pressed a soft kiss on her lips. "Sex is such a wonderful way to start the day."

Since they'd also started Friday morning with sex, Roni had to agree. "We haven't done much but eat, sleep, and have sex."

"I know." He grinned. "Ain't it grand?"

She laughed at the smug expression on his face. She had to admit he was right. Everything had been grand so far.

Jay rose up to his knees between her legs. He cradled her breasts, thumbed her nipples. "Want to go for a run before breakfast?"

They'd never run in daylight, only under cover of night. "Now?"

"Sure." Her concern must have shown on her face, for he smiled and tapped the end of her nose. "As humans, Roni."

"Oh." While she loved running as a wolf, running as a human didn't appeal to her at all. She wrinkled her nose. "Not really."

He shrugged as if it didn't matter. "Then what do you want

to do today? It's Saturday. There's no limit to what we can find to do in the city."

His thumbs made a pass over her nipples again. Each touch sent that little zing to her clit. "Keep that up and we'll never get out of bed."

He flashed that boyish grin at her. "Works for me."

Jay's cell phone on the nightstand belted out an old Doobie Brothers song. "That's Troy." He squeezed her breasts and lightly pinched her nipples. "I hate to let go of you to answer it."

"I'm not going anywhere."

Leaving one hand on her breast, Jay reached over and snatched up his cell phone. "Hey, man."

Roni watched Jay's eyebrows draw together. "Today?" He looked at her. "I have plans today. . . . Well, yeah, I know I said that, but . . . Okay, sure. . . . Give me an hour or so. I haven't showered yet. . . . Bye."

"Is something wrong?" Roni asked as he replaced the phone on the nightstand.

"Troy's run into a problem and wants to talk to me about it. He said it can't wait until Monday."

"He works Saturdays?"

"Sometimes, when we're pushing a deadline. We're introducing our new computer line in August and still have some bugs to fix." He stretched out on top of her. "That's a secret, so you can't tell anyone."

She made a motion over her lips, like turning a key in a lock. "I won't tell a soul."

"I'm sorry to mess up our weekend. Troy wouldn't bother me unless it was really important."

"You aren't messing up anything." She wrapped her arms around his neck. "You can drop me at a mall or shopping center, go do your business, then pick me up when you're through."

Jay smiled. "Sounds like a plan. Then I'll take you to dinner on the waterfront."

Roni cradled his face and kissed him. "Perfect."

Jay found Troy in the dungeon, a half-full mug of coffee at his elbow and a scowl on his face. He slapped his cousin on the shoulder. "You're supposed to play on Saturday, not work."

"Yeah, well, you'll be glad I'm so dedicated when I tell you what I found." He swiveled his chair around to face Jay. "We have a hacker, cuz."

Instead of the panic Jay knew his cousin would expect, he shrugged. "We track a lot of hackers, Troy. It's usually just kids trying to show off to their friends. No one ever actually gets past our firewall."

"They did this time."

Shocked at his cousin's statement, Jay sank down into the chair next to Troy's desk. "What?"

"I discovered it early this morning. But get this. Now there's no sign anyone was ever in our system. All traces I found right before I called you are gone." Troy tapped one fingertip against his monitor. "Whoever did this is very, very good."

Jay looked at Troy's monitor. He saw nothing but code for their operating system. "Are you sure? Maybe you only thought you saw something."

"I managed to get a couple of screen shots before everything disappeared. There's no doubt someone got past our firewall."

Jay rubbed his forehead. In the eight years since he and Troy had formed JEMATAR, no one had managed to get into their system. "We need to get our security team on this."

"Already on their way. I called them right after I called you."

"Good."

Troy leaned back in his chair, laced his hands over his stomach. "So, where's your lady friend?"

Since JEMATAR was so close to announcing the new line of computers, Jay would normally never take any time off. He'd told Troy that Roni was coming for a visit when he decided to take off Thursday and Friday. "I dropped her off at Fisherman's Wharf so she could do some shopping while I came here."

"Everything going smoothly?"

"Better than smoothly." Jay smiled. "She's the one, Troy. My mate. We bonded as wolves Thursday night."

Jay didn't receive the smile or the "that's great" he expected from his cousin. Instead, Troy's scowl returned. "You bonded and yet you know nothing about her."

"Troy—"

"It's the female's decision when to mate. How interesting that she was willing to move her tail the first time you met."

Jay scowled at Troy's crudeness. "Look—"

"Where does she work? Do you even know that?"

"Will you let me finish a sentence?"

Troy waved a hand in Jay's direction, as if to give him permission to speak.

"She works for her family's business in Dallas."

"What kind of business?"

Jay didn't know, nor did he care. "It doesn't matter to me."

"It matters to *me*." Gripping the arms of his chair, Troy leaned forward. "Your father is our Alpha. You're next in line to lead our pack. Not only do I love you and swear to protect you because you're my cousin and business partner, but because you'll lead us someday. I won't let anyone hurt you, Jay . . . not even the wolf you think is your mate."

"She *is* my mate, Troy."

"How do you know she isn't a spy from a competitor? Or someone out to trap you? You're worth a lot of money, cuz."

"She isn't interested in my money. She may not have as much as I do, but she isn't hurting. She lives in Highland Park.

That's a very ritzy part of Dallas. Besides, a wolf can't fake the call of its mate. As soon as I heard her voice, I knew we belong together."

Troy stared at him long enough that Jay was about to snap at him when he tapped his monitor again. "You're thinking with your dick, Jay, not your brain. I'm not satisfied with the little bit you know about Veronica St. James. As soon as I get this security situation straightened out, I'll do that investigation on her."

Whatever Troy thought he might find about Roni wouldn't make any difference in the way Jay felt about her. He knew she had nothing to hide. "Fine. Investigate away. You won't find anything wrong with Roni. I know that for a fact."

Roni could tell something bothered Jay, something he hadn't told her. He'd seemed fine when he'd met her on Fisherman's Wharf. He'd even gone through some of the souvenir shops with her and helped her pick out T-shirts for her sisters. But he'd been quiet and withdrawn ever since they arrived at the restaurant.

She reached across the table and covered his hand with hers. "What's wrong? You haven't said three words since we sat down to eat."

He laid his fork on his plate next to his barely touched steak. "I'm sorry. I'm thinking about the mess at JEMATAR. Troy is going nuts with this hacker thing."

Roni wondered if she should offer Clint's services. If someone had tried to hack into Jay's company, she had no doubt her brother could find him. Clint could not only find a needle in a haystack, he could find a needle in the whole hayfield.

Jay continued before she could make the offer. "Troy called in our security team. They'll work nonstop to plug the leak, if there is one."

"Is your security team good?"

"The best." His gaze turned sharper. "Why do you ask?"

"Because I can recommend someone if you need help."

"Who?"

"My brother."

Jay slowly sat back in his chair. "Your brother."

Roni didn't understand the flat tone of Jay's voice. "Yes. That's what our family business is—computer security. I'm here to finalize the contract with Parks Bank. They're our newest client."

When he said nothing, but continued to stare at her, Roni squirmed in her chair. Tension seeped off Jay, a tension she didn't understand. She had no idea why he would be upset at the mention of her brother. "Did I say something wrong?"

He smiled, but Roni thought it seemed forced. "Of course not." He reached across the table and laid his hand over hers. "I'm letting business get in the way of our time together. Troy will take care of the hacker problem. I want to concentrate on you for the rest of the time you're here."

His words should've relieved her, yet they didn't. Something bothered Jay that he couldn't—or wouldn't—tell her. "I want that, too."

"Then that's what we'll do. No more talk of work or problems. We'll just concentrate on us." He picked up his fork again and stabbed a piece of steak. "We can go to the movies after dinner, or go back to my house and watch a DVD."

It sounded like an ordinary thing to do, but Roni still suspected something wasn't quite right with Jay. For now, she decided to go along with him and hope he would confide in her later. "Do you have popcorn at home?"

"Absolutely. A movie isn't complete without popcorn."

"Then I vote for the DVD. Your father and Flora can watch it with us."

"Deal."

* * *

Jay stood at the window to his office, looking out at the softly falling rain. The weather matched his mood. He'd been down and depressed ever since Roni left Sunday morning.

He'd thrown himself into work the last two days, working with Troy and the design team to be sure all would be ready for the August first release. The few bugs Troy had mentioned had been resolved. Everything looked good for their newest babies to be released on time.

The fact that things had come together so smoothly made him happy, but didn't satisfy him. Nothing would satisfy Jay until he could be with Roni again.

It had to be a coincidence that she came into his life when JEMATAR started having hacker problems. Just because her family worked in computer security didn't mean she had anything to do with the attempted assault on JEMATAR's system. She would never do anything to hurt him.

He'd bet his life on that.

Warning bells had gone off in his head when Roni told him her family's business had to do with computer security. Who better to get *into* a computer than someone who knew how to keep people *out* of it? He'd soon realized he'd let Troy's suspicions put doubts in his mind . . . doubts that he had no right to feel. No matter what Troy believed, Jay knew better. His mate wouldn't betray him.

He'd spoken with her every night on the phone since she'd left Sunday. Not wanting to wait until tonight to hear Roni's voice, Jay unclipped his cell phone from his belt and entered Roni's number. She answered after the second ring.

"Hi."

As always, the sound of her voice went straight to his cock. "Am I interrupting anything?"

"Never."

He smiled at the pleased sound in her voice. "That's good to know."

"You're calling earlier than you usually do. Is something wrong?"

"No. I just wanted to hear your voice. I miss you."

"I miss you, too," she said softly.

His wolf pawed and growled. It wanted its mate *now*. "I can't stand being away from you. Come back." He hurried on before she could argue with him. "It's Memorial Day weekend. You could fly back here Friday and stay until Monday. I'll make the flight arrangements and pick you up at the airport." He gripped his phone tighter. "Please, Roni. I need you."

"Buying a ticket only two days before the flight will be very expensive."

"I don't care about the cost. Hell, I'll go buy a private plane and come for you if that will get you here."

She laughed, low and throaty. "I'm flattered you would go to so much expense for me."

"There isn't anything I wouldn't do for you. Will you come?"

"I'm sure I will as soon as you put your hands on me."

Jay groaned and his cock twitched. "You're evil, do you know that?"

"You left yourself wide open with that question."

"Guilty as charged." Her giggle made him smile. "So is that a yes?"

"Yes."

The smile spread across Jay's face. He stopped himself before he pumped his fist in the air. "I'll make the reservation right now and call you back with the details."

"I don't mind taking the red-eye Thursday night."

It pleased him that she was as eager to see him as he was to see her. "I'll do my best. I'll call you tonight."

"Okay. Bye."

Still smiling, Jay disconnected the call. He crossed his office and stuck his head out the door. April looked up from her desk at him.

"I need you to make a flight reservation for me. DFW to SFO. Tomorrow night or early Friday morning." His smile widened. "My mate is coming back."

Malcolm removed the earphones and took the sound amplifier from his dash. With his contacts, he was always able to get the latest and greatest toys. This particular toy let him hear through glass as clearly as if the person stood right next to him. He only had to point the amplifier at Jamieson Millington and he heard every bit of his conversation.

He'd had other . . . items to take care of before he could come to San Francisco. Now that all those other details were out of the way, he could concentrate on Millington. He smiled when he thought of the sweet commission he had been paid to kill this guy.

Millington expected company tomorrow or Friday. That meant he'd be occupied with his . . . whatever she was, and wouldn't be on guard.

Malcolm's smile widened. Perfect.

9

Jay watched people file by him on their way to pick up their luggage. Roni should've been close to the front of the line. He'd bought her a ticket in the first-class section so she could get off the plane quickly. He wanted her back in his arms as soon as possible.

It had been really stupid on his part not to talk to Roni about their future before she went back to Dallas. He had been high on love and hormones and finding his mate. He didn't think about how much he would miss her, or how much his wolf would miss its mate. It had snapped and growled ever since Roni left.

Jamieson had come to visit Jay, but also had business here in the Bay Area. Jay's stepmother, Tara, had stayed behind in England. Jay didn't know how his father did it, how he managed to stay away from his mate for so long. By the time Jamieson returned to England, he'd be away from Tara for almost two weeks. Five days away from Roni had Jay feeling lost and completely alone.

A flash of dark hair caught his eye. Jay stood taller, trying to see if that dark hair belonged to Roni. She stepped from behind a man and into Jay's direct line of vision. He would swear his heart swelled to twice its size at the sight of her. So did his cock.

She wore a long-sleeved gray dress with a droopy cowl collar. The soft material flowed over her curves to just above her knees. He admired the hint of her nipples through the fabric and the way her breasts gently bounced as she walked.

He had plans for those amazing breasts this weekend. And every other part of her.

Her gaze locked with his. With a gentle smile curving her lips, she walked toward him. He met her halfway, slipped one arm around her waist. He couldn't kiss her senseless the way he wanted to in front of all these people, so settled for a soft peck on her lips.

"Hi."

She smiled. "Hi."

"Is this all of your luggage?"

"Yes."

Relieving her of the wheeled carry-on she rolled behind her, he took her hand and led her toward the exit. "How was your flight?"

"Wonderful. I didn't know you were going to put me in first class."

"Nothing but the best for my lady."

He held the door open for her. Roni blinked at the bright sunshine. She pulled Jay to a stop. "Wait. I need my sunglasses."

While she removed her glasses from a case in her purse, Jay took the time to study her profile. Her breasts looked large and lush. He could see more than just a hint of her nipples now. She either wore a very sheer bra or none at all.

Blood surged into his cock at the thought of Roni riding on a plane, walking through the airport, with only a thin layer of fabric covering her breasts. "Are you wearing a bra?"

She turned her head toward him. He couldn't see her eyes through the dark lenses, but he saw the vixen's smile on her lips. "No."

"Panties?"

"No."

Jay had to clear his throat before he could speak again. "You aren't wearing *anything* beneath your dress?"

"Not a stitch."

"Fuck," he muttered.

"That's what I had in mind."

He grabbed her hand. "C'mon."

Roni's laughter tickled his ears as he tugged her through the parking lot toward his SUV. He'd brought it instead of his car, for he didn't know how much luggage Roni would bring. Now he had a much better use for the large vehicle with the tinted windows.

Luckily, he'd already lowered the backseat to make more room in the rear.

Jay pressed the button on his key fob to unlock the back door. After placing Roni's carry-on inside, he faced her. "Your turn."

She flashed him that vixen's smile again before climbing into the back of the SUV. She sat on her heels, her hands on her thighs, looking prim and proper. Jay knew looks could be deceiving. He could already smell the delicious musk from her arousal. He followed her, closing the door behind them. He wasted no time in drawing her into his arms for a long kiss.

The soft moan from Roni's throat went straight to his balls. He drew her up to her knees, cupped her ass with one hand to hold her against him. She slipped one hand between their bodies and squeezed his cock.

His control shattered. Jay jerked off Roni's dress and tossed it aside. She did the same with his pullover. Not wanting to take the time to completely undress, Jay unfastened his belt and jeans. By the time he pushed them past his hips, Roni lay on her back, her legs spread wide. Hooking her knees over his elbows, he entered her with one thrust.

There would be time for lovemaking later. Now Jay wanted to fuck. The way Roni dug her fingernails into his ass and met every thrust proved she felt the same way. He pounded into her wet channel and it still wasn't enough. It wouldn't be enough until he felt her beautiful cunt clamp onto his dick as if she never wanted to let him go.

"Come for me, babe." He nipped her earlobe, nibbled the sensitive spot beneath her ear. "I want to feel your pussy grab my cock when you come."

He'd barely said the last word when Roni shuddered beneath him and released a keening wail. The bite of pain from her fingernails in his ass gave him the final push he needed to follow her into mindless pleasure.

"That was certainly a nice welcome."

Jay managed to push himself up on shaky arms so he could look in Roni's face. "I aim to please."

Her smile reminded him of a woman who'd just devoured a huge piece of dark chocolate. "You aim very well."

"I promise we'll make love later."

"Several times."

He liked her attitude. "I do love the way you think."

The sex had been hard and fast. The kiss he gave her was tender and gentle. "I missed you."

Tears filled her eyes. "I missed you, too."

"We have a lot to talk about." He kissed her again, wiped away a tear that slid down her temple. "My father is in Monterey and I gave Flora the day off. She prepared one of her incredible casseroles and a huge Caesar salad before she left to spend the night with her sister. We'll be all alone to talk."

"That sounds wonderful."

Jay's soft cock slipped from her channel when he pulled

away from her. Her feminine lips shone with her cream mixed with his cum. "We made a mess."

"We always do." She motioned toward her carry-on. "There are some wet wipes in the outside pocket."

"I like a woman who's prepared."

"I thought the no-underwear thing would get to you."

"It definitely got to me."

He cleaned himself first, then gently bathed Roni between her legs. Clothes once again righted, Jay helped Roni from the back of the SUV and walked her to the passenger side. After giving her one more soft kiss, he rounded the hood and climbed in behind the wheel.

"Are you hungry?" he asked once he'd started the motor.

"Not yet, but I'd love a cup of coffee."

"Do you want me to stop for it or make a pot at my house?"

"I vote for your house."

Reaching across the console, Jay laid his hand over hers. "Since we'll be all alone, there's no reason for us to wear clothes."

"I hadn't planned to."

Jay groaned, his cock jerked in his jeans. "Do you realize how many mental pictures just flashed through my mind?"

She took his hand, molded it to her breast. "I hope they were all X-rated."

"Every one of them."

Roni chuckled, a wicked sound that made his cock jerk again. He squeezed her breast, pinched her nipple. "Okay. Clothes off as soon as we walk in the front door."

"Does that mean you're going to fuck me in the foyer?"

"Probably every room in the house before the weekend is over."

"Mmm, sounds good. I'll definitely have more fun than my sister."

"Your sister?"

"Samantha. I was scheduled to fly to Minneapolis yesterday for a meeting with a prospective client. I asked Sam if she'd go instead and I'll take the next trip."

"She was okay with that?"

"She was more okay than my brother. He'd already made flight and hotel reservations in my name, so had to scramble to change everything. Sometimes Clint can be way too serious."

"Clint. That's your brother?"

"The oldest. I have two others, Vince and Dean. We tease Dean about being an accident since he's eight years younger than Samantha. The rest of us are only a year or two apart."

Jay smiled at her joke, but the smile quickly disappeared. Clint. He knew that name from somewhere. Maybe someone he went to school with, or a brand-new employee. He did his best to learn the name and face of every employee at JEMATAR, which wasn't easy since the company employed hundreds of people.

Mentally shrugging off the nagging feeling, Jay turned into his driveway. Wanting the quickest way possible into his house, he pulled up in front instead of parking in the garage. Roni had already stepped down from the SUV by the time he made it to her side. Hand in hand, he led her toward the door.

The music of "Long Train Running" came from his cell phone. Jay stopped and groaned.

"Troy?" Roni asked.

"Yeah. I'm sorry. I have to answer it."

Smiling tenderly, she touched his cheek. "Go ahead. I'm going to walk to the back and enjoy the view of the water."

Jay watched the gentle sway of her hips while reaching for his phone. "What's up, cuz?"

"I've traced the hacker. He tried to get in again today, but I was ready this time. I traced him back to St. James Security in Dallas."

The nagging feeling came back with a vengeance, striking

Jay between his shoulder blades. The guard from Highland Pack, the one who had sworn revenge for the death of their Alpha two years ago, had the same name as Roni's brother.

"That's Roni's family's company, Jay."

"I know."

"You know," Troy said flatly. "Funny how you forgot to tell me that."

"I didn't forget. I didn't think it was important."

"The rivalry between our pack and hers goes back four hundred years, Jay. That's a lot of family history. Roni has to be behind this. She's keeping you occupied with sex while her brother tries to destroy our company."

Jay rubbed his forehead. Roni couldn't be involved in anything this evil. She loved him as much as he loved her.

A memory flashed through his mind from last week. Roni had dropped her purse. When Jay bent down to help her retrieve the spilled items, he'd seen a small pistol. She'd told him she had a permit and carried the gun for protection since she traveled so much on her own. That made perfect sense to him and he hadn't given the gun another thought.

Until now.

"What are you going to do?" Troy asked.

"I don't know." All his thoughts were one big jumbled mess. "Let me think about it."

"What do you want *me* to do?"

"Nothing yet. I'll call you later."

Jay disconnected the call and slowly walked toward Roni. A wolf's instincts were never wrong. His instincts told him she was his mate. Yet he couldn't deny the hacking incidents had increased shortly before he and Roni met. And her brother carried the same name as the one who had threatened Jay via phone calls and letters.

As if she felt his approach, she turned and smiled at him.

Emotion clogged his throat at the sight of her beautiful smile. She couldn't be behind any of this mess. She simply couldn't.

Roni fought to keep her smile from slipping when she saw the serious expression on Jay's face. Something Troy had said must have upset Jay. She took a step toward him, stopped when she heard the whizz of a bullet. Jay's body jerked and a shocked look filled his eyes. Two more bullets slammed into his back, one right after the other. Roni screamed as Jay fell facedown on the ground.

Using her enhanced wolf's vision, she saw movement in the trees. The shooter was getting away. She longed to shift and go after him, tear him apart with her wolf's canines. Jay had to come first before her urge to destroy the one who hurt her mate. She ran to him and dropped to her knees beside him. With tears streaming down her face, she jerked off his shoes and socks.

"Jay! You have to shift." She knew he would heal much faster as a wolf if he could manage to shift. "Help me get your clothes off. Jay, please! You have to shift to save yourself."

The sight of the blood seeping into his shirt made her tears fall faster. "Jay, *please!*"

"My . . . phone. Call doctor. Bri-Brian Hutton."

Roni frantically looked over the ground, searching for Jay's cell phone, which had flown out of his hand when he fell. Finally locating it, she hurried back to Jay. He'd managed to roll to his side and unfastened his belt and jeans. His normal olive complexion had turned a chalky white, his eyes dull and pain filled. Roni finished the job of jerking off his jeans. She cringed when she carefully removed his shirt and saw the three bullet holes in his upper back.

"A-alarm code for . . . back door. One zero one ni-nine two nine."

His voice trailed off as he shifted. He looked at her with those dark wolf eyes, then they slid shut.

Pawing through his jeans pockets, Roni located Jay's keys. She found Brian Hutton's number on the cell and pressed the button to place the call while she ran toward the house.

"Hey, Jay, what's up?" a friendly male voice answered.

"Dr. Hutton, this is Veronica St. James. Jay has been shot."

No longer friendly, the voice shouted, "What?"

"Please hurry! We're at Jay's house."

"Who the hell is this?"

She fumbled with the key ring, searching for the right key while trying to keep the phone on her shoulder. "I'll explain when you get here. Please *hurry!*"

"I'll be there in twenty minutes."

Roni stumbled into the house. Her fingers shook as she entered the code to turn off the alarm. She ran up the stairs to the linen closet she'd discovered last weekend when she'd snooped around Jay's house. Tugging three blankets off a shelf, she ran downstairs and back outside to Jay. He lay on his side, eyes closed, his breath shallow.

"Hang on, Jay. The doctor is on his way. Hang on!" Her breath hitched when the tears started again. "I can't lose you."

She covered him with the blankets and crawled beneath them, too, offering her warmth to help him heal.

Clint picked up his cell phone from his desk at the tone of an arriving text message. No number showed in the window, but he knew who had sent the message as soon as he read the two words.

Job done.

Sitting back in his chair, Clint smiled. Finally. Jamieson Millington was dead. Highland Pack's Alpha could rest in peace.

The tone announced another incoming message. Clint flipped through pictures Malcolm Lander sent of the shooting. He saw

Millington falling, blood already soaking the back of his shirt. The second picture showed Millington lying facedown on the ground.

Clint sat up straight when he saw the third picture. Damn it, there was a woman with Millington. She knelt beside him, tears running down her cheeks. Tapping the picture to enlarge it, he peered at the woman's face. She looked like . . .

His sister.

"Goddamn it!" He caught himself before he threw his phone across the room. "What the *hell* are you doing with Millington, Roni?"

It didn't surprise him not to receive an answer when he called Lander's cell. The assassin had told Clint that once a job was done, he disappeared without a trace. So Clint had no way to know for sure that Millington was dead, short of calling Roni. If she'd convinced the guy to shift, Millington might still be alive.

He had to know for sure. He didn't want to hurt his sister, but his first priority was revenge for his Alpha.

Clint removed the company credit card from his wallet and opened his browser to the American Airlines website.

10

Roni jerked when she no longer felt fur beneath her cheek. She quickly lifted her head and looked down into Jay's human face. More tears flooded her eyes as she touched his cheek with a shaky hand.

"How do you feel?"

"Like I've been shot."

"The doctor is on his way. He should be here any minute."

"I may need some help walking to the house."

She'd do anything for him, surely he knew that. Tossing aside the blankets, she helped Jay to stand. Once he was on his feet, she wrapped one of the blankets around his body to conserve heat. She dragged one of his arms over her shoulders and slipped her other arm around his waist to help him walk.

"I can feel two bullets in my back. One must have passed straight through."

"The doctor will remove them as soon as he gets here."

"They'll work themselves out, eventually."

"No. We aren't waiting. Those bullets are coming out today."

"You're sure bossy."

"Damn right. You have no idea how bossy I can be." She ushered him through the back door. "Can you climb the stairs?"

"Take me to the kitchen."

"The kitchen? Don't you want to lie down?"

"No. I'll straddle a chair at the kitchen table. That'll make it easy for Brian to check my back."

She didn't agree with his decision, but knew arguing wouldn't help. Turning a chair at the table around, she helped him straddle it. Even through the dried blood, she could easily see the three bullet holes. The one in his shoulder appeared to be already healing. The two in his back still oozed a bit of blood. She saw two small bumps beneath the skin at the holes, as if the bullets were working themselves out of his body, as Jay said they would.

After draping the blanket around his hips, she hurried to the refrigerator for a bottle of water. "Drink."

"Yes, ma'am." He opened the bottle and drained half of it in one gulp while looking at her. "You have blood on your dress."

"I don't care." She ran her hand through his hair. "I only care about you."

The sound of the doorbell pealed through the house. "I'll get that. You drink the rest of the water."

Roni answered the door to see a man in his mid-forties, dressed casually in a T-shirt and jeans, carrying a large brown leather bag. His scent announced him as wolf.

"Where's Jay?" he asked without bothering with introductions.

"In the kitchen."

Brian Hutton headed toward the kitchen as if he'd been in Jay's house many times. Roni shut the door and hurried after him.

"Who'd you piss off, Jay?" the doctor asked, setting his bag on the table. He withdrew a pair of latex gloves and snapped them on his hands.

"And a good day to you, too, Brian."

"At least you waited to get shot on my day off."

"I didn't want to interfere with your golf schedule."

Jay flinched when Brian touched the two protruding bumps. Roni clasped her hands together at her waist to keep from snatching Brian's hands away from Jay. She knew the doctor would help Jay, yet she couldn't stand anyone hurting her mate.

"I'm going to give you a couple of shots to deaden the area so I can remove the bullets." Brian looked at her over his shoulder. "Veronica?"

"Roni. People call me Roni."

"Would you get a bowl of warm water and a washcloth for me?"

It made her feel better to be helpful. By the time she returned with the items Brian requested, he had removed one bullet from Jay's back.

"You're lucky you were able to shift." He dropped the bullet in an empty coffee mug Roni assumed he'd taken from a cabinet. "If you'd passed out as a human, these babies would've done lots of nasty things in your chest."

"Roni helped me."

Brian looked at her again. "I see that. I assume that's your blood on her dress?"

"Yeah." Jay gazed at her, too, but Roni couldn't read his expression. She sensed . . . discomfort from him, and she didn't think it had anything to do with the bullet holes.

"Got it." Brian dropped the second bullet in the mug. Dipping the washcloth in the bowl of water, he gently cleansed the blood from Jay's back. "I'll bandage the wounds. Even though they're already healing, there might be some seepage. You should be fine by tonight. Until then, take it easy, okay?"

"Sure."

"I'll make sure he takes it easy," Roni told Brian.

"Good." He kept looking at her as he pulled off his gloves and dropped them in the trash can at the end of the cabinets. "I'll want the full story about you two when he's better."

Somehow Roni managed a slight smile. She liked Brian Hutton. He had kind eyes and gentle hands. Plus he'd helped her mate, which put him way at the top of her like list.

A quick glance at Jay found him gazing at her, that unreadable expression still on his face. Apprehension formed a knot in her stomach. Something obviously bothered him, something more than the gunshots.

Brian touched Jay's shoulder. "Call me if you need anything."

"I will. Thanks, Bri."

"I'll walk you out," Roni said.

"Don't bother. I know my way." He smiled. "Nice to meet you, Roni, although I would've preferred nicer circumstances."

"Me too."

She waited until she heard Brian leave before she turned back to Jay. He leaned against the cabinets, one hand clutching the blanket around his waist. "What's wrong?"

He drained the last bit of water in his bottle before answering. "I got shot."

She crossed her arms over her stomach since it still churned. "I have a feeling it's more than that, especially since you won't look at me."

He turned his head and peered at her with eyes that were flat. The apprehension in her stomach turned to fear. "Are you angry at me?"

"Why did you go to the cliff, Roni?"

His strange question surprised her so much, she didn't know how to answer it at first. "To give you time to answer your call from Troy. I wanted to give you privacy."

"But why the cliff? Why so out in the open?"

"It's a sunny day. I wanted to look at the water. I didn't think anything about . . ." She stopped when realization hit her. With that realization came pain more intense than she'd ever experienced. "You think I *lured* you out in the open so you could be *shot?*"

"Hackers have plagued JEMATAR ever since the first time we spoke on the phone, Roni."

She splayed one hand over her chest. "You think *I* had something to do with that? How could I? You called me first!"

"Your company certainly had something to do with it. That call from Troy was to tell me he tracked the hacker back to St. James Security."

Shock left her speechless. The man she loved, she man she hoped would father her children, stood there and accused her family of trying to destroy him and his company. "Jay, you can't be serious. No one in my family has any reason to hurt you."

Jay straightened his shoulders and faced her. Anger filled his eyes. "I've received threatening letters and phone calls from a man named Clint the last two years. Is that your brother?"

"I don't know anything about my brother sending you threatening letters and calls. Why would he?"

"Because he's a guard in your pack and is angry that your Alpha died."

"*You* had nothing to do with that!"

Jay scowled. "*I* know that! But apparently he doesn't care about that minor point." His eyes narrowed. "Are you helping him, Roni?"

It surprised Roni to discover she could still stand and breathe when her heart had completely crumbled. The pain was so excruciating, she couldn't even cry. "I don't know why my brother would want to hurt you. I don't know why you believe *I* would want to hurt you. You're my mate, Jay. I love you."

He said nothing, only continued to stare at her. Right then,

Roni knew they would never make it together as a mated pair. There couldn't be love—*true* love—without trust. And Jay no longer trusted her.

Or perhaps he never had.

She had never begged anyone for anything in her life. She wouldn't start now. "I need to borrow the bathroom to change my clothes before I leave."

He motioned with his hand toward the downstairs bathroom, but still said nothing. Head held high, Roni left the house to retrieve her suitcase from Jay's SUV. She called information for a taxi service while stripping off her bloodstained dress. After slipping on faded jeans and a comfortable sweater, she dropped the dress in the small trash can.

The taxi arrived as Roni came out of the bathroom, pulling her carry-on behind her. She stopped when she saw Jay in the foyer. He still clutched the bloody blanket around his hips. She would've gone to him if she'd seen any evidence of love in his eyes. She saw nothing but emptiness.

Not bothering to say good-bye, she walked out the front door and out of Jay's life.

Jay gave up trying to sleep at five a.m. He'd gotten totally shitfaced after Roni left, throwing down shot after shot of bourbon to forget that he'd let his mate walk away from him. He finally stumbled to his bed shortly after two. For three hours, he lay awake and stared at the ceiling while calling himself every kind of fool.

He remembered the pain in Roni's eyes when he'd accused her of being the hacker, the shock when he'd suggested she'd lured him to a spot on the cliff where he could be shot. Thinking of how much he'd hurt her tightened his gut with regret. He couldn't believe he'd been so stupid! He loved her and knew she would never do anything to hurt him.

Forcing himself out of bed, he drew on jeans and a long-sleeved T-shirt. He stumbled down the stairs and to the front door. Opening it wide, he stepped out on the small porch and inhaled deeply. He could sense Roni, feel her nearby. She was still in the city.

Which meant he could find her and tell her what an ass he'd been.

Jay slammed the door and ran back upstairs for socks and shoes. Grabbing his keys from the foyer table, he threw open the front door again. A man stood there, one Jay had never seen. He instinctively sniffed the air and caught the scent of wolf . . . and Roni. That meant this man belonged to Roni's pack.

"Can I help you?" Jay asked.

"Jamieson Millington?"

Jay nodded. The man's deep voice sent a shiver up Jay's spine. Before Jay could slam the door in his face, the man withdrew a pistol from his jacket pocket and pointed it at Jay's chest. "You're supposed to be dead."

"Sorry to disappoint you. You must be Clint St. James."

He didn't even bat an eye that Jay knew his identity. "I am."

Jay walked backward a few steps while trying to decide what to do. Clint followed, the hand holding the pistol steady. "I paid a hell of a lot of money to have you killed. I'm not happy my man didn't do his job."

That's it, keep talking. As long as you talk, you won't shoot. "Oh, he did it. My doctor dug two bullets out of my back. The third one went straight through."

"Why was my sister here?"

"What makes you think she still isn't?"

Clint gave Jay a look that clearly said Jay should know better than to question Clint's intelligence. "I know Roni's scent. I don't smell her."

"So this is all your doing. The hacking, the murder attempt. Roni had nothing to do with it."

"Of course she didn't. I don't want my sister involved in anything . . ." He trailed off, as if searching for the right word.

"Dirty?" Jay supplied. "Illegal? Immoral?"

Clint scowled. "You talk too much, Millington." He lifted the gun another inch, flashed a wicked smile. "It's time for me to end that."

"*What the hell is going on?*" Jamieson roared.

Jay and Clint both whirled to watch Jamieson stride toward them from the dining room, leaning heavily on his cane. The instinct to protect his father and his Alpha made Jay step in front of Jamieson. "Dad, this is between Clint and me. Please leave."

"He's a wolf. I'm not going anywhere." He moved out from behind Jay and pointed a finger at Clint. "Why are you holding a gun on my son? And why aren't you kneeling before an Alpha?"

"I won't ever kneel before *you*," Clint said with a sneer. "You're the father of the man who killed my Alpha."

The anger faded from Jamieson's face. He sighed deeply. "No, son, Jay didn't kill your Alpha. *I* did."

Jay glanced from his father to Clint. Roni's brother appeared as shocked as Jay felt. He looked back at Jamieson. "What?"

"Clint's Alpha—Benjamin—and I both loved Tara. She loved me, but Benjamin wasn't willing to accept that. He challenged me for her. I had to accept the challenge."

"Why?"

"It's the pack way, Jay. To turn him down would be to appear weak to my pack."

Jay knew nothing of a challenge between his father and another Alpha. His mother had died when he was three. He barely remembered her. He did remember how lonely and lost his father had been for years, until he met Tara. She'd always loved Jay as if he were her own son.

Clint rubbed his forehead. "Jamieson Millington killed my Alpha. That's him."

"It's *both* of us," Jamieson said. "I'm the senior, Jay is the junior. We carry the same name."

Still looking confused, Clint's hand holding the gun wavered a bit. Jay decided to make a move to grab the pistol when Clint straightened again and frowned.

"I don't care which Millington killed him. He has to die. Now."

"*Clint, no!*" Roni screamed.

Jay jerked at the sound of Roni's voice. Clint whirled around, the gun in his hand now aimed at his sister. The wolf in Jay leaped and growled, ready to defend its mate.

Before he could move, Roni snatched the pistol from Clint's fingers. "What are you doing? You aren't going to shoot anyone!"

Clint pointed at Jamieson. "He killed our Alpha!"

"In a fair fight, Clint! I wasn't able to get a flight back to Dallas yesterday, so I spent last night researching our packs' history in my motel room. Benjamin challenged Jamieson. He had no choice but to fight."

"He didn't have to kill him!"

Roni slipped the pistol into her jacket pocket, moved closer to Clint. "It's the pack way, Clint. You know that as well as I do. Jamieson did nothing wrong." She gripped her brother's hands. "He defended himself and was hurt doing so. He wasn't able to get help quickly enough to stop permanent damage. That's why he walks with a cane."

Clint's shoulders slumped. "I was his guard, Roni. I was supposed to protect him."

"You couldn't. No one could. A challenge is to the death and *no one* can interfere. You *know* that."

Clint looked over his shoulder at Jay and Jamieson. Jay saw the regret in Clint's eyes, the helplessness. He understood that. If someone challenged Jamieson now, Jay would do everything in his power to protect his father, pack law or not.

Jay stepped forward. "Maybe it's time to put the past behind us, Clint, and start fresh. I'm in love with your sister. If she'll forgive me for being such an ass yesterday, I plan to marry her."

A soft smile curved Roni's lips. "I have three brothers. I know about men being asses." Looking back at Clint, she took the pistol out of her pocket and held it out to him. "Are you good with starting over?"

He nodded, took the pistol, slipped it back in his pocket. Turning to Jamieson, he lowered his head, placed one fist over his heart, and dropped to one knee. "Sire."

Jamieson touched the top of Clint's head. "Rise, Clint. We have a lot to celebrate. Our packs will soon become one."

Clint rose to his feet, held out a hand to Jay. "I, uh, apologize for . . . everything."

"It's over." Jay accepted Clint's hand. "Fresh start begins now."

Clint nodded again, then drew Roni into his arms for a hug. "I'm sorry," he whispered.

"I know." She cradled his face in her hands. "I can feel the tension still in you. Why don't you go take a walk or something and come back later for dinner?"

A grin lifted one corner of his mouth. "Trying to get rid of me?"

"Jay and I need to talk privately. Plus he owes me a *big* apology. I plan to take a very long time to accept it."

Jamieson clasped Clint's shoulder. "If you don't mind hanging out with me, I'll buy you breakfast." He glanced at Roni, then Jay. "Maybe lunch, too."

Jay followed his father and Clint to the front door. He closed it, turned the dead bolt. When he faced Roni again, his heart jumped up to lodge in his throat. She stood with her arms crossed beneath her breasts, her chin high. The soft smile she'd given him earlier had disappeared.

"Exactly how big is that apology supposed to be?"

"Pretty damn big."

"Would chocolate help?"

He thought he saw her lips twitch. "It would help, but it isn't enough."

"Yeah, I figured that." Jay walked toward her. She uncrossed her arms, let them hang at her sides. Taking her hands, he raised them to his mouth and kissed her palms. "I'm sorry. I'm so sorry for hurting you. I never should have doubted you."

Her eyes softened, love shining from them. "It's over. Clint agreed to a fresh start. It'll be one for us, too."

He kissed her with all the love, all the desire, he felt for her. "We have a lot to talk about, Roni. What happens now, where we'll live, your family, my family—"

A fingertip to his lips stopped him. "I agree we have a lot to talk about, later. Right now, I want the rest of my apology."

Jay struggled not to grin. He had a feeling he knew exactly what she meant, but pretended he didn't. "Do you want more words, or should I take you to bed and show you how much you mean to me?"

"Actions speak louder than words."

Jay couldn't stop the grin now. "I do love the way you think." He scooped her up in his arms and headed for the stairs.